Praise for
The Hanover Square Affair

(Top Pick!) With her vivid depiction of the era,
Gardner brings her novel to life, from the streets
inhabited by the destitute to the mansions of the
wealthy. — *RT BookReviews*

In the tradition of Anne Perry, Ms. Gardner's
debut delivers an emotional and compelling
historical mystery. — Suan Wilson, *The Best
Reviews*

With a brisk narrative, credible characterizations,
a challenging mystery, and an authentic period
atmosphere, Ashley Gardner has created a
winner. — *Book Loons*

The Hanover Square Affair is an intricate web of
mysteries which Gardner skillfully combines with
the personality of [the] protagonist—*The New
Mystery Reader*

The Hanover Square Affair

Ashley Gardner

Captain Lacey Regency Mysteries
Book 1

This book is dedicated to the long-time readers of the Captain Lacey Regency Mystery series, who gave me the support and encouragement to continue.

Chapter One

London, April 1816

Sharp as a whip-crack, a shot echoed through the mists in Hanover Square.

The mob in the square boiled apart, flinging sticks and pieces of brick as they fled the line of cavalrymen who'd entered the far side of the square. I hugged a rain-soaked wall as people poured past me, bumping and shoving in their panic as though I weren't six feet tall and plenty solid.

The square and the streets that led to it had been bottled with traffic all afternoon: carts, carriages, horses, wagons, and those on foot who'd been running errands or passing through, as well as street vendors crying their wares. The mob had stopped traffic in all directions, trapping inside the square those now desperate to get out. They scrambled to get away from the cavalry and their deadly guns, and bystanders scrambled to flee the mob.

I scraped my way along the wall, rough stone tearing my cheap gloves, going against the stream of bodies that tried to carry me along. Inside the square, in the eye of the storm, the cavalrymen waited, the blues and reds and canary yellows of their uniforms stark against the fog.

The man who stood in their gun sights had led the mob the better part of the afternoon: shouting, cursing, flinging stones and pieces of brick at the unfortunate house that was number 22, Hanover Square. Now he faced the cavalrymen, his back straight, his gray hair dark with rain.

I recognized the lieutenant in charge, Lord Arthur Gale of the Twenty-Fourth Light Dragoons. A few years before, on a Portuguese battlefield, I'd dragged young Gale out from under a dead horse and sent him on his way. That incident, however, had not formed any camaraderie between us. Gale was the son of a marquis and already a social success, and I, the only son of an impoverished gentleman, mattered little to the Gale family.

I did not trust Gale's judgment one whit. He had once led a charge so hard that he'd broken through a solid line of French infantry but then found himself and his men behind enemy lines and too winded to get back. Gale had been one of the few who'd returned from that charge, leaving most of the others, horses and men alike, dead.

"Gentlemen," the old man said to the cavalrymen. "I thank you for coming. We must have him out. He must pay for what he's done."

He pointed at the house—number 22, ground-floor windows smashed, front door's black paint gouged.

Gale sneered down at him. "Get along, man, or we'll take you to a magistrate."

"Not I, gentlemen. *He* should face justice. Take him from his house. Bring him out to me. I beg of you."

I studied the house in some surprise. Any man who could afford to own, or lease, a house in Hanover Square must be wealthy and powerful. I assumed he was some peer in the House of Lords, or at least a rich MP, who had proposed some unpopular bill or movement, inspiring a riot against him. The rising price of bread, as well as the horde of soldiers pouring back into England after Waterloo, had created a smoldering rage in those who suddenly found themselves with nothing. The anger flared every now and then into a riot. It was not difficult these days to turn a crowd into a violent mob in the space of an instant.

I had no idea who lived in number 22 or what were his political leanings. I had simply been trying to pass through Hanover Square on my way to Brook Street, deeper into Mayfair. But the elderly man's quiet despair and incongruous air of respectability drew me to him. I always, Louisa Brandon had once told me, had a soft spot for the desperate.

Gale's eyes were dark and hard. "If you do not move along, I will have to arrest you for breach of the King's peace."

"Breach of the King's peace?" the man shouted. "When a man sins against another, is that not a breach of the King's peace? Shall we let them take our daughters while we weep? Shall I let him sit in his fine house while mine is ruined with grief?"

Gale made a sharp gesture to the cavalryman next to him. The man obediently dismounted and strode toward the gray-haired rioter.

The older man watched him come with more astonishment than fear. "Is it justice that I pay for his sins?"

"I advise you to go home, sir," Gale repeated.

"No, I tell you, you must have him out! He must face you and confess what he's done."

His desperation reached me as white mists moved to swallow the scene. The blue and red of the cavalry uniforms, the black of the man's suit, the bays and browns of the horses began to dull against the smudge of white.

"What has he done?" I asked.

The man swung around. Strands of hair matted to his face, and thin lines of dried blood caked his skin as though he'd scratched himself in his fury. "You would listen to me? You would help me?"

"Get out of it, Captain," Gale said, his mouth a grim line.

I regretted speaking, unsure I wanted to engage myself in what might be a political affair, but the man's anger and despair seemed more than simply mob fury over the price of food. Gale would no doubt arrest him and drag him off to wait in a cold cell for the magistrate's pleasure. Perhaps one person should hear him speak.

"What has the man in number 22 done to you?" I repeated.

The old man took a step toward me, eyes burning. "He has sinned. He has stolen from me the most precious thing I own. He has killed me!"

I watched madness well up in his eyes. With a fierce cry, he turned and launched himself at the door of number 22.

Chapter Two

I'd heard such a cry of despair once before, in Portugal during the Peninsular campaign, when a corporal had watched his best friend—some said his lover—be gunned down by a French soldier. He'd hurled himself, with that same cry, at the Frenchman, and had fallen onto his friend's body with the Frenchman's bayonet piercing him. I'd shot the Frenchman who'd killed them both.

The battlefield receded and Hanover Square came back into focus. The young cavalryman next to me stepped back, brought up his pistol, and fired it straight into the gray-haired man's back.

The man jerked as the ball penetrated him, and blood blackened his coat. With another cry of anger and misery, he fell slowly to his knees.

I caught him as he collapsed. Blood coated his rain-soaked worsted suit, and his eyes were wide, bewildered. I lowered him gently to the cobbles then glared up at the cavalryman. "What the devil did you do that for?"

The officer was young. His face was round and babyish, his eyes as gray as the clouded sky. His insignia told me he held the rank of cornet, the cavalry's version of ensign, and his eyes told me he'd never seen battle, or a French soldier, or death.

His fine nose pinched. "He is a madman. Railing at his betters."

The old man still breathed. The stones beneath him were slick with that afternoon's rain and filthy with mud and horse droppings, ground in by the wheels of carts and carriages. I pulled my coat from my shoulders, wadded it, and slid it under the man's head.

His coat, now ruined, had been well made, if it was a bit out of date, and a tear on his sleeve had been carefully mended. Beneath blood and mud, his gloves were whole and finer than mine. The dark gold rim of a watch peeped from his waistcoat pocket.

"He's not working class," I said. "A clerk or a Cit, possibly a solicitor's or banker's assistant. A man used to soft work."

Leather creaked as Gale dismounted. He moved to stand next to his cornet, and studied me in dislike. "Weddington, this is Captain Lacey. Of the Thirty-Fifth Light. Self-appointed expert on all mankind."

"Indeed, sir?"

"Indeed. He is ever fascinated by who a man is and why he does what he does."

I ignored him. Gale had never forgiven me, a mere nobody, for saving his life.

"Who lives here?" I asked, gesturing at number 22.

The house was no different from the others in the square—fine, modern, elegant, large. Two large multipaned windows, now broken, sat to the right of the door, and two more rows of windows marched across the first and top stories. Doric columns flanked the door, and arches above the windows relieved the plain facade. The number "22" hung on one of the columns. The door, painted black, sported a shining brass knocker, an indication that the family within was in residence. If they'd chosen to spend this spring elsewhere, the door would have been bare.

A curtain moved in the upper floor of the house next door, but number 22's windows remained tightly muffled.

"Damned if I know," Gale growled. "My commander told me he'd had a personal complaint about a disturbance in Hanover Square, and would I see to it? 'Yes, sir' was all I thought to say. I obey orders."

I hid my wince by straightening the dying man's coat, but old pain rose, fast and bitter. I wondered briefly if Gale were taunting me, but dismissed it. He could not know. We'd said nothing. That had been the agreement.

The gray-haired man began to shiver, and his eyes shifted back and forth beneath his waxen eyelids. "He'll die if we do not help him," I said.

"He'll die in Newgate then," Gale offered.

I looked at number 22. "We can take him in there."

"To the house he's been chucking bricks at? Find a cart and drag him out of here if you must."

My white-hot temper began to rise, and I briefly regretted not shoving Lieutenant Lord Arthur Gale back under that horse in Portugal. The dying man meant less to these fine gentlemen of the Twenty-Fourth than a trampled insect.

I got to my feet. I would take the man home. As an officer on half-pay, with no private income, I struggled to make ends meet, and this perhaps gave me more affinity with my poorer neighbors. Let Gale return home to receive his evening port on a silver tray. This man had no one to help him.

Another cry filled the air as a woman pushed through the edges of the now curious crowd and stumbled toward us. She was elderly too, with long gray hair escaping from her cap, her eyes as wide and wild as the dying man's. "Charles," she cried. "Husband."

Her basket fell from her arm, and fruit and paper parcels skittered across the wet cobbles.

The cornet started for her. I put a heavy hand on his arm, and he swung around, eyes lit with anger.

"Let it go," Gale ordered. "Mount up."

The cornet and I shared another glance of hostility before I finally released him. He turned from me, rubbing his wrist.

He caught his horse and climbed into the saddle, his movements angry. At a signal from Gale, the cavalrymen wheeled as one and trotted out of the square, leaving me alone with the dying man and his wife.

*** *** ***

I persuaded a good-natured drover to take them home. He didn't want to, having a load to meet near Hampstead, but I promised him a crown for his trouble. We made our unknown gentleman as comfortable as possible in the bed of the wagon, and his wife crawled in beside him. She neither looked at us nor thanked us, but merely crouched beside her husband, holding his hand as if she could pour her own life into his waning body. I had a devil of a time getting a direction from her, but finally she mumbled the name of a lane, which the drover recognized as one near the Strand.

I gathered up her basket. The fruit in it was rotten, as if she'd carried it with her for days. I threw away the fruit and unwrapped the parcels. Each contained lace, a fine skein of it, each identical to the others. I put them back into the basket and tucked it beside her. She scarce seemed to notice.

I accompanied them. My purpose in Mayfair that afternoon had been an appointment with the wife of my former commander, at their Brook Street house, but I was just as happy to climb into the cart and let it take me in the opposite direction.

Louisa would be annoyed when I sent my regrets, but I welcomed the chance to avoid the meeting. I had a feeling I knew what she wanted to speak to me about, and I wanted nothing to do with it. Also, her husband might be home, the man who had once been my mentor and closer to me than a brother. That same man had ended my career and very nearly my life.

The drover made his slow way through the traffic, still bottled, to Swallow Street, a narrow artery south. Plans were underway to widen this street into an elegant thoroughfare so that the Prince Regent would be able to travel a more or less direct route from a park that would be built north of Oxford Street to his opulent Carleton House just below Pall Mall. There the Prince, who'd been Regent for five years now, dwelled in splendor, while his father, King George, slowly lived through his madness in his padded rooms in Windsor. The rest of us used Swallow Street simply to leave graceful Mayfair for the darker regions of London.

The fog lowered. By the time we reached Haymarket, the rain had ceased, but the blanket of mist enveloped us. I held the man steadily against the bumps of the cobbles and the sway of the wagon. His wife simply sat, staring at nothing. Farther south, in Charing Cross, a street puppet theater had attracted a fair number of watchers, who, despite the darkening, chill weather, cheered or booed with enthusiasm.

The drover turned his cart into a small lane that opened from the Strand. The lane was narrow and dark, rather like the one in which I had lodgings, but the tall houses crowded here were painfully neat and respectable. The drover found the house and stopped his wagon before it.

I had to pry the woman's hand from her husband's and lift her to the pavement. The drover watched me, pity in his eyes. "Poor sods. 'Ow'd they get all the way to 'Anover Square?"

The same question had occurred to me.

The door of the house burst open, and a thin woman in maid's garb dashed out. "Madam? What has happened?"

"Help me with her," I said.

The maid's eyes flicked from the woman to the old man in the cart, and her already white face paled. "God above. Where did you find them?"

"Hanover Square," I said.

The dismay in her eyes told me that my words did not surprise her, that she'd been expecting something like this. The gray-haired woman turned instantly from me and flung her arms about the maid's waist, as though sensing she'd found someone stronger to pass her burden to.

"Did Mr. Horne shoot him?" the maid asked.

The question surprised me, but the drover interrupted before I could ask what she meant.

"What about 'im, guv?" The drover jerked his thumb at the wagon. The maid turned away without waiting for me to answer and led the clinging old woman into the house.

"Can you lift him?" I asked the drover.

"Aye, I've carried 'eavier loads than 'im, man and boy."

The house opened right onto the street. I followed the drover, who carried the old man through the open door into the dim hall of a small, but respectable house. The faded wallpaper was clean and uncreased, and competent, if unimaginative, landscape paintings dotted it. At the end of the narrow hall, a staircase rose to the upper floors. The banisters were free of dust, the runner straight and clean. The sconces on the landing held unlit candles, half-burned.

The maid reappeared as we stepped onto the first floor, and led us to a small front bedroom. The drover deposited his burden on the bed there and returned to me in the hall.

"'E's not long for this world, poor sod," he said. "Now, then, guv, I'm off to 'Ampstead."

He didn't exactly hold out his hand, but I took a crown from my pocket and dropped it into his calloused palm. I could ill spare it, but he had gone out of his way when he had no reason to.

The drover touched his forelock and departed, finished with the business.

I returned to the small, neat bedroom. The old man, barely alive, lay face up on the bed. The maid, her hands visibly shaking, was peeling his ruined waistcoat from him.

The ball had torn a heavy gash through his middle. Bone, white and obscene, poked through the hole, and his chest rose and fell with his shallow, rasping breaths. But I knew enough about gunshot wounds to know that this one was clean. The bullet had passed clear through him.

"He needs a surgeon," I said.

The maid answered without looking up. "We can't afford the likes of that."

I removed my coat. "Get a basin of water and plenty of cloths. Are you willing to help?"

"Help what, sir?"

"Patch him up if nothing else. That's all a surgeon could do. He may live if the wound doesn't sicken."

She stared at me. "Are you a doctor?"

I shook my head. "I've bandaged plenty of wounds. Including my own."

The maid was brave. She brought the basin and a pile of towels and stayed for the whole messy business. Alice, she said her name was, and she'd been doing for the master and mistress—Mr. and Mrs. Thornton—for twenty years. She steadied the

basin and handed me towels and held Mr. Thornton
to the bed when I came to the tricky business of
cleaning the wound.

In the heat of Spain and Portugal, during the war
against Napoleon Bonaparte, which had ended only
the year before, surgeons had used water to clean
wounds when they could no longer obtain healing
concoctions. They continued to use water when they
discovered that wounds cleansed with it tended to
heal more swiftly than those smeared with ointment.
I put that theory to the test now, sensing that these
people could not afford ointment from an apothecary
in any case.

I wrapped his torso in bandages, and Alice bathed
him. The room had gone dark, and I lit a lone candle.
Mr. Thornton had fallen into a stupor and lay still,
but his breathing continued—smooth, clean
breathing, with no bubbles of blood.

"Do you have laudanum?" I asked.

She nodded. "A little. I've given the mistress a few
drops."

"Give him some when he wakes. He should stay
utterly still for some days."

"I'll look after him, sir. I always do."

I wiped my hands and lowered myself to a hard
chair, sighing in relief as I removed the weight from
my injured leg. "Who is Mr. Horne?" I asked.

Alice spun around, cloths dripping watery
crimson onto the bed cover. "I beg your pardon, sir?"

"The first thing you asked when you saw your
master was whether Mr. Horne had shot him. Does
he live in number 22, Hanover Square?"

She swallowed and looked away, and I thought
she was not going to answer me. Finally she lifted

her head and met my gaze, her intelligent eyes keen and clear.

"He has committed an unspeakable crime, sir," she said. "A horrible thing, worse than murder. And I'd give anything, anything in the world, to watch him swing for it."

Chapter Three

At eight that evening, I reached Hanover Square again and made for number 22.

I'd retraced my route via a hired hackney from the Strand, and as I'd neared the elite environs of Mayfair, carriages, horses, and dwellings had become more and more elegant. Sturdy cart horses gave way to elegant, well-matched, fine-blooded teams pulling closed carriages painted anything from modest dark brown to bright yellow. A gentleman passed in his cabriolet, his white-swathed neck stiff with pride at his two-wheeled rig and the high-stepping horse pulling it. A small boy in livery, known as a tiger, clung to the perch in the back.

I'd sent a message to Louisa Brandon earlier, giving her my apologies for missing my appointment that afternoon. She'd demand an explanation when I saw her again, and I'd give her one in due time.

Someone had nailed boards over the ground floor windows of number 22, and the door still sported scars from rocks the mob had flung. Otherwise, the house was still, as calm as if the rioting had never taken place. The railings flanking the stairs to the kitchens remained whole and upright, the columns to either side of the front door were unblemished. The cobbles onto which Mr. Thornton had fallen had been trampled by horses and carriages and foot traffic, his blood already erased.

Despite the afternoon's excitement, number 22 was an ordinary house, no different from its neighbors to either side. But I had come to pry out its secrets.

I stepped up to the scarred door and plied the knocker. In a few moments, an elderly retainer with a hook nose opened the door and peered out.

"I would like to see Mr. Horne, if he's in," I said.

The door closed to a sliver. "We are much indisposed at present, sir."

"I know. I saw what happened to your windows." I thrust my card through the crack. "Give him this. I'll wait."

The retainer lifted the card to his rheumy eyes, studied it carefully, and opened the door a little wider.

"I will inquire, sir. Please follow me."

He let me inside, ushered me to a high-ceilinged reception room at the back of the house, and left me there.

I looked about after he'd departed and decided it a pity that the windows hadn't been smashed in this room as well—it would have made an improvement. The chamber was decorated in garish crimson, gold, and green in the faux Egyptian style, with divans, chairs, and ottomans upholstered with cheap fabric meant to look like brocade. The gilded frieze that marched around the top of the walls had been sloppily done, and depicted nude Egyptian maidens adoring fortunate, and well-endowed, Egyptian males. Under these scenes of debauchery hung incongruous landscapes painted by someone attempting—and failing—to imitate Turner.

I paced beneath these bad paintings trying to decide what I would say to Horne if he agreed to see me. He didn't know me, I had no appointment, and we'd never been introduced. He could very well have the butler toss me out again, and my errand would be for naught.

But I'd been driven here as sure as January wind drives the snow, because the maid Alice had told me about Jane Thornton.

Jane was the Thorntons' daughter, an ordinary girl of seventeen: pretty, quiet-spoken, dreaming of a husband and family of her own. Sometimes Jane would visit a young lady in Mayfair, daughter of a family called Carstairs. The young lady would frequently send her father's carriage for her poorer friend so that the two could enjoy a visit or an outing. One day Jane and her maid, Aimee, had set off to meet the young lady for an afternoon of shopping. They'd never arrived. When the carriage reached the young lady's home, Jane and her maid had not been in it.

The coachman had professed shock and astonishment and appeared as baffled as anyone else. Traffic in London streets often slowed to a crawl or halted completely; the two girls could have descended at any time without the coachman's knowledge. But for what reason? It made no sense for a girl to leap from a carriage into the perilous streets of London instead of allowing herself to be safely taken to the home of her friend. A search was made, but Jane and Aimee had never been found.

And then, weeks later, Alice had been walking with Mr. Thornton along the Strand, nearing St. Martin in the Fields church. A carriage had passed them, and its window had framed the face of Jane Thornton.

She had not called out, she had not waved, she'd only gazed at them sadly before another hand had pulled the curtain closed, hiding her from view. Alice and Mr. Thornton had pursued the carriage, with difficulty, all the way to Hanover Square, where it had stopped before number 22.

But when Mr. Thornton had thumped on the door and demanded admittance, the household had denied that Jane was there. Mr. Horne, the widower who occupied the house, even offered to let Thornton search the house for his daughter. Mr. Thornton had looked, but Jane was not to be found. He'd grown confused, his grief overcoming him, and Alice had taken him home.

Alice still believed Jane was at number 22. This morning, Mr. Thornton had persuaded Alice that he would take Mrs. Thornton shopping. Mrs. Thornton had convinced herself that Jane was away buying clothes, and she took refuge in shopping for her return. Mr. Thornton must have left her in Oxford Street and made his way to Hanover Square. He'd returned there a few times before, the Watch dragging him home again. He'd promised Alice after the last incident that he would not go again.

And so, here I was.

The story had awakened in me a dangerous anger, one that had led me to trouble countless times in my past. I had served as a light dragoon for the entire Peninsular campaign, from the time we'd landed in Portugal in 1808 to France's retreat in 1814. I'd felt no anger against the French in general; they were soldiers performing their duties, much as I was. Their infantry did their best to shoot me, their artillery did their best to destroy my men, and their cavalry charged us, sabers drawn, but that was all part of the great game of war.

No, what commonly enraged me beyond reason were the things others might consider small: the subaltern who'd beaten a prostitute nearly to death; my own soldiers committing horrific acts after the siege of Ciudad Rodrigo; and a toad-like colonel who'd made improper and unwelcome advances to Louisa Brandon, my commander's wife. I'd relieved my temper in the first two incidents by ordering floggings, the last, by calling out the colonel in question.

Dueling had been punishable by death in the army, but I'd cheerfully risked my career and my very life meeting the colonel at dawn in the company of my seconds. The duel was never completed, because the colonel had turned coward and begged pardon at the last minute. Louisa had been furious with me. Brandon, who'd been absent at the time, had scolded me for my impetuousness, all the while giving me looks of mixed envy and admiration. I hadn't known then about the anger smoldering deep within him. The fact that I, rather than he, had defended the honor of his wife had grated on him for a very long time. It still did.

The sitting room door opened and a maid rustled in. She stopped short and stared at me. Wisps of mouse brown hair stuck out from under her mobcap, and her eyes were small and dark.

"Who are you?" she blurted.

I found her rudeness irritating, but perhaps Mr. Horne had sent her down to query me, since I'd arrived without invitation, a similar act of rudeness.

"Captain Gabriel Lacey," I said. "Here to see Mr. Horne."

She moved close to me. "You've come from Mr. Denis, then?"

Before I could decide how to answer this, she stood on tiptoe and put her lips to my ear. "It's all right. Safer this way, ain't it? I know all about it. But I don't say nothing."

Her breath smelled of onions. She took a step back and looked at me expectantly.

Questions welled up inside me, beginning with who the devil was Mr. Denis, but the old retainer returned before I could speak.

"Grace," he snapped. "Get off to the kitchens, girl."

Grace flashed a look at me then scurried from the room.

The butler became correct again. "I beg your pardon, sir. Mr. Horne has said he will speak with you. Please follow me."

I thanked him and obeyed, slightly surprised that Mr. Horne had agreed to see me at all.

When we emerged into the hall, Grace had disappeared. The retainer led me to the back of the house and up stairs that folded alongside the reception room. More dreary paintings adorned the garish wallpaper. I tried not to look at them as the butler led me to the first floor and down a short passage.

He opened a door into a study. The yellow carpet was the only cheerful note in this room; the furniture seemed haphazardly arranged, and was mismatched. A mahogany kneehole desk stood near a window, and a chaise longue had been placed before the fireplace. A wardrobe stood, incongruous and alone, against a wall, and a satinwood table with tapered legs reposed near the door. The wallpaper bore only one painting, this one of yet another wretched landscape.

Mr. Horne rose from behind the desk and came to me with hand extended. He was about six inches shorter than I was and possibly a decade past my own age. Gray streaked his black hair and lines creased the corners of his eyes. His nose was small and sharp, his mouth wide like a woman's. Whatever muscle he'd ever possessed had gone to fat, though he was soft and fleshy rather than stout. He had a double chin just hidden by the stock that covered his neck.

He shook my hand, his palm slightly moist. "How do you do, Captain? I have heard of you. You are a friend of Mr. Grenville's."

He spoke the name with relish, and I realized now why he'd admitted me. Society had discovered this spring that Lucius Grenville had befriended me. Grenville was their darling. The man had traveled the world, he was the confidant of royalty, and he possessed exquisite taste in art, wine, food, horses, architecture, and women. He was much imitated; his acquaintance, much sought. A hostess had only to say "I've got Grenville," and her gathering was certain to be a success.

Why Grenville had decided to take up my acquaintance, I did not yet understand. He was not much younger than I, but he exhibited an exuberance for life that twenty years of campaigning had drained from me. Because of him, I now received invitations to sought-after gatherings and had been placed on the guest lists of prominent hostesses. I knew the beau monde wanted only to assess me and wonder why Grenville had decided to so honor me, but I sometimes enjoyed the outings even so.

"I have his acquaintance, yes," I answered neutrally.

"It must be all to your advantage, I imagine."

I didn't like Horne's wispy voice, his taste in art, and his implication, but I said, "Indeed."

His eyes almost twinkled. "Well, what can I do for you, sir, that your connection with Mr. Grenville cannot?"

I thought about the maid I'd met downstairs. "Mr. Denis," I hazarded.

He stopped twinkling. He hesitated a long time, as if deciding whether to admit recognizing the name, then he nodded. "Of course. Of course. I understand completely. Let us sit and discuss it."

He led me to the two chairs near the fireplace. He rang for the butler, who eventually wandered in with a bowl of punch—warmed port, sugar, water, and lemon—filled glasses for us both, then departed.

I sipped from my glass and tried not to make a face. I didn't like the sweet addition, and the sugar couldn't hide the fact that the port was cheap. I reasoned that Horne must have money, because only a man of wealth could afford to reside in a house in Hanover Square, but whatever he spent his money on, it was not drink or art or interior decoration.

"So you are interested in Mr. Denis," he said once we'd made the obligatory remarks about the weather, the state of London streets, and Princess Charlotte's upcoming wedding to Leopold of Saxe-Coburg-Saalfeld. "Why did you think to come to me?"

I shrugged. "I took a chance."

He chuckled, his chins bouncing against his neckpiece. "Well, well. Excellent for you that you did. If you were not vouched for by Grenville, you know, I would not speak of it. But Grenville knows all about it, doesn't he? He is, as are you and I, a connoisseur."

I hid my distaste, amazed that this man put himself in the same sphere as the refined Grenville.

"What is your interest, eh, Lacey? Wine? artwork? or something, shall we say, softer?"

I swallowed bile. If Jane Thornton had spent five minutes with this man, I would throttle him.

I took another sip of the disgusting punch. "Young women, you mean?"

His eyes widened. "Devil a bit, but you're blunt, Captain. I suppose it is the army in you. Do not be blunt with Denis. He will throw you out on your ear."

I waited, letting him watch me. "But he can help me?"

"Oh, I believe he can. I believe he can."

So who was this Denis, I wondered. A procurer? Was he responsible for abducting Jane Thornton? Any decent gentleman would have shown me the door had I asked the question I did. But Horne sat smirking and bridling, and my temper boiled to the breaking point. I toyed with the idea of removing my sword from my walking stick and running him through then and there. Perhaps that would erase his smirk.

I willed myself to cool. I had no proof that he had Jane Thornton, not yet. But if I found it, if I found Miss Thornton in his power, I would break him.

I cleared my throat. "When?"

"I will have to write him, make an appointment, convince him to see you. He does not see just anyone, you know. Mr. Grenville's name should speed things along."

I shook my head. "Do not mention Grenville. I do not want to presume." I imagined myself having to explain to Grenville why I'd used his name to gain an appointment with a procurer. I had no right to presume upon his patronage, nor did I want to drag him into something without his knowledge.

Horne looked disappointed. "Very well, but it might take longer. Though my vouching for you will help. Give me your direction, and I will write to you."

I told him to send missives to the bakery beneath my rooms in Covent Garden. It was definitely not a fashionable address, but he did not blink.

Horne took a sip of punch, which left a red line around his lips. "You were wise to come to me. If you'd gone to Mr. Denis with your blunt ways, you would have come away the loser. He wants a delicate touch, does Mr. Denis. Who directed you to me, anyway? Was it Grenville?"

I looked him in the eye. "Jane Thornton," I said.

The words dropped into the room like bullets into a barrel.

Horne stared at me blankly. "Who?"

"You do not know her?"

"Never heard of her. Did she send you to me?"

I sat back, doubt creeping into my anger. "There was rioting today in the square. Your front windows were broken."

"Indeed, yes. We were in much confusion here."

"The riot was directed at you."

Horne raised his brows. "Do you think so? Nonsense, it could not have been personal. My political opinions are far from radical. No, it was some lunatic escaped from Bedlam stirring the crowd. My life, alas, has not been very exciting."

"You did not know the gentleman?"

"Should I have? What are you on about?"

He seemed puzzled, in truth. My fury abated enough for me to assess my position. I realized I had only the word of the maid, Alice, as to Horne's involvement in Jane's abduction. Though Horne had already irritated me in every way possible, I knew I must go carefully. A man who lived in Hanover Square would have the wherewithal to bring suit against me for slander, which could ruin me completely and not help the Thorntons one bit.

"I am on about nothing," I said. "Merely making conversation. As you observed, I am not skilled at it."

Horne laughed again. "Indeed, you are not. Perhaps you should cultivate Mr. Grenville's acquaintance more thoroughly, Captain. He sets an excellent example in manners."

*** *** ***

I went home by way of another hackney. To a captain on half-pay, the shilling-a-mile fare was dear, but rain had begun to pelt down in earnest again, and I knew I'd never make it on foot without much pain.

The driver dropped me at the top of Grimpen Lane, a tiny cul-de-sac that opened from Russel Street near Covent Garden square and paralleled Bow Street. My landlady, Mrs. Beltan, who let rooms in the narrow house to me and another tenant, kept a bake shop on the ground floor. Passersby willingly made the trip to the tiny court for her yeasty breads, which went down well with a jar of ale.

At this hour, the bake shop was shut, and the windows above it were dark. The second floor was let to an actress, the pretty Marianne Simmons, who, between roles, sometimes paraded about the Covent Garden or Drury Lane theatres, looking for a protector for a fortnight or two. But she was discreet, and I rarely saw the gentlemen who took her up.

The house had been grand a century ago, with a high-ceilinged staircase that ascended one side of the house. The staircase walls had been painted with a mural of a lush landscape that rose to a soft sweep of blue overhead. Painted clouds and slightly out-of-proportion birds dotted it. Years and grime had faded the painting, and only bits of the landscape protruded through the haze, so that candlelight fell on the branch of a tree here, a shepherdess in charming yellow there.

Tonight, I did not bother to light a candle. I groped my way up in the dark, one hand on the cool wall, the other on my walking stick. I lived on the first floor, one story above the ground floor. The rooms, one in front and one behind, had once been the house's drawing room and grand bedchamber, and the ceilings were high, a drawback in the cold of winter. Plaster arches, once carved to resemble vines twisting around pillars, crumbled a little more each day. Bits of plaster were apt to float down and land in my coffee.

When I opened the door to the front room, I found a single candle glowing there, and to my surprise, Louisa Brandon sat in my armchair.

Chapter Four

We stared at one another for the space of a moment, then I closed the door and stripped off my gloves.

"Did you not receive my message?" I asked.

She rose to her feet in a rustle of silk. "I did. But I wanted to see you."

I came to her, and she raised her cheek for a kiss. Her light perfume touched me as I pressed my lips to her smooth skin.

I wanted to grow angry at her for presuming to seek me out, but I could not. I always felt a lightening of the heart in the presence of Louisa Brandon, despite what was between her husband and myself, and after the events of this day, my heart needed soothing.

I released her hands. She'd stirred the fire, but it burned feebly, so I knelt and shoveled more precious coal into the grate. "Does your husband know you're here?" I asked as I worked.

"He knows I have gone to the opera."

I gave the fire a cynical poke. "In other words, he knows you are here."

Louisa resumed her seat with a graceful sweep of skirt. "Aloysius does not keep me, Gabriel."

I rose from the fireplace and tried to speak lightly. "I will send for coffee if you want it, but I do not guarantee you will like it. I suspect the landlady at the Gull brews it from old boots."

"I did not come for coffee," she said. "I came to talk to you."

I did not answer. I knew why she'd come.

Nineteen years before, my mentor and greatest friend, Aloysius Brandon, then a captain, had introduced me to his bride. She'd been a fresh-faced girl of twenty-one, with white blond hair and eyes of gray. Her hair was still as yellow and her eyes still as clear, but her face bore lines of grief, etched there by the loss of her three children, none of whom had lived past their first year.

My own dark hair had threads of gray in it, and my own face held lines of pain. Louisa had been there for every single one of them.

I rested my arm on the crumbling mantel and let the fire's warmth ease the ache in my leg. I waited for her to begin, but she simply watched me, while rain beat against the windows like grains of sand.

"I have had a trying afternoon, Louisa. I know you've come to reason me into accepting your husband's apology, but don't bother. I'm not yet ready."

"He wants to see you."

"The hell he does," I said.

"He wants everything the way it was before. He's told me."

Something tightened in my chest. "Well, it cannot be. I've lost my trust in him and he in me. We will never look at each other the same way again."

"You agreed to at least make a pretense."

"I agreed to too damn many things. Look at me, Louisa. My career was the only thing in my life I had done right, and now I do not even have that."

"He wants to help."

My jaw hardened. Brandon had offered his charity a few times since we'd returned to London, but the look on his face when he'd done so had enraged me further. "I'll not take help from your husband."

"You loved him once," Louisa said.

A piece of coal broke and slithered to the hearth. "I have changed. And he has done things that are unforgivable. You know that."

Louisa would try, I knew, for the rest of her life to reconcile us. But I had made a devil's bargain with Brandon to keep our mutual shame hidden, to quietly leave the army and say nothing. I'd taken half-pay so that I could have at least a meager income, but I doubted I'd ever take up my commission again. With the end of the war and so many officers redundant, few regiments would be interested in a fortyish, wounded captain. And so here I was, washed up on London's uncaring shores, a commander with no one left to command.

"Did you soil your slippers in Grimpen Lane tonight to tell me this?" I asked after a time. "You ought to have spared yourself the journey."

She spread her hands but gave me a smile. "I had to try. And my slippers are in a box in my carriage."

"Which I did not see outside. I refuse to believe your devoted coachman dropped you at the end of the lane and bolted for Brook Street. What are you up to?"

"If you'd seen my carriage and known I was here, you might have gone away until I gave up and went home."

"I might have, yes."

She looked at me. "I ought to have known you wouldn't come to the house. I have the devil of a time seeing you in private these days."

"Can you wonder why?"

"I know why, Gabriel. I just wish you wouldn't."

We shared a long look. Firelight touched her sleek hair, golden as sunshine. Her nose was slightly crooked, a fact I'd noticed the moment I'd met her.

I relented. "Forgive my temper, Louisa. As I said, I had a foul afternoon."

"You've not told me what happened to keep you from our appointment. I assumed you simply did not want to come."

I ran my hand though my hair, noting that it was growing long again. I needed to crop it. "It was too complex to explain in a note," I said.

"Then explain now, if you please. Are you all right?"

I sat on the room's remaining chair and rested my elbows on my knees. I had thought to spare her the sordid details of Thornton's shooting and Horne's household, but I would welcome Louisa's clarity of reason. So I told her. All of it.

I realized, as I related the tale, how little I'd truly learned from Horne. I'd discovered the existence of Mr. Denis, a man to whom one went when one wanted artwork or women, but I'd discovered little else. I could have demanded to search the house, but it had done Jane's father little good. The possibility also existed that Alice and Mr. Thornton had mistaken the house. Jane could have gone into number 23 or number 21, or to a house on a different side of the square altogether.

I wanted Horne to be guilty, I guessed, because I'd disliked him. But I had no more proof than Thornton had — only the evidence of an obscene faux-Egyptian frieze and a feeling in my bones.

Louisa's eyes glinted in outrage. "Lieutenant Gale ordered the poor man shot?"

"I don't know if he gave the order. The cornet who did it was young and green, and maybe he simply took it into his head to fire. Gale did not even know why he'd been sent instead of a magistrate." I paused in disgust. "He never questions an opportunity to parade about in his uniform and look important."

Louisa sat forward, her gray eyes alight. "Do you plan to continue looking for the girl?"

"I want to find her. You did not see the Thorntons, Louisa. She was all they had."

"How will you search for her?"

I had debated this while I rode home in the stale-smelling hackney. "Put up notices. Go to Bow Street. Pomeroy, one of my sergeants, became a Runner. I can pry information from him even if I can't afford to hire him."

"Offer a reward," she suggested.

I opened my hands. "I have nothing to offer. But I can question the neighbors and Horne's servants. Someone must know something about her."

Louisa moved to the edge of her seat, familiar determination on her face. "I will supply the reward. We can offer five pounds. That will be enough to bring people out of the woodwork."

"A good many people, I'd imagine."

"And give me the Thorntons' direction. I will go to them. I might be able to help them."

"They do need it." I reached forward and took her cool hand in mine. "Your kindness, Louisa, always astonishes me."

She looked at me in surprise. "Why should it? Being charitable is a duty. You must find that poor girl, Gabriel." She hesitated. "But let it end there."

"That means what, exactly?"

"You know what it means. I know what you are like."

I gave her a half-smile. "What you mean to say is, don't pursue Horne and Denis and make them believe in the wrath of God."

"Yes. Leave it be."

I released her. "They might be safe from me. They may have had nothing to do with the abduction. I have not yet decided. I saw no sign of a young woman at Horne's today, except for the maid, and I do not think she was Jane. She was definitely working class, and decidedly odd."

Louisa watched me. "If they do have something to do with it, what will you do?"

"I have not decided that either."

"There is not much you can do, even if they are guilty."

I grew annoyed. "Why are you adamant about sparing Horne? He is an oily bastard and up to something. The maid hinted as much."

"Because the last time I saw you go off with this much fervor, *that* happened." She pointed to my left knee.

It twinged, reminding me it still ached and would punish me the rest of the night for abusing it. "The last time, I was a damned fool, and I trusted your husband and his honor. That was my great mistake. I'll not make the same again."

Her voice softened. "It has been two years, Gabriel."

I'd known I could not divert her from her original purpose for long. "And every day of that two years has reminded me what I gave up. When I agreed to leave the army, I had no idea I would be living this"—I gestured to my barren rooms—"this half-existence."

Her gray eyes darkened. "Has it been that?"

"You know it has."

"You have many friends—you have the acquaintance of Mr. Grenville."

"Yes, yes, everyone believes that being smiled upon by Mr. Grenville is the same thing as being touched by God."

"But because of him, you are invited everywhere."

"Only so that the *ton* can peer at me and wonder what Grenville sees in me. And I never thought you believed that a person's worth was derived from how many invitations he receives."

Louisa smiled. "I am trying to point out that you are more than your army career. The war is over anyway. Most army men no longer have careers."

"Many of them had something to return to. I never did. That is why I followed your husband in the first place." I clenched my hand. "I believe I have done enough for the Brandon family without you forcing me into a false reconciliation."

Louisa's eyes were clearest gray, like the sea under clouds. The firelight picked out the flat gold buttons on her spencer, a jacket of almost military rigidity. "You must have loved him once," she said, "to spare his honor as you did."

"I did not do it for his honor, Louisa. I did it for yours."

Louisa stared at me in shock. "You never told me that."

I pressed my fist tightly against my thigh. "I would not have. But I want you to understand. When Brandon worried so about his honor, he never once spoke of the fact that his disgrace would also be yours. You would suffer as much or more indignity than he, and worse, you'd be pitied. Your own misery never occurred to him, and for that, I will not forgive him."

She drew a sharp breath, lips parted, and I wished I had not spoken. The last thing I wanted to do was make Louisa Brandon believe that my current state was her fault. It had been my choice. I could have sunk Brandon and taken Louisa with me to Canada. But she loved the undeserving idiot, and I couldn't have borne to hurt her.

She rose in agitation and made for the door. I reached it before she did and blocked her exit. "Where are you going?"

She would not look at me. "To the opera, as I said. I am meeting Lady Aline."

"I'll fetch your carriage and escort you."

"You need not come with me."

I thought of Jane Thornton, riding alone with her maid, stolen from a Mayfair family carriage. "The devil I'm letting you run about Covent Garden alone. I will take you. And if your husband disapproves, he can call me out. "

She looked up at me then, and I saw in her eyes not guilt, but a mixture of pity and anger. I turned from her and strode into the cold staircase hall, slamming the door behind me. The last thing I wanted from Louisa Brandon was her pity.

*** *** ***

"Josiah Horne," Milton Pomeroy wrote in careful capitals on the back of my card. "Who's he when he's at home?"

"A gentleman who lives in number 22, Hanover Square," I answered.

"Never heard of him. What's he done, exactly?"

Pomeroy had a shock of yellow hair, which he slicked back with a cheap pomade that smelled faintly of oil of turpentine. He had a square, sturdy body and clear blue eyes and a voice that could bellow across battlefields. He knew nothing of the circumstances of my departure from the Peninsula; Pomeroy himself had followed the Thirty-Fifth Light Dragoons to Waterloo, then home again, to find himself at a loss for what to do.

By accident, he'd stumbled upon the lair of a thief who had been methodically working his way through London. Pomeroy had followed him, catching him in the act. The former sergeant had made the arrest himself, as citizens had the right to do, grabbed him by the neck, and hauled him off to

Bow Street. His persistence had impressed the magistrates, and when an older Runner retired, they'd hired him on.

Pomeroy was well suited to life in the Bow Street Runners, an elite body of men who investigated crimes, tracked down wanted criminals, or searched for persons gone missing. They were allowed to keep whatever reward was posted for the criminal's capture and conviction, and Pomeroy applied himself with his ruthless sergeant's efficiency to gain as many rewards as he could. I frequently observed him tramping the streets near Covent Garden, some unfortunate in his grip, his sergeant's voice roaring above the crowd: "Now then, lad, you're for it. Show some dignity, son. Stand on your feet and face the magistrate like a man."

Constables, who often performed their duties only with reluctance, made arrests or looked into disturbances, but the Runners got the glory. If we found Jane Thornton, Pomeroy would land the reward, not me. Chasing criminals and searching for lost young women were not considered jobs for a gentleman.

Pomeroy and I stood together in the dingy hall of the Bow Street magistrate's court amid unwashed, half-sober men and women awaiting whatever judgment would be thrust upon them. I'd walked here after waiting about my rooms all the morning for a reply to a letter I'd sent to Grenville.

I wanted to pry from Grenville any information about Josiah Horne, because Grenville knew everything about everyone in London. He'd certainly be familiar with any gossip surrounding a wealthy gentleman like Horne. No reply came, to my irritation, so after an early afternoon meal of rolls from Mrs. Beltan's shop, I sought out Pomeroy instead.

My head felt thick. I'd stayed with Louisa in her box at the opera the night before until Lady Aline Carrington had arrived at the interval. That spinster had given me a good-natured grin, and I'd bowed stiffly and left Louisa in her redoubtable care. I'd gone home and taken three glasses of gin before retiring.

Despite my headache, the gin had successfully staved off the melancholia I'd sensed creeping over me. I'd suffered from the malady since my youth, and sometimes a dark depression would blanket me, depriving me of the strength even to rise from my bed. I'd learned to prevent the circumstance by immersing myself thoroughly in some interesting situation, but sometimes only gin and a night's rest would keep the darkness from me.

I made myself reflect carefully before answering Pomeroy's question about Horne. The former sergeant had the tenacity of a cardsharp, though not the wit. I did not want to set him on Horne until I had proof the man had done something.

"There was a riot before his house in Hanover Square, yesterday," I said at last. "His windows were broken."

Pomeroy peered at me with wary curiosity. "I heard of the riot. Didn't get there meself."

"What about the girl, Jane Thornton?"

Pomeroy gave a firm nod. "Her family reported her missing, that they did. Around February, I believe it was. We never found her, and the family couldn't offer much reward. Nasty business, but it goes on. Young ladies snatched off the streets. Can only be one trade for them after that, can't there, poor beggars?"

"She did not turn up as a suicide?"

"No, sir. I looked when I got your letter this morning. No Jane Thorntons fished out of the river as far as I know."

I wondered how many anonymous girls *had* been recovered from it. Or whether Jane was still lying in the Thames, her young body slowly being torn apart by tides and fishes.

I thanked Pomeroy, who agreed to notify me if he discovered anything. I pushed past the defiant or hopeless women and men waiting in the hall, and left the Bow Street house.

I made my way to a printers in the Strand off Southampton Street, and told them to print notices of a five-pound reward for anyone with information regarding a girl called Jane Thornton, who had disappeared between the Strand and Hanover Square two months before. A notice had long odds of succeeding, but it was one of the few resources I had to hand.

Louisa had given me money to fund this enterprise. I'd swallowed my pride and accepted, knowing she'd offered for the Thorntons' sake, not mine.

After I'd finished this business, I walked westward along the Strand to ask questions of the vendors who lingered near the lane I'd brought Thornton home to the day before. Most answered me with poor grace because I stood in the way of paying customers, but a few were willing to chat. An orange girl who worked there most days remembered the posh carriage that used to wait at the end of the lane for a young lady, but she could not swear to it standing there a certain day two months ago or to who got into it.

Common practice was that the coachman would pull up and wait. The young lady would come with her maid, and one of the boys who waited about to sweep the street clean for nobs would assist her into the carriage, and then the carriage would roll on. The coachman never got down, or bought an orange, or had a chat, but the lady was always polite and sometimes bought something from her or the strawberry girl.

I gave the young woman a few pennies, and walked home with an orange in my pocket.

It was growing dark again when I approached the market at Covent Garden. The rain had slackened. Carts wound through the square, and housewives thronged the stalls, looking for last-minute bargains before the vendors shut down for the evening. Strawberry sellers, street performers, beggars, pickpockets, and prostitutes thronged among them. Cries of "Sweet strawberries, buy my ripe strawberries" vied with "Knives to grind, penny a blade."

A girl sidled up to me and tucked her hand through my arm. "Hallo, Captain," she said. "Fancy a bit?"

Chapter Five

I looked down. Black Nancy, so called because of her long, dyed, blue-black hair, sauntered along beside me, grinning at me to display her crooked teeth. A few of her colleagues sashayed just beyond her.

Nance could not have been much more than sixteen, and my constant rejection of her offers was a great puzzlement to her. She pursued me with a doggedness almost comical, I suppose assuming that one day, she would eventually wear me down. In her world, she was considered to be growing elderly—in mine, she was still a child.

She wore her favorite gown today, a worn russet velvet cut to show off her generous bosom. She'd topped it with a blue wool jacket at least ten years out of date. She was good-humored, but she hunted her flats—the gentlemen she lured to her—with a ruthlessness that made Napoleon Bonaparte's campaign to conquer Russia look like a frivolous Sunday outing.

"I'm a poor man, Nance," I began, embarking on the familiar argument.

She winked. "I know. Maybe I fancies ya."

One of the other girls laughed. "He likes ladies as bathe, Nance. You ain't had a bath in a twelvemonth."

"Shut your yap, Margaret. I seen him first."

Nance tucked her arm more firmly through mine. The other girls grew bored with teasing me and dropped away, turning to likelier marks. Nance lingered, strutting along beside me, smiling with her red-painted mouth.

"Ain't seen ya in a few days, Captain. You hiding from me?"

"I've been busy." I stopped, thinking. Every day and well into the night, Nance moved all over Covent Garden, up and down the Strand, and everywhere in between. If anyone was likely to observe things there, it was she.

"What're you thinking, Captain?" she asked. "Your eyes go all dark when you do that. Do you really know how handsome you are, or are you just teasing me?"

I ignored her. "What would you say to earning a few shillings?"

Her eyes lit, and she melted against me. "Ooo, thought you'd never ask."

I frowned. "Not for that. I am looking for a coachman. Do you speak to the ones who wait at Covent Garden Theatre?"

She gave me a look of disappointment and pushed herself away. "Sometimes. They share a nip of gin when the weather's cold. What you want with one of them? You don't have a coach."

"I am looking for one in particular, a coachman for a family called Carstairs. Do you know him?"

Carstairs was the name of the family who'd sent their coach for Miss Jane Thornton and her maid that fateful afternoon, so Alice had told me.

Her look turned sly. "I could find him for ya. For a price."

"I can give you a shilling now, and another when you find him."

She smoothed the lapel of my coat. "You keep your money, Captain. I'll find this coachman to a gentry-cove. You pay me then. If I don't find him, you're out nothing." She slanted me an inquisitive look. "What you want him for?"

"I need to ask him something. You find him and tell him to visit me in my rooms."

"Now you got me curious. Ain't you going to tell me? I won't peep."

"I'd rather not until I speak with him."

Her fingers drifted down my coat. "You know how to string a girl along. I'll find him for you, Captain. Maybe you can pay me another way." She glanced at me from under her lashes.

I tried to give her a severe look. "I am old enough to be your father."

She cackled, but withdrew her hand. "You're older than me dad, but you're that much prettier."

"You are too kind. Now I am hungry. Let me go and have my dinner."

She obeyed, uncharacteristically. I felt her small hand on my backside as she departed, and I watched her dart away, her hair swinging in a black wave.

As I walked on toward the Gull at the end of the square, I surreptitiously checked my pockets to make sure that all my coins were intact.

*** *** ***

Much later that night I was wandering Cockspur Street near Charing Cross, on foot, in my regimentals.

My coat was a deep blue, with white facings and silver loops and braid. This uniform—which had cost me almost a year's pay—I had kept fine for social occasions, but on the Peninsula, I had worn another like it to ruin with sweat and mud and blood. With a carbine on my saddle and a saber at my side, I and the light and heavy dragoons had charged at everything: French cavalry, squares of French infantry we wanted to scatter, and even artillery. We'd been trained to draw our sabers at the last instant before our lines merged and met—the sound of ringing steel and the sight of a glittering forest of sabers were meant to strike fear into the enemy. But I never discovered if the enemy even noticed this spectacle, because at that very moment, they had been busy trying to shoot us, bayonet us, or slice us to pieces in return.

Now I fought a different battle, one for social acceptance and good public opinion. Both Louisa and the loathsome Horne had been right when they'd told me that recognition by Grenville was an advantage to me. Those who might not have spoken to me or even noticed the existence of an obscure gentleman from a remote corner of East Anglia—a captain who'd made no famous name for himself on the Peninsula—now sent me invitations to some of the most sought-after events in the social season.

I had been correct, too, when I'd told Louisa that they invited me only to speculate why Grenville had taken up with me.

I'd met Grenville earlier that year, at a New Year's rout at his own house. Lady Aline Carrington, a spinster who loved gossip and Mary Wollstonecraft's *Rights of Women*, in that order, had persuaded Grenville to allow her to bring me along. I had escorted her and Mrs. Brandon to the rout, and there met the famous Mr. Grenville.

Admittedly, I had not thought much of him on first glance, dismissing him as a dandy too full of his own opinion. I believe he sensed that, because he was cool to me, though he did not actually turn me out of his house.

Things changed when I discovered, quite by accident, that several of the extra staff he, or rather his butler, had hired for the evening, had planned to rob him. Grenville kept rare artwork and antiquities in his private upstairs sitting rooms; only a privileged few were ever allowed to view them. The gang of thieves, led, as it turned out, by the butler, had arranged an elaborate scheme to carry off these artworks.

I had made so bold as to approach the disdainful Grenville and tell him my suspicions. To his credit, he dropped his pose, listened to me, then asked me why the devil I thought so. I told him, because the footman's livery did not fit him.

The staff hired for the night had not been allowed anywhere but the kitchens and the grand reception rooms on the ground floor. It turned out that several had laid out Grenville's large footman, Bartholomew, and one had stolen his livery in order to access the upper floors. They supposed that great gentlemen never noticed what their own footmen looked like—they were hired by butlers, housekeepers, or stewards. True, very few people at the rout looked into the faces of the servants circulating with champagne and macaroons.

But Grenville had hand-picked his servants—though, he confided later, he had made a grave mistake with the butler. When we found Bartholomew, trussed up, sore, and most angry, in a retiring room upstairs, Grenville had been furious. We had rushed to the sitting room and caught the thieves in the act. Bartholomew had returned the blows laid on him in a fine show of pugilism, and I of course had the sword in my walking stick.

The next morning, Grenville had sent his carriage for me, inviting me to breakfast with him and to discuss the incident. Thus had begun our interesting acquaintanceship.

This acquaintanceship with Grenville gave me another advantage—he knew nearly everything about everyone in London, being a cultivator of minute gossip about his fellow human beings. He'd know about Horne, and possibly the Carstairs family, and what he did not know, he could easily discover.

The advantage of his acquaintance at the moment seemed small, because I couldn't run the devilish man to ground. I'd written, and he'd not replied, and I refused to write again pleading to be allowed to speak to him. I would not reject his friendship, but I refused to be his sycophant.

However, I needed his knowledge, so I'd accepted an invitation tonight, issued by one Colonel

Arbuthnot, who was hosting a viewing of the latest work by an up-and-coming painter called Ormondsly. I'd accepted because I had every expectation of finding Grenville there.

Grenville was foremost in the art world, and artists cultivated his every opinion. The cream of society would wait, breaths held, as Grenville would lift his quizzing glass, candlelight glinting on the gold eyepiece, and run his slow gaze down the painting. I'd seen crowds biting lips, pressing fingers to mouths, or shifting from side to side while Grenville cocked his head, pursed his lips, backed a few steps, and then started the process all over again. At last he would render his judgment—he would either pronounce the painting a work of genius, or an abysmal failure. With his words, an artist would be made, or broken. He'd be certain to be at Arbuthnot's.

Before I could leave my rooms for the outing, my upstairs neighbor, Marianne Simmons, opened my door and tripped blithely inside. "Got any snuff, Lacey?"

Unsurprised, I took up my gloves and pulled them on. "In the cupboard." I nodded at the aging chest on frame that stood against the wall next to the door. Grenville had recently given me a fine blend from his suppliers in Pall Mall, complete with ornate ebony box inlaid with mother-of-pearl. I did not take much snuff, nor did I smoke the small cigarillos or larger cheroots that many army men did. It was an odd gentleman who did not like tobacco in some form or other, but I'd always found I could take it or leave it alone.

Marianne did not even thank me. She moved to the chest and began rummaging through the drawer in which I usually kept my supply of snuff. She'd caught up her yellow ringlets in a ribbon, á la greque, a style a little out of date, but one that suited her childlike face. Her prettiness made her liked on stage and popular with gentlemen offstage. And she was certainly pretty. Even I, who'd come to know her well, could still appreciate her round bosom, her wide blue eyes, and the slender turn of her ankle.

But I'd come to see that behind her prettiness lay the hardness of a woman who had looked upon the world and found it unkind. Where Black Nancy bantered with her mates and faced her hardships with good nature, Marianne Simmons could be hard and cold and ruthless.

Knowing I was poor, she spoke to me only when she wanted to borrow coal and tapers or a few pence for tea. That is, when she did not simply help herself. She also considered me a convenient supply of the snuff she was addicted to but could not afford.

She pulled out the ebony box. "If this Grenville is so rich, why does he not simply give you money?"

When Marianne had discovered that the famous Lucius Grenville had taken me under his wing, she'd pestered me with questions about him, although she seemed to know more about him than I did. I imagined that the gentlemen she took up gossiped heavily about him.

"A gentleman does not offer money to another gentleman. "

"Bloody inconvenient for you." She clutched the box to her chest. "I suppose he does not take up with actresses?"

"He does." In fact, I'd seen him the night before at the theatre with Hermione Delgardia, the latest sensation on the Continent, who was visiting England for a time.

Marianne wrinkled her nose. "None who dance in the chorus, I'd wager. No, he sets his sights loftier, does he not?"

I ushered her out the door without asking for the box back. "I couldn't say."

I shut the door and locked it with a key. I did not miss Marianne's disappointed look that she would not be able to creep back downstairs and filch candles while I was out.

As it turned out, I would not be able to query Grenville that night about either his taste in actresses or his opinion of Josiah Horne, because he never appeared at Arbuthnot's. The party there consisted of a duke, another actress of considerably more note than Marianne, several other people I knew only slightly, Lady Aline Carrington, and a very pretty young widow called Mrs. Danbury. The latter mostly ignored me, though I attempted to include myself in any conversations around her.

I waited most of the night, but Grenville never arrived. The painting hadn't much to recommend it either.

Tired, annoyed, and at the last of my resources, I took a hackney as far as I could afford the fare and ended up in St. James's. I strolled along, hoping I'd chance upon Grenville arriving at or departing from one of his clubs, but the man remained elusive.

I'd walked slowly down to Pall Mall and onto Cockspur Street, making my weary way back toward

Covent Garden. As I approached Charing Cross, a man hailed me.

"Captain Lacey, is it? It's me, sir, remember? Sergeant-major Foster?"

I looked down into a leathery face and twinkling blue eyes. I hadn't seen the man in three years, but he'd been a mainstay of the Thirty-Fifth, rising through the ranks quickly until he attained his final one of sergeant-major. I knew he'd gone to Waterloo but had heard none of him since.

"Of course." I held out my hand.

He grinned at it, then took a step back and saluted. "Can't get used to civilian life, sir, that's a fact. Once a sergeant, always a sergeant. And you, sir? I heard you'd hurt yourself bad and came home to convalesce."

I smiled faintly and tapped my left boot with my walking stick. "I did. Still a bit stiff, but I get around all right."

"Sorry to hear it, sir. You were a fair sight on the battlefield, you were, riding hell-for-leather and screaming at us to stand and fight. An inspiration you were." His grin widened.

"I suspect 'inspiration' was the kindest of the words used."

Foster chuckled. "You always were a sharp one, sir, begging your pardon. Ah, here is someone else you might remember. Mrs. Clarke, here's our Captain Lacey."

The plump young woman who'd been peering into dark shop windows a little way away from us turned and stepped back to the sergeant-major. The polite smile I'd put on my face in expectation of a half-remembered acquaintance froze.

I hadn't known her as Mrs. Clarke; I'd known her as Janet Ingram, and seven years ago, she'd briefly been my lover. I hadn't seen her since the day she'd left the Peninsula to return to her dying sister in Essex. She smiled into my eyes and I felt the years between us slide away, as if the pain, the betrayal, the empty ache of them, had never existed.

She looked little different now than she had all those years ago and all those miles away in Portugal when she'd been a corporal's widow. Her waist was as plump, her arms as round, her hair, now adorned with a flat straw hat, as richly auburn. Her brown eyes sparkled as they had of old—the sparkle of a woman who faced life on her own terms, whatever it dealt her. Our affair had lasted only six months, but every day of those months was sharp and clear in my memory.

I don't know if Sergeant-major Foster remembered the circumstance of our acquaintance. He stood by, beaming and grinning, as if he'd played a joke on me. My throat was paper dry, and I did my damndest to smile and politely tip my hat.

"Mrs. Clarke."

She bypassed my stilted politeness with a smile that took my breath away. "Gabriel." She ran her gaze from the dark brown hair at my forehead to the tops of my boots. "I am pleased to see you, though you do not look the same. What happened to you?"

"That," I said, "is a very long story."

Sergeant-major Foster rubbed his hands. "Well, well, quite a reunion tonight. How's the colonel, Captain?"

I dragged my gaze from Janet back to Foster's tanned and smiling face. "I beg your pardon?"

"Bless me, he's forgotten already. Our commander, sir. Colonel Brandon. Your best mate."

I flinched as the truth wanted to come out, but I masked it in politeness. "The colonel is in good health. As is his wife."

Janet cocked her head, her eyes skeptical, but she said nothing.

"Pleased to hear it," Foster said. "I've had a bit of luck meself. Me old uncle passed on and it seems he had quite a bit of money put by. All came to me. I'm thinking of going to Surrey and finding a nice little house in the countryside. What do you think of that for an old sergeant, eh, Captain?"

"I think it excellent news, Sergeant-major."

"When I'm all settled in, I'll send word, and we'll have a nice long talk over old times."

"I'd like that."

My mouth spoke the expected responses, but my thoughts, and eyes, were on Janet. She looked back at me, her smile pulling me to her and telling me all I needed to know.

"We'll let the captain get on now, Mrs. Clarke," the sergeant-major was saying. He saluted again, stiff and exact. "Good night, then, sir."

I saluted back. "Good night, Sergeant-major. Mrs. Clarke." I wondered who the devil *Mr.* Clarke was, but that question would have to wait.

Janet took my offered hand, and the brief, warm pressure sent a slight tremor through me. I realized then that although I'd sent Janet away all those years ago, I'd never truly let her go.

They said their good-byes and walked on together. My feet led me the other way, toward Long Acre. After I'd gone perhaps ten paces, I stopped and looked back. Janet walked beside Foster, equal to the small man's height. She turned her head and looked back at me.

She'd always been able to tell what was in my heart. I imagined, as our gazes locked, that she could tell what beat there now.

At last she turned away, and I walked on, but the world had changed.

*** *** ***

"Gossip is flying about you, my friend," Lucius Grenville said as his butler silently presented me a goblet of French brandy. I thanked him and sipped the fine liquid, my eyes closing briefly in appreciation.

We reposed in the upstairs sitting room of Grenville's Grosvenor Street house. The façade of the house was simple, almost austere, in the style of the Adam brothers from the later years of the last century. The inside, however, was lavishly furnished. This room in particular showcased items from Grenville's travels: carpets from the Orient piled the floor, a silk tent hung overhead. Ivory and bits of Egyptian jewelry filled a curio shelf near the door, and a gold mask of some ancient Egyptian adorned the fireplace mantel. Furniture ranged from a Turkish couch to mundane straight-backed chairs set at random around the room. Real wax candles, dozens of them, brightened the gloom and softened the colors around us.

I recalled the faux Egyptian room in Horne's house and wondered if the man had tried to emulate this chamber, though it was unlikely he'd ever seen it in person. If he'd meant to imitate, he'd fallen far short of the mark.

Grenville was a slim man a few years younger than I, with dark hair that curled over his collar, and sideburns that drew to a point just below his high cheekbones. His eyes were black in his sharp face, his nose long and sloping. He could not be called a handsome man, but there were hordes of women, respectable matrons and Cyprians alike, willing to forgive him for it.

In that morning's post, I had found a letter from Grenville, informing me that his carriage would call for me at eleven o'clock to carry me to his home. I was torn between annoyance and relief. He'd solved the problem of my seeking him by him seeking me, but his abrupt habit of summoning me whenever he wished to see me grated on my pride.

Horne had also written me that he'd had an answer from Mr. Denis, and would I call at number 22 that afternoon at five o'clock? I replied, answering in the affirmative.

I'd bathed and breakfasted and thought about Janet Clarke, who'd once been Janet Ingram.

Janet had been the widow of a young infantryman, left on her own very young, without money or protection. One night I discovered a card game in progress among my men—the winner would take Janet home with him. When I broke it up, she grew angry and demanded to know where I thought she was to sleep that night, if I were so clever. I said I supposed she could stay with me. Which she did, for six months.

She never spoke much about her past, although she did tell me she'd been born in a village on the east coast of England, near Ipswich. She'd had little to look forward to, she said, except backbreaking work on a farm or being pawed at by the local lads. When young Ingram had passed through her village, boasting that he was taking the King's shilling and going off to chase the Frenchies out of Portugal, Janet had seized a chance to escape her narrow life, and left with him.

Life following the drum was hard for a woman, as I well knew, but many of them, like Louisa Brandon, developed a resilience that any general would envy. They suffered loss and deprivation and hunger and exhaustion, and every battle, successful or not, brought much death. Wives so easily became widows; many more than once.

Janet herself had developed enough resilience to survive her husband's death and declare she would become the wife or mistress of whoever won the card game. My men were annoyed with me for taking her for myself, but I ever after rejoiced that I had. During those six months I was more alive then I had been in the decade before or the years since.

We never spoke of love, or later. During the war in Spain and Portugal, you had only now, because tomorrow, a battle or a French sniper could change your life forever. When Janet received word that her sister was dying, I'd sent her home, knowing she would not come back. We did not promise to write, or to meet again, or to wait. Time had passed, but she was still beautiful. Still Janet.

Grenville held up his forefinger, which was encircled with a diamond-encrusted ring. "First, you escort Mrs. Brandon to the opera, while her husband is conspicuously absent."

I said, "Any slander regarding Mrs. Brandon will be silenced at the end of my pistol."

Grenville grinned and shook his head. "Your honor, and Mrs. Brandon's, seems to be unquestionable. Though the most malicious tried valiantly to make something of it, that story was quashed."

He lifted his second finger alongside the first. "Second, you are putting up notices about a young woman I have never heard of, which means you are involved in something interesting."

"That is almost close to the truth."

Grenville raised the next finger. "Third, you single-handedly threw a dozen cavalrymen out of Hanover Square yesterday, where they were making a nuisance of themselves. Lieutenant Gale is fuming."

"Five," I said.

"I beg your pardon?"

I took another sip of brandy. "I threw only five cavalrymen out of Hanover Square."

Chapter Six

Grenville half smiled at me, as though he thought me joking. He wore monochrome colors today, his black and white suit as understated as the exterior of his house. A ruby stick pin adorned his white cravat like a drop of blood.

I continued to sip brandy, and his eyes widened.

"Good lord, Lacey, you are serious. You astonish me."

I settled myself on his Turkish divan, stretching my left leg to ease the ache in it. "Is that why you asked me to call on you? To discover which rumors were true?"

"Only in part. The other was to get your opinion on this brandy." He held up his glass, showing amber depths glowing behind crystal facets.

"It is truly remarkable," I conceded. "An excellent choice."

"I enjoy giving you food and drink, Lacey. You do not wait to discern what I want you to say before pronouncing judgment. If something truly disgusts you, you do not hesitate to declare it so. I appreciate your honesty."

"And I thought I was only being rude," I said. "I went to view Ormondsly's new painting last night. I was surprised you did not attend."

"Were you?" Grenville leaned against the mantelpiece, crossing one polished boot over the other. "What did you think of the painting?"

I had barely noticed the damned thing. My attention had been distracted by watching for Grenville, trying to keep up my part of the conversation, and staring at the lovely Mrs. Danbury. I shrugged. "It was . . . "

He gestured, diamond rings glinting. "Exactly. Ormondsly is young and talented, but unperfected. In a few years' time, he will amount to something—if he does not murder himself with his opium eating before then. If I praise his painting now, artists of more merit will be undeservedly ignored; if I slight his work or give it lukewarm praise, his career will be over before it begins. Best to pretend I regretted I hadn't the opportunity to view the work. I will see it in private, with him there, and tell him what I truly think."

He took a sip of brandy, finished with his lecture.

I said dryly, "It must be difficult to have such power."

For a bare instant, anger sparkled in his dark eyes, and I wondered if I'd gone too far. He'd summon his large footmen to toss me out, and I hadn't had the chance to finish this excellent brandy.

Then his good humor returned. "Society does put a value on my opinions that is far higher than it is worth. To save having to think up their own opinions, I imagine."

I took a sip of the precious brandy in relief. "In truth, it is your opinion I am seeking at this moment."

"Not about that painting, surely."

"No. I want to know about a gentleman who lives in Hanover Square."

Grenville gave me an inquisitive look, and I saw a gleam of interest in his eye. I told him the tale, stopping here and there to wet my mouth with the brandy.

During the story, Grenville frowned into the depths of his glass, then, when I related Horne's mention of Denis and my speculations that Denis was a procurer, he sat down abruptly on one of the straight-backed chairs.

When I'd finished, Grenville said, "My apologies, Lacey. I was eager for gossip and had no idea you'd been involved in something so tragic."

"No matter. What do you know about Josiah Horne? The Thornton family, including Alice, believe Horne abducted Jane. Is it possible?"

Grenville rolled his glass between his palms. "I've never heard anything against the man. Horne is an MP for Sussex. He's a widower who lives quietly, and as far as I know never raises a ruckus in Parliament. Not a political hothead. I rarely see him at social gatherings, and I can't name one person who truly knows him well." He sipped brandy. "You say he did not recognize Jane Thornton's name?"

"I would swear that he'd never heard of her. But maybe he knows her by another name."

"Or he could be telling the truth."

"But Mr. Thornton and Alice saw Jane go into the house."

"They may have mistaken the house," Grenville pointed out. "Or Horne may not have known she'd come there at all. Perhaps her meeting was with someone else—the butler, the valet, the maid you saw."

"Why are you trying to absolve him? He may have abducted the girl and ruined her. If she is not still with him, she will have nowhere to go but into a brothel or the streets."

Grenville lifted his hand. "Calm yourself, Lacey. I am merely pointing out possibilities. I know you disliked the man, and I cannot blame you for that if what you say is true. But before sending in the magistrate, you should first discover if he ever truly saw the girl at all."

I drummed my fingers on the table beside me. "Louisa Brandon said as much. I have an unfortunately rash temper."

"So I have heard. Did you know, a colonel who frequents my club told me you'd once put a pistol to the head of another colonel and demanded he rescind one of his orders." He regarded me with curiosity, as though hoping I'd regale him with the entire story.

"An order that would have killed all of my men. I would not sacrifice them so that he might claim courage."

I recalled that blustery winter day on the battlefield in Portugal, when my blood had boiled hot and a cavalry colonel had wet himself because he'd thought me insane enough to pull the trigger. Fortunately, the staff officers knew of the man's incompetence, and so I'd avoided an incident that could have wrecked my career. Watching my temper rise dismayed me—my vision would become clear and sharp, and a course of action, direct and plain, would present itself to me. Right and wrong became suddenly vivid; a complex situation would resolve into one bright point. Sometimes my rages cut right to the heart of a matter; at others, they only made things worse. Unfortunately, I could not always tell which was which.

Grenville rose and paced to the fireplace. "Speaking of your rashness, I am going to give you a bit of advice concerning this James Denis." He faced me. "Have nothing to do with him. Pursue Horne if you must, but leave Denis out of it."

I lifted my brows. "Why? Who is Denis?"

Grenville hesitated, while shadows played on his angular face. "James Denis is a dangerous man to know. Please take my word for it."

He wanted me to stop asking questions, which ensured that I simply wanted to ask more. "If that is so, why have I never heard of him?"

Grenville shrugged. "He lives quietly."

"So does Horne, you say."

Grenville regarded me uncomfortably, as though wanting to deny he had the information I wanted. Then he gave a resigned sigh and set his crystal glass on the mantelpiece.

"I do not know who James Denis truly is," he said. "His father is rumored to have been a footman and his mother a lady of quality. I'm not certain I believe that. But despite his origins, Denis is now one of the wealthiest men in England. Dukes know him. The Prince Regent has no doubt hired him; you know

what a mania the Prince has for art, especially when
he's told the thing in question is impossible to
acquire. I've asked the Prince point blank if he used
Denis to find some of his collection, but he only gave
me that coy look he has when he's trying to be
clever."

I'd never met the Prince Regent or seen him closer
than from the back of a crowd that watched his coach
travel down Pall Mall. The last time I'd spied his
coach passing, the crowd had booed him and mud
had splattered the side of his garish yellow carriage.
The Regent's daughter, Princess Charlotte, was
wildly popular, but the profligate Regent was barely
tolerated. Grenville had told me tales of dining at
Carleton House—on one occasion the dining table
had been surrounded by a sparkling trough of water,
through which fish had swum. Grenville had shaken
his head while relating the anecdote, his expression
pained.

"Well," I said. "I will meet Denis soon and
discover what he is for myself. Horne wrote that he'd
had an answer to our request for an appointment."

Grenville turned swiftly, eyes wide. "No, Lacey,
don't go, not even for curiosity's sake. Denis is
dangerous. Leave him alone."

The directive, of course, only fueled my
determination. "Explain to me what he is then. A
procurer? A smuggler?"

Grenville shook his head. "I wish I knew. The
man is elusive, even to someone as bothersome as
me. I know that he has procurers and smugglers
dancing his bidding. He obtains things, things that
might be out of reach of the ordinary person. He is
able to work seeming miracles to get exactly what

his, shall we say, *customer,* wants." Grenville paced again. "Whenever he expresses interest in a bill or discussion in Parliament, funnily enough, the vote always seems to coincide with his interests. But I have never heard that he actually controls anyone. You never hear anything directly against Denis. He is that discreet."

"Discreet enough so that his customer might not know the name of the young woman abducted for him?"

Grenville paced the length of the hearth rug then turned to me. "Lacey, I beg you, do not openly accuse James Denis of abducting Miss Thornton. You would never get out again."

"You speak as though you know him well. Does he have the honor of your acquaintance?"

Grenville colored. "No. I was a—customer—once."

The candle beside me guttered and died in a spattering of wax. "Were you, indeed? This sounds interesting."

"Yes. And, like you, I want to know all about a person before I commit myself. I made it my business to find out about Denis, and I did not like what I found."

"Yet, you hired him."

Grenville tapped his heel against a pattern of the rug. "I had no choice. I wanted a particular painting that was in France during the war. In Bonaparte's personal collection, as a matter of fact. It belonged to an exiled French aristocrat, painted for him specially, he told me, and the man had tried everything to get it back." Grenville continued to study the carpet. "I offered to help him, and I had heard of Denis. I hired Denis to find and deliver the painting. Denis did."

"Damned resourceful of him. How did he manage it?"

"I have no idea. And I never asked. The price was, as you might expect, very high."

For some reason, I suddenly thought of the screen that Colonel Brandon had brought home with him from Spain. Its three panels depicted scenes of the holy family, done in gold leaf and ebony. I had no idea where he'd obtained it, but it was very old, and he prized it above all possessions. Louisa told me he'd set it in his private sitting room behind his bedchamber, a room few were allowed to enter. I'd always wondered where he'd stumbled upon the thing, which looked valuable beyond compare. I wondered now if he'd obtained it from someone like Denis.

I pried my fingers apart. "So that is why Horne intimated that you knew all about Denis."

Grenville shook his head. "He did not hear such a thing from Denis. Or from me. I imagine my French acquaintance flapped his tongue. It might explain why he departed so suddenly for France." He hesitated, his dark brows lowered. "When you attend this appointment with Denis, I will accompany you."

I didn't want that. Grenville would want to handle everything very discreetly, while I would prefer to take Denis by the coat and shake him until I received the information I needed. Grenville would also, as was his habit, take over the conversation. I simply gave him a nod and decided I would not bother to mention the time and day of my appointment when I learned it.

Grenville snatched up his glass and crossed the room to the brandy decanter. "You've piqued my interest in this situation anyway, Lacey. Raise the reward to ten guineas. I will supply it; Mrs. Brandon can save her pin money. And advertise in newspapers. If Miss Thornton has gone to another protector, that protector might believe confessing her whereabouts is worth ten guineas. My carriage, also, will be at your disposal for dashing about London questioning people."

He filled his glass, then came to me and poured more brandy into mine.

"Why are you so interested in sparing me shillings?" I asked.

He shrugged as he returned the decanter to the exact center of the table. "The last time I was in a hackney, it smelled as through the previous passenger had relieved himself in the corner. You can't pretend that is preferable to my rig."

I had to shake my head. "I would think you'd want to stay out of such a sordid business."

He turned to me, hands restlessly cradling his glass. "I will tell you a secret, Lacey. The answer to why I traipse about the world like a vagabond and come home with these interesting trinkets. The reason I elbowed my way to the top of society and take mistresses of exotic and unusual backgrounds."

I finished for him. "Because you are hopelessly bored."

Grenville shot me a look of surprise and then laughed. "Am I so readable?"

"It is what I would do, if I had the means."

"You have uncanny perception, you know, Lacey. I discovered that shortly after I met you. I also discovered that anything you are involved in is certain to be interesting. That is why I brought you here and am plying you with brandy. I am making a rude attempt to satisfy my curiosity."

"So I thought."

I knew full well that Grenville's interest in me was entirely selfish. He sought to entertain himself, and paid me back by smoothing my way into a society that would normally have ignored me. I supposed I should be grateful, but what I mostly felt was irritation.

Colonel Brandon had been another man who'd smoothed my way for me, in this case, into an army commission when I'd had no money to purchase it. He'd convinced me to volunteer as an officer, which I could do as the son of a gentleman, and his influence slid me into the rank of cornet when one came open. I'd clawed my own way up the next few ranks to captain, moving more slowly than others because of my lack of wealth, but Brandon's influence, and money, certainly had helped me.

And then, in the end, he had completely and utterly betrayed me. The look on his face when I'd returned from the mission in which I was to have died had forever shattered any remnant of love and respect between us. Poor Louisa, blaming herself, had tried to sow the seeds of forgiveness, but neither of us had let her.

Small wonder that I never wanted to depend upon anyone again. I barely knew Grenville, despite the interesting circumstances of our first meeting. He must have the acquaintance of scores of officers from the Peninsular campaign, not to mention Waterloo, but he'd fixed his interest upon me.

Grenville confirmed my thoughts even as I had them. "I admit that I collect people," he said, "much as I collect art. I am interested in people like you, people who have lived. I've only played at living."

"You have explored Africa and much of the Amazon," I reminded him.

"A rich man relieving his ennui. You, on the other hand, have lived your life."

I warmed the goblet in my palm. "Yet, I would gladly trade with you."

Grenville shook his head. "You would not, in truth. I have done things that I regret."

"As have all of us."

Grenville fixed an intense gaze on me, but I could see that he saw something beyond me. "Have you?"

I simply drank my brandy. Grenville did not know the half of what I regretted, and I was not going to tell him.

*** *** ***

The afternoon had clouded over, and by the time I reached Hanover Square for my appointment with Horne, the sky was dark, rain spattering in little droplets. I descended from the hackney and knocked on the door, hoping the butler would hasten to answer.

I'd decided after speaking with Grenville to ask Horne point blank about Jane Thornton and her maid. If he were innocent, then he would have nothing to fear from me—I'd apologize and leave him alone. If he were not innocent, I'd put him to the question until I knew Jane's whereabouts. If she were in his house, I'd get her out of it, using violence if necessary. If she were elsewhere, I'd damn well make the man take me to her.

I was tired of polite evasiveness and roundabout methods. It was my nature to act. If I offended the man and he called me out, then he did. I'd borrow a pistol from Grenville and let Horne shoot at me while I fired into the air. If he were innocent, I'd deserve it.

The butler took his time. I plied the knocker again.

Instead of the butler, a young footman yanked open the door and peered out at me. I handed him my card. He looked me up and down, inspected my drab suit, then ushered me inside to the dim hall.

The hooknose butler entered from the back of the house as the footman took my hat and gloves. "Captain. Welcome, sir. My master is expecting you. I will inform him of your arrival."

He limped away and mounted the stairs. The footman led me to the same reception room with the same annoying Egyptian drawings and the same clumsy paintings. I did not sit down.

The footman moved to stir the fire. He shot me a few eager looks over his shoulder before he wet his lips and spoke. "Were you in the war, sir? At Waterloo?"

I was asked that often, but no. Brandon and I had chosen semiretirement before Napoleon's escape and return to power in 1815. While the last, glorious battle had been waging in Belgium, we'd remained in London, learning of the outcome only when the guns in St. James's Park had fired to celebrate the victory. "Not Waterloo," I answered. "The Peninsular campaign."

The footman grinned in delight. Already, the horrors of the war were fading, the brutal battles of

Vitoria, Salamanca, and Albuera had becoming distant and romantic tales.

"What regiment, sir?"

"Thirty-Fifth Light."

"Aye, sir? My brother was in the Seventh Hussars. He was batman to a colonel. The colonel died. Shot out of the saddle. My brother was that broken up. Narrowly missed ending up a Frog prisoner."

"My condolences for his loss," I said.

"I wanted to go. But I was only fifteen, and me ma wouldn't hear of it. What was to happen to her if both her sons died over in foreign parts? she wanted to know. So I stayed. My brother came back all right, so she worried for nothing."

My own father had forbidden me to go into the army; the fact that he could not afford a commission for me had been moot. We'd had day-and-night screaming rows about it, which included him cuffing me or beating me with a stick when I couldn't elude him. I'd no money of my own for a commission either, and I'd assumed I had no hope. Then, just after my twentieth birthday, I'd met Aloysius Brandon, who convinced me to come with him to India and volunteer.

Brandon had been a compelling man in those days and our friendship had deepened quickly. So I'd turned my back on my father and gone with Brandon to the King's army. I heard of my father's death the very day I'd followed Arthur Wellesley, the brilliant general who was to become the Duke of Wellington, into Talavera, in Spain. The next morning, I'd been promoted from lieutenant to captain.

We heard the butler returning, but he was running, clattering down the stairs. Somewhere upstairs, a woman began screaming.

The footman with his young exuberance gained the hall before I could. The butler swayed on the stairs above us, clutching the rail, his face gray. His gaze fixed on me and clung for a moment, then he doubled over and vomited onto the polished floor.

The screaming went on, winding down to wails of despair. Footsteps sounded on the lower stairs—the rest of the staff emerging from the kitchens to see what was the matter.

The footman charged past me and up the stairs. I came behind, my injured leg slowing me. On the first floor, in the doorway of the study in which I'd met Horne the day before, huddled the maid called Grace. Her cap had fallen from her brown hair, and her face was blotched with weeping.

The footman looked past her into the room, and his face drained of color.

The pretty yellow carpet had been ruined. A huge brown stain marred it, spreading from under the body of Josiah Horne. He lay face up, his eyes wide, his mouth frozen in a grimace of horror. The hilt of a knife protruded from the center of his chest, and a small circle of blood stained his ivory waistcoat.

But that wound had not made the dull brown wave that encompassed most of the carpet. Horne's trousers had been wrenched opened and his testicles sheared from his body.

Chapter Seven

The stink of blood and death coated the stuffy room. I pushed past the footman and made for the window, taking care to step only where the carpet was still yellow. I unlatched and opened the window onto the garden letting in the chill wind and rain. I gulped the cold air in relief.

When I turned back, Grace was clinging to the doorframe, sobbing wretchedly.

"Take her out," I told the footman.

The footman tried to coax Grace to her feet, but she remained in a heap, weeping. The footman grasped her under the arms and hauled her bodily up and away.

I made my way back across the room, barely feeling my stiff knee, my thoughts tumbling. In these moments of shock, when the world blurred for others, it became crystal clear for me. I saw the room with sharp edges, every piece of furniture, every shadow from the tiny fire, every fiber of carpet soaked with blood.

Horne's face was a mask of surprise. His mouth was wide open, his brown eyes round. He'd died without struggle, I could see from the way his hands lay open at his side. His fingers were curled slightly, not raised in defense. His testicles, bloody and disgusting, rested on the carpet between his spraddled legs. The knife in his chest must not have killed him instantly, but the mutilation of his body had spilled his life onto the bright yellow carpet.

I turned away, like a man caught in a dream, and found the butler in the hall. He leaned against a wall, his handkerchief to his mouth, his breathing shallow.

Here was one whose world blurred with shock; he'd be useless to me. My long habit of command seeped through me, and I straightened my shoulders. "Send someone for a constable. And a doctor. Keep the others from coming in."

The footman trotted back to us from the stair, his young eyes wide and excited. "A doctor's not going to do him any good. He's dead, ain't he?"

"A doctor can tell us how long he's been dead," I said.

"Can he, sir? Must have been a long time. Would have to be for all that blood to dry, wouldn't it?"

The butler whimpered, and I snapped my attention back to him. "When was the last time you saw Mr. Horne?"

He moved his handkerchief a fraction. "This morning, sir. In this very room."

"This morning? It is five o'clock. You did not speak to him all day?"

"He told me he did not want to be disturbed, sir."

"Was that usual?"

The footman nodded. "Aye, on account of his ladies. We were never to come nigh him when he was with his ladies. No matter what."

"Shut up," the butler wheezed.

"We weren't supposed to know. He kept it quiet like. But we knew."

I kept my gaze on the butler. "So you thought nothing of it when you never saw him from that moment to this?"

Both servants shook their heads.

I scanned the room again. An odd place for Horne to have a liaison. The desk was littered with books and papers and the chaise was too narrow to be comfortable. Odd places could be exciting, but Horne was older than I was, his body thickset. A man of his stature would long for a deep featherbed for anything more than a playful kiss.

I looked again at the wardrobe. It was of cheap mahogany, like the rest of the furniture, but its presence bothered me.

I went to it, again keeping to the edges of the carpet. It sported two keyholes, double locks like misshapen eyes. I ran my hand down the seam between the doors. Near the locks, the crack between the doors was nicked and chipped, small gouges in the finish.

I pulled on the handles. The doors did not move.

"Do you have a key for this?"

In the hall, the butler said, "I have keys for all the locks."

"Bring it to me."

Keys jingled as the butler sorted them in his shaking fingers. The footman carried one across the room and laid it in my outstretched hand.

I inserted the small key into one of the locks and pulled open the door. It swung on its hinges, noiseless as mist, and I stopped in shock when I saw what was inside.

Inside the wardrobe lay a young woman, her knees pulled against her chest, her hands twisted behind her back and tied. She lay motionlessly, her eyes closed, her pale lids waxen. A fall of yellow hair half hid her bruised face, and the brown tips of her breasts pressed the opaque fabric of a chemise.

I felt the footman's breath on my shoulder. "My God, sir."

I knelt and touched the girl's bare neck. Her skin was cool, but her pulse beat under my fingers.

"Who is she?" I demanded.

The footman stammered. "That's Aimee. I thought she'd gone."

Aimee. My heart beat thick and fast. *Jane Thornton's maid.* "Where is the other girl? Where is Jane?"

"Don't know any Jane."

"Damn you, the young woman she came here with."

The footman took a step back, dark eyes bewildered. "The girl she came with weren't Jane. She was Lily."

"Where is she?"

"Don't know, sir. She's gone."

I drew a short knife from my pocket. The footman looked at me in alarm, but I turned away and gently cut the cords that bound the girl's hands.

I rose to my feet. "Lift her."

"Sir?"

"I cannot carry her. You must. Is there a chamber we can take her to?"

"I suppose a guest chamber, sir, but Mr. Bremer's got the keys."

I assumed that Mr. Bremer was the butler. I glanced at the hall, but he'd crept away while we stared at Aimee.

"I'll find Bremer him. When did this girl named Lily leave?"

The footman's brow wrinkled under his white wig. "Oh, weeks ago it was now."

"Where did she go?"

He looked close to tears. "I don't know, sir."

I let it go. "Take her to a guest chamber. I'll fetch Bremer."

I left him lifting the girl in his beefy arms, looking down at her in undisguised awe. I found Bremer in the kitchen. He sat at a table, his head in his hands, the other staff gathered around him. They looked up at me, white-faced and anxious, while Grace's wails echoed from the dark doorway beyond.

A tall and bony woman, with an alert, almost handsome face, her apron dusted with flour, stepped in front of me. "Who are you?"

I ignored her and went to Bremer. "I need your keys."

He unhooked them from his belt and handed them to me in silence, the keys jangling as his fingers shook.

I pointed at a boy who leaned against a wall. "You. Run and get a constable. Then go to Bow Street and ask for Pomeroy. Tell him Captain Lacey sent you."

They all stared at me, and I clapped my hand around the keys. "Now."

The boy turned and banged his way out the scullery door into the rain. His thin legs flashed by the high window as he ran up the outside stairs.

The servants continued to stare at me as I turned my back and tramped away. Behind me, Bremer began to weep.

I found the footman waiting before a door in the upper hall. The young woman lay insensibly in his arms, her hair tangled on his chest. His wig had been knocked askew, which made him look still younger than his thick arms suggested—a child's frightened face on a man's body. The footman seemed unsurprised that I'd assumed command, and waited patiently for his next order.

The room I unlocked was neat and cheerful, the first one with those qualities I'd seen in this house. I told the footman to lay the girl on the bed's embroidered white counterpane and to start the fire.

I shook out the quilt that lay at the bottom of the bed and draped it over the girl. She lay in a swoon, but her breathing was better, her chest rising and falling evenly, as though she were simply asleep. The footman watched her, a mixture of pity and fascination in his eyes.

"Stoke the fire well," I told him. "And tell the other maid to come up and sit here with her. Not Grace."

The footman dragged his gaze from Aimee. "You want Hetty, sir? I'll fetch her."

"In a moment."

I limped out of the room and back to the study. I closed the door on the grisly scene and locked it with Bremer's keys. When I returned to the bedroom, the footman was tossing heaping shovelfuls of coal onto the grate one-handed. He'd built the fire to roaring, and heat seeped into the room.

For a moment, I wanted to sink to my knees and, like Bremer, press my hands to my head. I had come here to get the truth from Horne, by violence if necessary, but someone had beaten me to it. Someone had stabbed him through the heart, cheerfully perhaps. And then, not satisfied with that, the killer had mutilated him.

I could almost understand the murder. Horne was disgusting and self-satisfied, and by all evidence, he'd beaten this young woman and kept her tied and locked in a wardrobe. But what the murderer had done afterward lodged bile in my throat. That had been an act of anger, of vengeance, an act as disgusting as Horne had been himself.

Behind my disgust, my clear thoughts kept working to piece together what had happened. I felt a sudden need to order everything in my mind before Pomeroy arrived, though I couldn't have told myself why. It was Pomeroy's job to discover the culprit and arrest him, not mine.

I looked at the footman. "What is your name?"

He turned from the fireplace, still on his knees. "John, sir. I was christened Daniel, but gents mostly want a John or a Henry on their doors."

"If your master told Bremer he was not to be disturbed, why was Grace there?"

John thought a moment. "Sometimes he had Grace wait on him. When he wouldn't have us."

I remembered Grace kneeling in the doorway, staring in anguish at Horne's body in the stain of brown blood. "Was she there before or after Bremer opened the door?"

He looked confused. "I don't know, sir. I was with you."

I let that drop. "What is your job here? To stand by the front door?"

"Aye, sir. From the morning until I locks it last thing of the day. If a gent comes to the door what has business with the master, I put him in the reception room and give his card to Mr. Bremer. If it's someone as has no right to be here, I chuck him out."

"But you are not on the door all the time, are you?"

He looked confused. "Yes, I am."

"When I arrived yesterday, Mr. Bremer let me in. Not you."

"Oh. Well, I'm really the only man here, ain't I? Except Mr. Bremer, and he's too old. I help Hetty and Gracie carry the coal buckets up and down the stairs. Or a load of wood, or a tub of water to the scullery. No one else is big enough."

"So all day you or Mr. Bremer opens the door to visitors. No one comes in without you knowing it."

"No, sir."

"Who came today?"

His eyes widened. "Do you mean someone who came today might have stuck the master?"

"It is possible. Think back. Who came to visit?"

John's face screwed up with effort. "Well, there was one gent, thin, dark haired. You'll have to ask Mr. Bremer who he was. I was helping cook lug in the potatoes for dinner. I let the gent out."

"When was that?"

John wiped his sweating forehead on his arm, dislodging his footman's white wig and revealing cropped dark hair beneath. "Oh, maybe half past two."

"Was he the only visitor the entire day?"

"Excepting yourself, sir."

"What about the girl, Aimee? You said you'd thought she'd gone."

His gaze strayed to the bed. "Aye, sir. Weeks ago now. Her and Lily, they went."

"You saw them go?"

He thought. "No. The master said they were gone. Gracie was that glad. She had to wait on them. She didn't like them."

"The girl, Lily. Are you certain that was her name?"

"The master said it was."

"What did she say it was?"

He looked worried. "She never said. I never went nigh her. Wasn't allowed, was I?"

"Did he tell you why they went away?"

John shook his head. "They just went."

I leaned on my walking stick. John watched me with an anxious expression on his shiny face. I didn't know if his worry meant that he was lying or whether he simply waited for another difficult question.

"Go fetch Hetty. If you remember anything else, please tell me."

"Yes, sir."

John rose to his towering height and lumbered from the room.

The air had warmed, and the cold tension eased from my muscles a bit. I pulled a chair close to the bed and sat down. I itched to rouse the girl to ask her questions, but she was breathing evenly, sleeping well. Had Horne tied her and put her in the wardrobe before the murderer came, or had the murderer done that? Either way, Aimee might have seen something, heard something, enough to tell us who had killed the man in the library.

Pity moved me to let her rest. I had found at least one of the girls, and she still lived. Bruises, dark and angry, threaded the translucent skin on her face, throat and chest. Fury beat through me at the sight of them, fury at Horne and the murderer both. Dead, Horne could made no recompense for what he'd done, and I had a deep and aching need to make him pay. The murder had robbed me of that satisfaction.

The door opened and a maid I had seen in the servants' hall came in. Dark hair showed through the white cotton of her cap, but her face was not young. It was an intelligent face, with a sharp nose and rather narrow eyes.

She looked at the pale, sleeping girl on the bed, and her nostrils pinched.

"You sent for me, sir."

"Yes. Hetty, is it?"

"Yes, sir. I'm downstairs maid. And I help cook."

I gestured to the bed and kept my voice low. "Did you know that this young lady was in the house?"

"She's not a young lady, sir. And I didn't know until John told me a moment ago. I thought she'd gone."

I clamped down on my anger at her self-righteousness. "Do you remember when she first came here? She came with another girl, the girl Mr. Horne called Lily."

"Oh, yes, I remember."

"Was Lily the girl's real name?"

"How should I know, sir? They give themselves names, don't they?"

My fingers curled around the head of my walking stick. "How did they arrive here in the first place, Hetty? In a carriage?"

"I don't know, sir, I never saw. I was out shopping for cook the day they came. When I came home, cook was in a foul temper and said we had to make up for more people. She sent me right out again for more vegetables. She was that glad when they left again. What do you want to know, for?"

I held on to my patience. "Did you see them go?"

"I never did. But the master said they'd gone. Both of them."

"You knew why they'd come in the first place."

Hetty flushed. "Of course I did, sir. But it's not my place to say anything, is it? If the master wants to keep young ladies about, it's not my business."

"But you didn't like it," I prodded.

"No, sir. John laughs and says the master has lively appetites. But it's wrong, isn't it? John says I read too many pamphlets."

"Yet you stay," I pointed out.

Her eyes flickered. "It's a good place, sir. Hard to get another place with wages so good. And Lily spoke kind, for what she was."

"Would it surprise you to learn that Lily was in truth a respectable gentleman's daughter, brought here against her will?"

Hetty looked doubtful. "Indeed, sir, it would surprise me very much. I thought she was an actress or dancer or some such. Are you sure? She never tried to run away."

No, I wasn't sure. I wasn't sure of anything.

"Would you have stayed if you had known she was really a respectable young lady?"

Her voice dropped a notch. "I'm ashamed to say I don't know, sir. The wages is high."

I tapped my fingers on my walking stick. "If Mr. Horne was so generous, and this is such a large house, why aren't there more of you? You said you have to double as the cook's assistant."

Hetty shrugged. "Sometimes there's more. They come and go. Cook and Mr. Bremer, they've been here forever. I've been here the longest after that, then John, then Grace, then Mr. Horne's valet, Marcel. He's French. Henry—he's the boot boy—has only been here a sixmonth. He'll not last long, though. He doesn't like it." Her face grew mournful. "But we're all out of a place, aren't we, sir? Now that the master is gone. He's truly dead?"

I gave a short nod. "He is most definitely dead. Did anyone go upstairs to the master's chambers today, Hetty? After he gave orders not to be disturbed?"

She thought a moment. "Mr. Bremer and Grace. They're the only ones he lets. No one else. But most of the afternoon I was in the kitchens with cook and Henry, so I don't know who all went up and down in the front."

So Bremer had already lied. He'd told me he hadn't seen Horne since Horne gave orders not to be disturbed.

I said, "But there was a visitor earlier in the day. A thin gentleman. Bremer let him in."

Hetty nodded. "Oh yes, sir. I served him port in the downstairs sitting room. Mr. Bremer took him upstairs."

"Do you know who this gentleman was?"

"Yes, Mr. Bremer told me. He was a gentleman called Mr. Denis. A friend of the master's, Mr. Bremer said."

Chapter Eight

"Bury me cold," the constable breathed. "Look what they done to the poor bugger."

The constable for the parish, a round-faced young man, blacksmith by trade, stood in the doorway of the study and stared at the carnage within.

I sat at the kneehole desk near the window, leafing through Horne's collection of calling cards. Pomeroy planted his fists on his hips and surveyed the dead body, the pool of blood, and me rifling the desk.

"Did you find him, Captain?"

I didn't look up. "The butler found him. I was in the reception room. Bremer rushed down and fetched me."

"He's the gent you were asking me about, ain't he? Friend of yours? "

I chose my words with care. "He is a friend of a friend. I called to pay my respects."

"To be sure. And you found him like this."

"The butler found him," I repeated. "He fetched me, and I followed him upstairs. Horne was lying as you see him now."

Pomeroy advanced to the edge of the stain, pudgy fingers stroking his chin. "Bled like a pig, didn't he? Took a while for that lot to dry, though, wouldn't you say? Crows would be at him by now."

I said, "The butler and footman say Mr. Horne came into this room this morning and asked not to be disturbed. After that—" I spread my hands, indicating anything could have happened after that.

"Well, I'll be questioning the butler and footman, to be sure. Now, if you don't mind, sir, the constable and I will be at it."

I palmed the card of Mr. James Denis, slid it into my pocket, and closed the card box. "Carry on, Sergeant."

I crossed the room to the door and went out. The constable remained in the hall, staring at the body, his pasty face shiny with sweat.

I said kindly, "The footman can fetch you brandy or port."

"Them are the devil's drinks, sir."

Dear God, A London constable who was a Methodist. I silently wished him luck.

As I neared the staircase, Hetty put her mob-capped head out of the bedroom. "She's awake, sir. I told her the master was dead. She's a bit bewildered by it all."

I glanced back at the study, but Pomeroy and the constable were not watching me. Pomeroy's loud and cheerful tones floated down the hall. I motioned Hetty back inside the room, then stepped in quietly and shut the door.

The yellow-haired girl watched me from the bed, her dark eyes pools of confusion.

"Aimee?"

Her voice was a shallow whisper. "Yes."

I sat down in the chair I'd pulled close to the bed, and she flinched and closed her eyes.

"I'll not hurt you, Aimee," I said in the gentlest voice I could. "I've come from the Thorntons."

Aimee's face relaxed, and after a moment or two, her eyes drifted open. She had brown eyes, but the brown was swallowed up by the black of her pupils. I read shock there, and hurt so deep I could not reach it.

"My name is Captain Lacey," I said. "I've come to find you and Jane. Do you know where Jane is?"

Tears filled her eyes and streaked silently down her cheeks. "No, sir. She's gone. He sent her away."

"Do you mean Horne? Where did he send her?"

Aimee shook her head against the pillow. "He wouldn't tell me, sir, no matter how much I begged."

"I'm going to find her," I said.

Aimee's eyes remained hopeless.

I suddenly hated Josiah Horne with all my strength. I no longer gave a damn who had killed him, and I raged at them all—the nervous Bremer, the oblivious John, the self-righteous Hetty. They'd known their master for what he was, they'd known of Jane and Aimee, and yet they stayed and said nothing, silently consenting to what he did.

"I've sent for Alice," I said. "Do you remember Alice, the Thorntons' maid? I will stay until she comes."

Aimee nodded faintly and closed her eyes.

I rose, trembling with anger and helpless frustration. Hetty looked up, but I said nothing to her as I let myself out of the room, closing the door on the ruined creature on the bed.

*** *** ***

I searched for Bremer again and found him in the servants' hall. He'd moved to the long table and held a tumbler of clear liquid between his shaking hands. His eyes had lost focus. "I've never seen the like in all my days."

I had seen worse in the army, acts of atrocity not always committed by the enemy, but I did not tell him so.

I sat down next to Bremer, noting that the room boasted a comfortable fire and a sofa under the window. I'd discovered what Horne had spent his money on—high wages and comfortable furnishings for servants who would stay with him no matter what crimes he committed.

"The girl I found in the wardrobe," I said. "You know who she is."

Bremer exhaled a volume of gin-scented breath. "She's nobody, sir. Just a maid."

I resisted the urge to shove him off the chair. "When her mistress left, she stayed behind. How long ago did the other girl, Lily, leave?"

Bremer searched for inspiration in his glass. "Three weeks gone now."

I stared at him. "Three weeks? How could John and Hetty not know that Aimee hadn't left with her mistress? Aimee had to eat, to sleep somewhere. Are you claiming that half the household did not know your master kept Aimee here for three weeks?"

Bremer shrugged. "He had her in an upstairs room, where no one is allowed to go but me."

"And Grace."

"And Grace. Mr. Horne had to have someone see to her, didn't he? So Grace brought her meals and cared for her."

"And told no one? No whispering it to Hetty or John, no games that she knew something they did not?"

"Indeed, no, sir. Grace knows her place. He pays her extra wages. And me."

"The cook must have known," I said. "She would have to prepare meals."

Bremer shook his head. "Grace was sent out for her meals, and took them up to her. And the door to her room was always locked, and only I and Mr. Horne had the keys."

Damn the man. I had been angry with Hetty, but she truly had not known the extent of her master's crimes. Bremer had openly helped him. "And Aimee never raised an outcry? A healthy, young girl locked up in a room would make some noise. She would bang on the door or shout out of the window."

"Mr. Horne gave her opium to keep her quiet."

I sprang up, no longer able to sit. Here was Bremer, warmed by a good fire with a thick carpet under his feet, drinking from a crystal tumbler, while a young woman was fed opium and beaten and raped.

"Why did Horne send Lily away?"

"I don't know, sir."

"You do know, damn you. Tell me."

"I think because he'd got her belly-full."

I grabbed Bremer's tumbler from his hands and smashed it to the floor. "And you stood by. You knew what he was and what he did, and you said nothing. You did not tell the girl's family, or the magistrates, or anyone. You let him ruin a girl and her maid, right before your eyes."

Bremer choked out, "He paid good wages, sir."

I grabbed Bremer by his coat and hauled him onto the fine veneer of the table. "Damn your wages. He destroyed an entire family. I hope *you* murdered him, because it would prove you had one ounce of human feeling in you."

"I didn't," he gasped. "I didn't."

"But you know who did. You must. You are the only one who knows everything about this household."

"No."

Pomeroy's battlefield voice floated into the room accompanied by his heavy tread. "Not much to see up there. Just one very dead cove minus his ballocks. What are you doing, Captain?"

I eased my hands from Bremer's coat, and the butler slumped back into the chair, eyes bulging.

"Just having a word with Mr. Bremer," I said.

"Oh, aye? I know how that usually plays out. Don't break his neck yet, sir, I want to ask him some questions. Beginning with who was the girl in the wardrobe?"

Bremer opened his mouth, but I glared him to silence. "She has nothing to do with this. I am taking her home."

"She the young lady you were looking for?"

Pomeroy was always too tenacious for his own good. The constable looked on, his breathing shallow and rapid.

"No," I said. "Leave her alone. She's been through much."

"All right, sir, if you like. But she might have killed the gent upstairs."

"Unlikely. The wardrobe was locked from the outside and her hands were tied."

Pomeroy shrugged, as if such facts were mere inconveniences. "If she's ill, she'll not go far. Now then, sir, I want to talk to this butler before he's completely trimmed. I hope you won't take offense if I ask you to go. Your temper's a bit wild, and he can't answer me if you break all his teeth. Thank you, sir. I knew you were with me."

*** *** ***

I did not want to wait in Aimee's room for Alice, because I couldn't bear to look again into those hopeless eyes. I made my way to the kitchens, instead, which I found empty. The boy, Henry, was still out, and there was no sign of John.

The cook stamped into the room. She dumped a bag onto the flour-strewn kitchen table and began to pile things in it—knives, towels, spoons. She was a handsome woman, tall, large boned, and ample chested, a woman I might have found attractive in another circumstance. Now her brow was clouded in high indignation, and her lips trembled.

"Such goings-on in this house," she snapped. "I never heard the like."

I leaned against the dresser and folded my arms. "I assume Bremer or John told you about Aimee. Did you know she hadn't gone?"

"Well, how could I? I work down here all day and all night, don't I? Making his meals and baking his bread." She swept an angry arm across the table and flung abandoned dough and flour onto the flagstone floor. "And Grace helping him like his abbess. I gave her the sack, I can tell you."

I had wondered where Grace had disappeared to. "What about John? Where is he?"

She thrust a handful of towels into the bag. "How should I know? With his mates at the public house, I expect, filling their ears with the tale. Well, no more for me, thank you very much. I'm off to stay with my brother and his wife. They have an inn on the Hampstead Road, and she's got her hands full because he was always a shiftless lout."

"The constable will want to speak to you before you go."

"Well, I don't want to speak to him. Here I am in this kitchen all the day long, cooking dainties to please the master's delicate appetite. The dishes I created for him and him alone. He would come down those stairs some nights and thank me, smiling so friendly-like, and take my hand . . . " She stopped. "And now there's rioting outside the house one day, and murder inside the next." She picked up the bag, which clanked. "I'll have no more of it. Good evening to you, sir."

She marched past me, lips firm, head high, and out through the scullery. After a moment, I saw her climb the steps outside, gray skirt swirling to reveal shapely ankles and stout shoes.

I knew I ought to go after her, to escort her somewhere safely at least. A young woman walking alone, no matter how robust, in London, had much to fear. But somehow I sensed that any would-be assailant would get the worse end of the bargain in an encounter with her tonight.

No, I left her, I left Bremer sobbing in the servants' hall under the onslaught of Pomeroy's questioning, and I left that house.

Outside, fog rolled over me, thick and clammy, but I inhaled as if I stood in a fragrant spring night of Portugal. I leaned against the railings and let the rain beat on me, and was still there when Alice came, worry and relief on her work-worn face, to take Aimee home.

*** *** ***

Grenville's carriage stood at the head of Grimpen Lane when I arrived home, coach lights throwing a sickly yellow swirl into the fog and rain. Despite the weather, my neighbors had turned out to ogle it and the fine horses that pulled it, but the sight did nothing to relieve my temper.

Grenville sat in the same worn wingchair Louisa had occupied the night before, with something crumbly and bready in his hands. He had stoked the fire high and the room hung with heat.

"Ah, Lacey," he said as I entered. "Your Mrs. Beltan does a fine crumpet. I'd have her supply my house entirely, but my chef would never speak to me again. Thinks he's a genius with pastry." He peered at me. "Good lord, Lacey, what happened?"

I was soaked through, and my face must have been grim as an undertaker's. I moved to my bedroom and began peeling off my clothes.

I heard Grenville rise and follow me. "Are you all right?"

"Ask Mrs. Beltan to bring me some hot water," I said and slammed the door in his face.

Chapter Nine

I soaked in the steaming water for half an hour as the heat slowly leached into me. I heard Grenville and Mrs. Beltan in my front room, discussing me.

"He gets like this sometimes," she confided. "Won't speak to a soul. I've seen him take to his bed two days at a time, and not even look at me when I come to see if he's all right. Melancholia, they call it."

"What do you do?"

"Nothing, sir. I make sure he's well and leave him be. He comes out of it on his own and goes on right as rain."

I let them talk, although I could have told Mrs. Beltan that my mood did not stem from melancholia. I simply wanted to wash the evil of number 22, Hanover Square from my skin.

I knew evil existed in the world. I had seen men, fire in their eyes, thrust bayonets through other men they did not even know. I had seen scavengers swarm battlefields to take everything from the fallen, even the coats on their backs. I'd seen such a scavenger put a gun to the head of a soldier, who might have lived with a small amount of help, and pull the trigger, all so that the murderer might steal his boots. But never had I felt the clinging, clammy evil of Horne's household, the gruesome secrets that hid behind a mask of respectability. At least the evils of war had been committed in the open.

The gray shadows of my bedchamber chased each other over the carved posts of my bed as the day died and the water warmed me. The wooden flowers and leaves became eyes and mouths, open and round.

I rose from the bath, dried myself, and dressed. Grenville was alone again when I emerged.

"Horne is dead," I said before he could speak. "Someone murdered him."

Grenville stared at me in open-mouthed astonishment. "Good God. You didn't—Lacey, you didn't—kill him yourself, did you?"

"No. I only wanted to."

I told him everything. We sat in the darkening room, the firelight's shadows on the curved beams rendering the room a cavern of hell. I hadn't wanted to talk about Horne's murder at all, but the words came out of me, forced out as though another entity moved my mouth.

"No wonder you looked like you'd been wrestling the devil," Grenville said when I'd finished. "Did Pomeroy make an arrest?"

"I don't know. I didn't ask him."

"What about Aimee? Did she hear anything when she was inside the wardrobe?"

I sighed, suddenly tired. "I didn't ask her. I wanted to leave her alone. I'm rather more interested in the fate of Jane Thornton than with Horne's murderer."

Grenville touched his fingertips together. "They might be connected. You say Denis visited that day?"

"According to the maid."

"Odd, because he rarely visits anyone. One goes to him. Only with his permission."

I shrugged, not caring very much.

"A puzzle," Grenville said. "What about the butler—Bremer? Perhaps he had grown disgusted with his master and decided to stick a knife into him."

"I would swear his shock when we found the body was genuine. But any of them had time and opportunity to murder him. With only five of them to look after so large a house, each of them would have been alone for some stretch of time during the day. I didn't speak to the valet, because it was his day out."

Grenville pursed his lips. "Perhaps he returned, killed Horne, and left again."

"I suppose he must have a key. I imagine Pomeroy has asked questions about him. He's usually thorough."

Ploddingly, ruthlessly so. Pomeroy had hounded more than one poor soul to the gallows—guilty and innocent alike.

"What about the other maid? Grace?"

"I didn't speak to her either. The cook had sent her off."

He started to say something more, then stopped and stared at me. "I sense a lack of interest in you, Lacey. Or perhaps you believe Horne deserved what he got."

"No one deserves what was done to him."

"You say that out loud. But do you feel it in your heart?"

I did not answer.

Grenville tapped the arm of the chair. "Well, I'll not press you. The reason I presumed to call on you today is because I received an answer to one of your advertisements." He reached into his pocket and plucked out a letter.

I came alert. We had agreed that inquiries should be sent to the newspaper itself, but I had been too stunned by Horne's death and finding Aimee to stop for the letters tonight. "Someone has found Jane Thornton?"

"I don't know. The letter is from a man called Beauchamp, who lives in Hampstead. He saw the notices and the advertisement, and wrote to say a young lady from his household had also disappeared in mysterious circumstances."

I sat back. "Which may have nothing to do with Jane."

"Possibly not. But I would like to look into it. It seems a cousin of his wife's came to live with them a year ago. Her family is from Somerset. When her parents died, she had no living relatives but the Beauchamps, and she went to Hampstead to live with them. About two months ago, she left the house and never returned."

"About the same time Jane Thornton disappeared."

"Exactly. The two incidents may not be connected, but then again, they might. This young woman, Charlotte Morrison, is about ten years older than Jane."

"Denis might have procured her as well."

Grenville threw me a look. "Might, Lacey. Might. We should gather facts. Are you well enough to go to Hampstead with me?"

I did not have the energy to light a candle, let alone be dragged to Hampstead. But Grenville was ready to run there himself and probably frighten the life out of the worried family. "You don't have to go. I can call on them alone."

"I'd rather go. I am damned curious. Or do you think they'd be intimidated to have Lucius Grenville pay them a visit?"

I snorted. "They have probably never heard of you."

Grenville looked affronted, then he smiled. "Touché. You pay the call, and I'll follow along as an anonymous gentleman."

I studied the fire, not answering. Grenville waited, and I sensed his impatience. I looked up to find his dark eyes upon me and something in them that had lost friendliness.

"Very well," I said. "Let us journey to Hampstead."

*** *** ***

After Grenville left me, I let the fire die down. He'd stoked it with at least a week's supply of coal, with the zeal of a man who never had to think about the cost of fuel.

I sat in the wing chair he'd vacated and let my hands fall limply over the sides. I sensed melancholia, black, menacing, and watching, start to creep over me. I closed my eyes and willed it away. When it struck me, it often kept me abed for days, rendering me unable to move or eat. But I needed all my faculties at the moment. Jane Thornton was still missing, perhaps in danger, and I wanted to find her. I could give in to despair after that.

The murderer had cheated me out of throttling the whereabouts of Jane from Horne's throat. But the butler, Bremer, must know, or Grace, the maid. They were the only ones allowed to wait on the two girls, and a man could hardly spirit away one young woman and hide another without the help of his butler, valet, or coachman.

Pomeroy would bully most of the information out of Bremer, but I still wanted a go at the spindly butler. Pomeroy would not know the right questions to ask. I'd lost my temper today, but I'd get Bremer in my hands again and interrogate him coldly. He had to know something.

The valet was another matter. I would wait until Pomeroy tracked down the valet—which he would—then ask the man pointed questions. Grenville was right when he'd commented that the valet could very well have let himself into the house, slain his master, then let himself out again, without the other servants seeing him. He'd know who was likely to be where in the house, and perhaps he had been disgusted by Horne's proclivities. Or perhaps he'd been jealous and wanted Jane or Aimee for himself. Or perhaps the murder had nothing to do with Jane and Aimee whatsoever.

Someone knocked on my door, making my head throb with each rap. Only one person would think to pound on my door so late.

I called out, "Go away, Marianne. I don't have any candles to spare."

This was met with silence. Usually Marianne would make foul remarks about my stinginess and enter anyway.

The knock did not sound again. I supposed I should rise and see whether anyone stood on the stairs beyond the door, but I did not have the strength.

The handle moved, and the door swung open. Janet Clarke stood on my threshold.

The strength returned to my limbs in a rush. I was out of the chair and halfway across the room before she could step inside.

She smiled at me. "Hello, my dear old lad."

Chapter Ten

I caught Janet's hands and more or less dragged her inside. She drew a breath to speak, but I gathered her against me and held her in a crushing embrace. I had no idea whether she'd come to speak to me, or to say good-bye, or to talk over old times, but for that instant I needed her as she was, needed her to take me to the past where I'd been, for a brief moment, happy.

Janet raised her face from my shoulder. Her hair was mussed and her cheeks were flushed, but she still smiled. "That happy to see me, are you?"

I said hoarsely, "Yes."

She straightened the lapels of my coat. "Then I am glad I asked Mrs. Brandon for your direction. She was very gracious."

I smoothed Janet's hair. I had no right at all to hold her like this, to touch her, but I somehow could not let go. "Mrs. Brandon is always gracious."

"She told me about your injury. It hurts you, does it not?"

"The break never healed properly, but if I take care, it doesn't pain me too much."

Janet slid from my grasp and took a step back, looking at me with a critical eye. "I don't mean that. I was remembering the night I took ill and nothing would comfort me but coffee. You searched all over camp for some, and it was raining so hard I thought the sky would come down. You sprinted through the rain, holding that packet of coffee under your coat as though it were the most precious gold. I've never seen a man run so fast in all my life. But you did it, and you laughed. Someone took that liveliness away from you." She touched the hair at my temple. "Nor was this gray here when we parted."

"I was not an old man then."

Janet sat down on one of my straight-backed chairs, lacing her fingers. "You'd had better start telling me that story, if it's so long."

I sat in the chair facing hers. I stared at the flames on my hearth for a few moments, while I decided what to tell her.

In the end, most of it came out of me. I told her of the cold morning that Brandon and I had met one another with pistols drawn, until Louisa and several other officers from our regiment had persuaded us to settle our differences and shake hands. I'd thought the matter finished with, even if the topic of our falling out remained uncomfortable, and then had come Brandon's betrayal. I told her of the mission he'd sent me on, never meaning for me to return, glossing over our decision to leave the army behind to avoid disgracing ourselves, Louisa, or the regiment.

When I'd finished, I sat silently, as bereft as I'd been the day I'd left Spain to return to England. I made to smooth my damp hair and saw that my fingers trembled.

Janet reached across the space between us and caught my hand. "And what do you do now?"

I smiled. "Very little."

"Colonel Brandon ought to help you. He ought to find you a proper job."

I shrugged. "He tries hard to pretend nothing ever happened."

Her eyes glowed with anger. "You always told me how he was like a father to you, or a brother. Your years together should count for something."

"It is difficult for some to acknowledge a mistake."

Her face softened. "Oh, Gabriel. And you love him enough to let him do it."

She was wrong. I hated him. He had taken things from me, and I would not easily forgive him.

My anger must have shown on my face, because Janet squeezed my hand. "I'll not press you. You were always one for not knowing your own heart."

"You don't think so?"

Her brown eyes twinkled. "No, my lad, I do not. You have honor and duty and love all mixed up in that head of yours. That's why I'm so fond of you."

I leaned forward and touched her face. "And I am fond of you, because you are not afraid of the truth."

"I am sometimes. Everyone is."

We shared a look. A thump sounded upstairs, as though Marianne had dropped something to the floor. A few flakes of plaster wisped down and settled on Janet's hair.

"You have not told me your story," I said. "What happened to you after I sent you off with my smitten lieutenant?"

She smiled. "Your smitten lieutenant was a perfect gentleman. He only made three or four propositions and took it well when I turned him down."

"Poor fellow."

"Not a bit. We parted as friends when we reached England. I went to Cambridge and stayed with my sister until we buried her." She hesitated. "I met a gentleman there."

"Mr. Clarke," I said.

"He was my sister's neighbor. A kindly man. He succumbed to influenza three years gone now."

I suddenly felt shame for wallowing in my own self-pity, and pure compassion for her. Janet ever found herself alone. "I am sorry."

Her eyes softened. "He was kind to me to the end. He left enough for me to get by. And I have friends."

"Like Sergeant-major Foster?"

"I speak to him from time to time. He frequents a public house near the Haymarket, where I buy my ale."

"He is a good man," I said. "And a good sergeant."

The room went silent. Wind groaned in my chimney, and upstairs, Marianne dropped something else.

Janet rose and came to me. Her cotton gown smelled of soap and clean things. "I remember the first time I saw you. You were ready to murder those soldiers for playing cards for me."

"They had no right to."

"You had no right to break up the game before I found out who won."

I chuckled. She leaned down and brushed my lips with hers.

I put my arms around her waist. My mouth remembered hers, my hands remembered her body, and we came together as though the seven years between this kiss and our last had only been seven days.

I took her to my cold bedroom and stoked the fire there, putting to flight my plan of conserving the rest of that week's coal. We sat on the bed and touched and kissed each other, our hands and mouths discovering again what we had once known so well. I eased the hooks of her dress and chemise apart and slid my hands to her bare torso. She nuzzled my cheek, and my desire stirred, pressing aside my darkness.

Not long later, we lay tangled together in the firelight that spilled across the bed, the heat warming our skin. My senses embraced her—the smell of her hair, the sound of her breathing, the press of her body, the remembered taste of her mouth. I hadn't known how much I needed her. I lay for a long time in her arms, managing to at last find a small bit of peace in that stark bedroom in the April night.

*** *** ***

The Beauchamps occupied a small house in a lane not far from Hampstead Heath, in a quiet turning with brick houses and tiny gardens. The afternoon sky was leaden as we approached, but a steady breeze kept mists from forming.

The sweet sounds of a pianoforte drifted from the right-hand window as Grenville and I approached and cut off when I plied the knocker to the black-painted door. A middle-aged man in butler's kit opened the door and stared at me inquiringly. I gave him my card.

"Who is it?"

A woman, small and plump like the marsh thrushes from my corner of East Anglia, hovered on the threshold to the room with the pianoforte.

The butler held the card close to his eyes. "Captain Gabriel Lacey, madam."

She looked blank. Grenville fished the letter from his pocket and held it up. "We've come in answer to your husband's letter. About Miss Morrison."

"Oh." She peered at both of us in turn. "Oh dear. Cavendish, go and fetch Mr. Beauchamp. Tell him to come to the music room. Would you follow me, please, gentlemen?"

I limped after her to the music room, which was dominated by the pianoforte. A violin and bow lay on a sofa, and sheets of music littered the floor, the tables, the top of the pianoforte.

"Please sit. My husband will be here directly. I knew he'd written you, but I did not expect an answer so soon."

I moved aside a handwritten sheet of musical notes, with "Prelude in D; Johann Christian Bach," scribbled across the top.

"We were anxious to speak with you," Grenville said as he sat on a divan and smoothed his elegant trousers. "So we thought it best to come right away."

I eyed him askance but said nothing. Mrs. Beauchamp hastened to me and took away the violin and sheets of music. "I beg your pardon. We are a very musical family, as you can see."

"I heard you play as we arrived," I said. "You have much skill."

She blushed. "It does for us. Charlotte—Miss Morrison—plays a beautiful harp. Many's the night we had a trio here, with me on the pianoforte, Mr. Beauchamp on the violin, and Charlotte there." She glanced at an upright harp covered with a dust cloth. Her face paled, and she bit her lip and turned away.

"Gentlemen."

Mr. Beauchamp stood on the threshold. He was small and plump like his wife, putting me in mind of two partridges in their nest. He went to Mrs. Beauchamp and dropped a kiss on her raised cheek then held his hand out to me.

Both Beauchamps were past middle age, but beauty still lingered in the lines of Mrs. Beauchamp's face, and Mr. Beauchamp's eyes held the fire of a man not docile.

"You received my letter," Beauchamp said without preliminary. He drew a chair halfway between me and the pianoforte and sat. "I saw that you were looking for another young lady, and thought you could help us."

Grenville folded his hands and took on the look of an examining magistrate. "We are helping a family whose daughter has disappeared. She vanished in London under mysterious circumstances. Your letter hinted that your cousin, Miss Morrison, has also vanished mysteriously."

"She has that," Mrs. Beauchamp said. Her plump face held distress. "She went off to the market, a basket on her arm, and never came back."

"When was this?" I asked.

"Two months ago. On the twentieth of February. We made a search when she did not come home that night. We asked and asked. No one had seen her after she left our house. No one knew anything." Her eyes filled with tears, and she blinked them away.

"There was no question of an accident? Or that she'd gone to meet someone?"

"What are you implying, sir?" Beauchamp growled.

"I imply nothing. She might have arranged to meet a friend, and perhaps something befell her when she went to that meeting."

"She would have told me," Mrs. Beauchamp said. "She would have spoken of an appointment if she'd had one. No matter what."

"She did not know many around Hampstead," Beauchamp put in.

"She had been here a year, you said in your letter. She had no friends here?"

"She had us."

I subsided. I'd angered them, and I did not know why.

Grenville broke in smoothly. "She came from Somerset, correct?"

"Oh, yes." Mrs. Beauchamp seemed eager to talk, though her husband relapsed into glowering silence.

Charlotte Morrison had lived in Somerset all her life. Two years before, her aging parents had both fallen ill, and she'd nursed them until they died. She'd corresponded with the Beauchamps regularly, and when Charlotte found herself alone, Mrs. Beauchamp proposed she travel to Hampstead and live with them.

Charlotte had complied and arrived shortly after. She had seemed content with life here. She wrote often to friends in Somerset and was a quiet girl with polite manners.

I digested this in silence and growing frustration. Charlotte had known no one, had met no one, and yet, one afternoon, she'd vanished into the mists. I did not even have a coachman to question, or a Mr. Horne to pursue. She had simply walked away.

"Did you advertise?" I asked.

"To be sure, we did," Mrs. Beauchamp said. "And offered a reward. We heard nothing."

"Then why do you suppose we can help you?"

Beauchamp stirred. "Because we both want the same thing. To find a missing young lady. Perhaps the two are connected, and if we find the one, we'll find the other."

"Possibly."

"I will do anything to bring Charlotte back," he said. "She belongs here."

His wife nodded.

"There was no question of her returning to Somerset?" Grenville asked.

"Why should she return to Somerset?" Beauchamp demanded. "This is her home now."

"She might have taken a whim to go there, visit her old friends," Grenville said.

"I tell you, she would have told us, not walked away," Beauchamp said. "Why do you question her character? Someone took her from us and that is that."

Grenville lifted his hands. "I beg your pardon. I did not mean to upset you. I am trying to establish possibilities. If you assure me that Charlotte would not have left of her own accord, I will believe you."

I was not as sanguine, but I said nothing.

Mrs. Beauchamp looked pensive. "There *was* something odd."

Her husband scowled. "Odd? What do you mean? I know of nothing odd."

"A week or two before, she—well, she seemed to fade a little. I cannot be more forthcoming than that, because I did not notice it at the time. But several times she started to tell me something, something she was worried about, but she would stop herself and change the subject."

"It probably had nothing to do with her disappearance," Beauchamp said. "Nothing at all." His face was red, his eyes glittering.

"She missed Somerset, though," Mrs. Beauchamp said. "She loved it. Her letters to us before she came here were filled with the delights of it."

"She would not have gone there without telling us."

His wife subsided. "No."

Grenville broke in. "We do need to prepare you. The other girl we are looking for was abducted, we believe, by a man called Horne."

"Or Denis," I put in.

Grenville shot me a warning look.

Both Beauchamps remained blank. "I have not heard either name," Beauchamp said. "But we are not much in London. Who are these gentlemen?"

"Mr. Horne lived in Hanover Square," Grenville said. "He had our young lady in his keeping for a time, and we are trying to discover what became of her. Miss Morrison's fate might be similar."

Mrs. Beauchamp bowed her head. "I thought of that—that she might be ruined. But I only want her back. I only want her safe."

Beauchamp regarded his wife a moment, his face unreadable. "My wife and I were never blessed with children. We quite looked upon Charlotte as our daughter. No man could be prouder of his own offspring."

"Or woman."

Tears stood in Mrs. Beauchamp's eyes. I felt like a fraud. I had no help to give.

"The letters she wrote," I said. "Would you permit me to read them?"

Mrs. Beauchamp looked up, hope lighting her face. "Indeed, yes, Captain. She wrote beautiful letters. She was a dear, sweet girl."

Beauchamp wasn't as happy. "What good will it do to read her letters? She made no indication in them that she wanted to leave us."

"She might have met someone that she wrote about, might have known someone in Somerset, someone she might have gone away with."

"I tell you, there was no one."

Mrs. Beauchamp rose. "No, I want him to read the letters. So he'll understand what she was like. And he might see something we missed. We don't know that."

She passed me in a swish of skirts and a waft of old-fashioned soap as Grenville and I got politely to our feet. Mr. Beauchamp also rose, but he crossed to the window and stood with his back to us. Beyond him, the rain dripped down the gray windows.

I said, "I will do everything in my power to discover what happened to Miss Morrison."

Beauchamp turned, his stance dejected. "I will not lie to you, Captain. Writing to you was my wife's idea. She holds out too much hope. She will not even voice the possibility that Charlotte is lost to us forever, as I believe her to be."

"Dead, do you mean?" I asked gently.

"Yes. Because she would have written to us, otherwise. We are her only family. Why would she go away? She would have explained."

Tears hovered in his eyes. I wondered very much what he had truly felt for Charlotte—the love of a father? Or something else? And did he even realize it himself?

Mrs. Beauchamp fluttered into the room and thrust a lacquered wooden box at me. "I've kept all the letters she'd written me in the year before she came to us. She also copied out a few that she sent to a friend in Somerset since then. Read them, Captain. You will come to know her through them."

I took the box. "I will return them to you as soon as I can."

"Take all the time you like. I ask only that you do not lose them. They are dear to me."

"I will take very good care of them," I promised.

They hovered, but I knew that the interview was over. "Thank you for seeing us," I said, then Grenville and I bowed and took our leave.

As we rode away in Grenville's carriage, the box tucked beside me, I looked back. Mr. and Mrs. Beauchamp stood at the wide ground-floor window, watching us depart.

*** *** ***

We spent the night in Hampstead. While we'd talked with the Beauchamps, the rain had increased, until black water fell around us and cold rose from the Heath. It was Grenville's idea to find a public house to stay the rest of the evening and drive leisurely back to London the next day.

I'd thought the public house would be too rustic for the wealthy Lucius Grenville, but he laughed and said that he'd slept in some places in the wilds of Canada that made Hampstead positively palatial.

He obtained private rooms at the top of the public house that proved snug. A sitting room in the middle opened to a bedroom at either side, luxurious accommodations by my standards. The publican's wife, a cheerful, thin woman, trundled us a supper of roasted chicken, thick soup, greens, cream, and bread. After the penetrating damp outside, we both fell upon it heartily.

The publican's wife lingered, inclined to talk. "I'm afraid it's only the leavings and the soup from yesterday's beef and vegetables, but it will fill the stomach. I know gentlemen are used to much finer, but you won't get better in Hampstead."

"Madam, it is admirable," Grenville said around a mouthful of chicken.

She gave him a modest look. "You'll have fresh eggs in the morning. I suppose you gentlemen are from London, then?"

We replied in the affirmative.

"Journalists, are you?" she asked. "Have you come about our murder?"

Chapter Eleven

I nearly choked on my soup. I coughed and pressed my handkerchief to my mouth then hastily seized my glass of stout.

Grenville finished chewing and swallowing without expression. "We know nothing of a murder. It happened here?"

"Oh, aye, they found her off in the woods, torn to bits, poor lamb."

"When did this happen?" Grenville asked.

The woman leaned on the table, her eyes bright in her bone-thin face. "A week or more, now. Maybe two weeks. I don't remember. That's when they found her. One of the blacksmith's lads, he had gone to do a spot of fishing. Didn't half give him a turn."

"Who was she?"

"That was the funny thing, sir. They didn't know at first. Turns out she's kitchen maid up at Lord Sommerville's big house. She'd gone missing sometime back. Near two months."

"They were certain she was the kitchen maid?" I asked.

She looked at me in surprise. "Oh, yes, sir. Her brother came from London and said it was her."

I sat back, wondering if we'd just discovered the whereabouts of Charlotte Morrison, even in spite of the brother's identification. If she'd been torn to bits, he might not have been able to recognize her.

The publican's wife chattered on, leaning on her hands until white ridges appeared on the sides of her palms. "She'd been dead a long time, they said. I didn't go to the inquest, but my husband, he's always one for gossip. He went out of interest. Whole village did. Poor thing had lain there nigh on two months. Not much left of her."

"Why did they think it was murder then?" Grenville asked. "She might have taken ill, or fallen, or some such thing."

The woman pointed at the nape of her own neck. "The back of her head was bashed in. They said she died of that, then was torn up and dragged out there to the woods. I don't know how they know these things meself."

"Lack of blood where they found her," I said woodenly.

"Truly, sir? It's a bit gruesome, I say. But we had a few journalists come. Not very many." She sounded disappointed.

"Did they discover who did the murder?" Grenville asked.

She shook her head. "And it does give one a shiver of nights, knowing that went on not two miles from your own house. No, the girl's young man was in London when she ran away, and he can prove it.

She'd probably run off with some other man what promised her money or jewels or such nonsense. Lured her away and killed her. We've been on the lookout for strange young men since then, but we've not seen a one."

Grenville oozed sympathy. "It must have been a frightening thing to happen."

"It does make one think. Not much wrong with the poor girl but silliness. She didn't deserve to be killed. Now then, gentleman, I've kept you long enough with my talk. You enjoy your supper, as little as it is. I or Matthew will bring breakfast in the morning. We keep country hours here, so you gentlemen will want to be early to bed."

Finished with her gossip, the publican's wife clattered a few dirty plates onto a tray and departed with a rustle and a bang of the door.

Grenville raised his brows. "I was half afraid for a moment that our errand was for naught."

I picked up my spoon. "I wonder if the girl was another victim of Mr. Denis."

"It is possible, of course. This soup, Lacey, is almost excellent. Remind me to tell our lively-tongued hostess. But remember, girls run away or are lured away all the time, though not all of them come to such a tragic fate. Either their families can give them nothing, or they're told they can't have a luxurious life, and they can't resist seeing whether there is something more in the world for them. James Denis cannot be responsible for them all."

I didn't answer as I sopped up my soup with the heel of the loaf. Perhaps Grenville was right—the girl had gone away with a predator who had murdered her. The back of her head had been crushed, the publican's wife had said. I hoped she had not known death was coming.

My heart burned for her, as it did for Jane Thornton. I wondered savagely why civilized England was so much more dangerous for a young girl than the battlefields of the Peninsula had been for soldiers like me.

*** *** ***

I took Charlotte Morrison's letters to my bedchamber with me, tucked myself under the cozy quilt with bricks to warm my feet, and read them. I laid them out chronologically, and read through the last two years of Charlotte's life.

It seemed she'd been happy in Somerset, content with domestic life and her small circle of friends. She described her journeys to the moorlands and to Wales in poetic terms, painting a picture of the wild lands that was both beautiful and stark. She had been worried for her ill parents and anxious to give them every comfort. She expressed concern for what would happen to her once they died, but without complaining. The curate, she said, had taken some interest in her, but a subsequent letter explained it had come to naught. The curate felt himself too poor to take a wife.

Charlotte wrote with sorrow of her parents' death, then with anticipation of moving to her new home in Hampstead. She spoke of closing up the house, selling the livestock, and preparing for her journey.

The letters ended in the April of the previous year. After that were copies of a half dozen letters to a Miss Geraldine Frazier in Somerset. Charlotte described her arrival in Hampstead, her gratitude to the Beauchamps. She seemed to like Hampstead, though she missed the remoteness of Somerset. "It is never possible to be truly alone, here. Always there are carriages and horses in the streets, and families from London who come to picnic on the Heath of a Sunday. But the woods and hills are pretty, and my cousins and I take many walks. They are kind people."

Two letters, one from November and one from January, interested me. In them, Charlotte said something curious:

"Pray disregard the incident I wrote to you of before, and please do not write me of it! It may be all my fancy, and I do not wish to slander. They say that looking into the eyes bares the soul, but when I do so, I am only confused. I cannot tell what is what, or the difference between what I imagine and what is real."

I searched the previous letters again for any mention of a curious or sinister incident, but if she had described such a thing, she had not copied out the letter that contained it.

The next letter, dated January of that year, reintroduced the theme:

"I wake in the night, afraid. Perhaps some step jars my sleep, or perhaps it is fancy, but my heart beats hard, and it is a long time before I drift off again. No, please do not worry, and do not write of it; my cousin would think it odd if I did not share your letters."

She said nothing more on the subject. The January letter was the last.

I read them through again, wondering whether I'd missed something, but I found nothing else. I folded the letters into the lacquer box and laid them on the bedside table.

I wondered what had frightened Charlotte and if it had anything to do with Jane Thornton. Had Charlotte met someone she suspected had sinister designs on her? Or was she simply unused to living so near London?

I wanted to speak to the friend she'd written the letters to. I'd write to her, though I did not like the prospect of a journey to Somerset. It would be long and expensive and my leg already ached from the short excursion to Hampstead. It would also take time from my searching for Jane Thornton, and I feared that every day might be her last.

I put out my candles, lay back, and tried to sleep. But the pain in my leg kept me awake, as did my thoughts. I went over the publican's wife's tale of the murder of the girl in the woods. Why had she been killed? A quarrel with a lover? Or had she seen something — the abduction of Charlotte Morrison perhaps?

Sleep would not come. I tried to still my thoughts by thinking of Janet and loving her. She had turned up exactly when I'd needed her, and I greatly looked forward to seeing her again.

But visions of her face flitted from me and I could only remember Horne in the pool of dried blood and Aimee locked inside the cupboard with dark bruises on her face.

The quiet of the room irritated me. I was used to city dwelling now, and even in the depths of Portugal and Spain, I had lived with the army, in noise and chaos and without privacy. I tossed for a time under the blankets, then I gave in to my restlessness.

I rose, took up my candle, and padded to the sitting room. The door to Grenville's bedchamber stood open. I crossed to close it, not wanting to wake him with my restlessness.

I stopped. Grenville's bed was empty. The sheets lay smooth and undisturbed, turned down for the night by the chambermaid who had scuttled in as we finished our repast. Grenville had not slept there, and he was nowhere in sight.

*** *** ***

I returned to bed, and despite my disquiet about where Grenville had disappeared to and why, I slept again.

In the morning, he turned up for breakfast as though he had been there all along. I nearly asked him where he had gone, but decided I would not pry. I would pretend, as he did, that he had gone nowhere until he chose to tell me otherwise.

We decided that I would return the letters to the Beauchamps myself, and Grenville would ride to visit with Lord Sommerville before we departed for London. Grenville was acquainted with the elderly viscount and said he would drop a few questions about Sommerville's kitchen maid the publican's wife had reported to us was found dead in the woods.

After breakfast the hostler's boy hoisted me onto a mare Grenville had hired. I could still ride a horse, if it were an even-tempered beast and someone boosted me onto the bloody thing. She was about seventeen hands, a bit larger than the horses I'd charged about on in the cavalry. For a country nag, her conformation was surprisingly fine, her gaits smooth. Her hocks bent and lifted with precision, and her eye was alert, her going, sound.

I had ridden fine horses in Portugal and Spain, but I'd forced in myself a certain detachment to them. Horses died at three or four times the rate of men, and though I took care, I lost more than my heart cared to. I'd seen cavalry officers weep as their horses, wounded, thrashed furrows into the bloody ground, the stench of death and fear covering them. More than once, I'd shot the poor beasts for them, as the officers stood, helpless, rocking in grief and sorrow. Dead horses, mounded with crows, had littered the battlefields. Detachment, I'd found, was best.

I turned the mare to the road that led to Beauchamp's modest house. The clouds lowered and threatened rain again. I nudged my horse into a faster trot, and pulled my hat down over my forehead as the first drops touched me. My route led me through an open field, and the road dipped.

A young man rose up from the low hedge beside the road and grabbed my horse's bridle. The horse snorted and danced, and I slid halfway from the saddle.

"What the devil— ?"

The youth abandoned the bridle, grabbed me by the arm, and yanked me from the saddle. My stiff knee protested, and I landed hard on the packed earth.

My assailant came at me, arms wide. I struggled upright and waited. He lunged. I tucked my body together, ducked to one side, and caught his outflung arm.

He was strong, heavy, young muscles determined, but he was inexperienced. I jerked with my weight and flipped him neatly over onto his back.

He made a "ha!" noise as the air whooshed from his lungs, and he lay still a moment, like an insect on its back. I sprinted the distance to the horse. I knew I'd never mount without assistance, so I snatched my walking stick from the saddle.

I yanked the sword from my cane just as two huge arms closed around me from behind and the lad half lifted me from my feet. I swung my sword behind me in an arc and slapped him hard on the leg.

He yelped. I slapped again. His hold loosened. I pulled my elbow close to my body and slammed it backward.

"Oop—" he gasped.

I slid from his slack grip, whirled, and faced him, my sword level with his heart.

"Odd place for a robbery, here on an open green in the middle of the day."

He did not answer. His mouth opened and closed a few times, his face red with his returning breath. His eyes held no belligerence, only surprise, as though he had not counted on a victim who would fight back.

The youth stared at my sword a moment then whirled and fled, straight for the horse.

"Damnation." I limped after him as fast as I could. The horse, as I'd said, was an even-tempered beast who did not fear humans. She shied a little as the big lad approached but allowed herself to be caught. Instead of mounting, the boy dug into the saddlebag, pulled out the lacquer box, released the horse, and ran from me across the green.

I cursed again, running and hobbling after him, my knee spreading white-hot pain up my spine. I had told Mrs. Beauchamp I'd take care of the letters, and now they moved farther and farther away in the beefy hands of an unknown boy.

"Lacey!"

I turned and saw Grenville cantering toward me on his bay horse. "What happened? Did you take a fall?"

"Go after him." I pointed at the silhouette of the lad fast disappearing into the mist and rain. "Hurry. Get the box from him."

Grenville nodded curtly, wheeled his mount, and galloped away.

I caught my horse and led her in Grenville's wake. Dividing my weight between the walking stick and the mare, I was able to hobble along without hurting myself too badly, although the horse tried to take a bite out of my jacket from time to time.

I reached the top of a small rise and looked down the slope that slid smoothly to a gray pond, dull under the rain. The lad made for it, Grenville only a few strides behind.

A small black object arced from the young man's hands and landed with a silent splash in the water. The lad leapt from the bank into the water, and Grenville's mount danced backward from the fountain that erupted from the impact. The boy swam the narrow distance to the other bank, pulled himself quickly out, and ran on.

"Grenville!" I shouted through cupped hands. "Get the box!"

Grenville slid from his horse, then stopped among the reeds, his hands on his hips. I ran forward, dropping my horse's reins. The box bobbed in the still water, not yet saturated enough to sink. I slipped in the mud on the bank, and caught myself in time from falling in.

"What the devil happened?" Grenville demanded. "Who was that?"

"I don't know."

I leaned out over the pond, extending my cane. The box floated just beyond my reach. "Hold on to me."

"Blast you, Lacey, you'll go in, and then I'll have to fish you out."

"Do it!"

Grenville looked at me in exasperation but nodded.

I lowered myself to my stomach in the mud. Grenville grasped my ankles while I inched toward the water. The box floated, half-submerged and bobbing on the gray surface. I thrust my walking stick toward it. The handle slapped the water, and the box danced away. I slithered forward, praying Grenville had a good grip on my legs, and reached again.

I touched the box. The end of the cane shook as I gingerly hooked the gold head of the stick on the edge. I raked the box toward me. It came, dragging on the surface, its top glistening with water. When the box bumped the bank, I tossed my walking stick to the ground beside me, plunged my hands into the chill water, and dragged the box out.

Water poured from the seams. I rolled over, dislodging Grenville's hold, and squirmed to a sitting position on firmer ground. I sat holding that damned box, my coat and breeches plastered with mud. I turned the box around in my hands, depressed the catch that opened it, and stared in dismay at the sodden mess inside.

"Anything salvageable?" Grenville asked.

"I have no idea." I lifted a paper, gently separating it from the others. Peeling off his muddy gloves, Grenville reached a long-fingered hand into the box and pried out another paper. I related the tale of the young man's surprise attack and his theft of the box.

Grenville frowned. "Notice that he threw the *box* into the pond."

I glared up from the wet paper in my hand. "Yes, I had noticed."

"I mean that if he were simply afraid of being caught, he could have flung the box down and fled, or thrown it across the pond to pick up when he reached the other side. But he deliberately chose to send it into the water. As though he wanted to destroy the letters rather than risk you getting them back."

"Or he thought we'd stop and try to retrieve it, giving him time to run away. What would he want with Charlotte Morrison's letters?"

"What indeed?"

I glanced at him, but he had bent to the task at hand again.

Grenville caught the horses while I patted the papers with my handkerchief and folded them carefully back into the box, now lined with Grenville's handkerchief. Grenville boosted me onto my horse, tucked the box back into the saddlebag, then mounted his own horse. I couldn't help looking warily into the scrub that lined the road as we turned onto it.

"I doubt he'll be back," Grenville said. "He expected to pluck his pigeon easily, not be pummeled by you and chased by me." He chuckled. "I am sorry I missed the first part."

I didn't bother to answer. I was cold and muddy and annoyed and my leg hurt like fury. Grenville, on the other hand, even in the rain, looked dry and elegant and ready to step into a drawing room.

We parted again at the crossroad, me to ride on to the Beauchamps, Grenville to continue to Lord Sommerville's.

I had to explain to Mrs. Beauchamp what had happened to the letters. She hugged the box to her chest as she listened, her brown eyes round.

"Whoever would want to steal Charlotte's letters?"

"He may not have known the letters were inside," I said. "He saw a pretty box and thought it would contain something valuable."

I knew that was untrue. The box had been out of sight, in the saddlebag. The lad had deliberately looked for it.

"I am so sorry, Captain. Thank you for rescuing them."

"I ought to have taken better care of them."

"You cannot blame yourself."

She wanted to be generous. She gave me some hot tea laced with port and let me dry out near her fire. She chatted to me of life in Hampstead and of Charlotte and their life together.

Her husband waylaid me as I made my departure. On the walk in front of the house, Beauchamp seized my arm and looked up into my face, his dark eyes glinting. "Did the letters help?"

"That remains to be seen," I said. "You may be right that she is dead."

"If you find her—" His voice caught. He cleared his throat. "Please bring her home to us."

"I will."

Beauchamp did not offer to shake hands, nor did he bid me farewell. I turned back to my horse, let his footman boost me aboard, and rode back to the public house to await Grenville's return.

*** *** ***

The drive back to London was quieter and wetter than the journey out had been. For the first part of it, I told Grenville what had been in Charlotte's letters, and he described his visit with Lord Sommerville. Grenville had managed to bring up the death of the kitchen maid. Lord Sommerville, as the local magistrate, and also distressed that one of his staff should come to such an end, had made an inquiry, but it had turned up nothing. The young man she customarily walked out with had been in London on the night in question, visiting his brother and nephews. According to servants' gossip, the maid Matilda, had apparently been cuckolding the young man with a new suitor, but Lord Sommerville did not know who the new suitor was. In the end, the death was put down to Matilda's having met a footpad in the woods.

After Grenville's recounting I dozed, still tired from my adventure. Grenville remained pensive and talked little. He mostly read newspapers, which each gave a lurid account of the murder of Josiah Horne. The *Times* speculated whether the brutal killing would reintroduce the question of creating a regular police force in England, such as they had in France.

Grenville gave me no explanation of why he'd disappeared from the inn the night before, and I did not ask him about it. His coachman left me at the top of Grimpen Lane, and I walked home. Again my neighbors streamed out to ogle Grenville's coach and fine horses. Mrs. Beltan handed me a stack of letters that had arrived for me in my absence. I bought one of her yeasty, buttery buns and retired upstairs to read my correspondence.

Among the constrained and polite invitations to social gatherings was a letter from Louisa Brandon, telling me that she was doing what she could for the Thorntons. She also mentioned that she would host a supper party on the weekend, making it plain that she wanted me to attend. I tucked the letter aside, my mind turning over what excuses I'd come up with for refusing her invitation.

Another letter, which I lingered over for a time, was from Mr. Denis himself, setting an appointment with me for two days hence at his house in Curzon Street. The tone of the letter conveyed that Horne's dying was only an inconvenience and should not stop a transaction of business. I wrote out a reply that I'd come.

The last of the post was a folded square of paper with my name on it in capitals. Unfolded, the note read: "I arrested the butler. Magistrate made short work of him. Pomeroy."

Chapter Twelve

I flung down the letter. I'd washed my hands of Horne's household and his death, but I did not think Bremer had killed his master. I'd left them to Pomeroy's mercy, and he had been his usual ruthless self.

After shaving and downing the bun, I walked to Bow Street and the magistrate's court. Inside the drab halls, the dregs of the night's arrests lay about waiting to appear before the magistrate. The smell of unwashed bodies and boredom smote me. For some reason, I scanned their ranks for Nance, but I didn't see her. Most game girls bribed the watch to look the other way, but occasionally, one chose to pick the wrong gentleman's pocket or got caught in a brawl.

The pale-faced bailiff accosted me and demanded my business. I sent him looking for Pomeroy. While I waited, a small man with wiry hair latched his fingers on to my cuff and began a barely intelligible, one-sided conversation, washing me in gin-soaked breath.

"Get on with you," Pomeroy boomed. He cuffed the little man, who howled and ran back to the wall. "Captain. Good news. I arrested the butler. He goes to trial in five days."

There was no privacy to be had in that hall. I motioned Pomeroy away from the crowd, but still had to raise my voice to be heard. "Why Bremer?"

"Stands to reason, doesn't it? He's the last one to see his master. He stabs him, cuts off his bollocks, sticks the knife back in the wound, leaves the room, and tells everyone the master asked not to be disturbed. You turn up later and won't go away, so he legs it upstairs and 'discovers' the body. Nothing mysterious about it."

"But why should Bremer kill Horne?"

"Because by all accounts that cove Horne was a right bastard. Jury won't be sympathetic, though. Be wondering if their own manservants will get the idea to cut off *their* bollocks."

I stood my ground. "Horne paid very high wages. Surely Bremer would put up with a difficult master for that. Or give notice if he truly disliked the man."

Pomeroy shrugged. "No doubt he'll confess his motives at the trial."

"And why mutilate Horne? Why not stop at simply killing him?"

"Damned if I know, Captain. I didn't ask him."

"What did he tell the magistrate?" I asked.

"Not much. Kept babbling that he didn't do it. Magistrate asked him *then who did*? But he couldn't answer. Just gibbered."

I shook my head. "Think, Pomeroy. Whoever killed Horne had to best him. Horne was younger and stronger than Bremer. It couldn't have been easy to stab him."

"Even the weak and frightened can do damage when they're riled enough." Pomeroy gave me a patient look. "Magistrate wanted a culprit. I gave him one."

"Horne had another visitor that day. No one saw Horne after the visitor left, not even the butler."

"Oh, yes? Who was that then?"

"Mr. James Denis."

Pomeroy snorted. "And it ain't likely I'm going to run 'round and arrest him, sir, is it? He's a toff that no one's going to touch, least of all the likes of me. What would he kill Horne for anyway?"

"Perhaps Horne owed him money, and Denis was angry that he hadn't been paid. Perhaps Horne slighted him. Perhaps Horne knew something that Mr. Denis didn't want put about."

Pomeroy considered this. "All those things could have happened. All the same, I'm not arresting the man. And you'd do best to let him alone, Captain. He's a one what likes his privacy. Pretend he never went to that house, and you know nothing about it."

"I already have an appointment to speak to Mr. Denis."

Pomeroy looked me up and down then spoke in a slow voice. "You know, Captain, when we were on the line, opinion in the ranks was that you were one of the bravest officers in the King's army. The bravest and the best. But sometimes, we thought you went too far. You were so crazy-brave, you expected all the rest of us to be, too. Like charging a hill loaded with artillery. We thought we should truss you up and toss you in the baggage carts. Meaning no disrespect, sir."

I looked him in the eye. "We won that hill, Sergeant. Which allowed our infantry to move through."

"It didn't make you any less insane. This is another case you ought to be trussed up, sir. Don't have nothing to do with Mr. Denis. You'll regret it something powerful. Let Bremer be the culprit. Easiest on everyone."

Except Bremer, I thought. I changed the subject. "What do you know about the murder of a young woman in Hampstead?"

Pomeroy's eyes gleamed. "Someone else has been murdered?"

"The body was found about a week or so ago, in the woods. A young woman. She'd been there a while."

"Hmm, I think I remember hearing about it. A maid or some such?"

"A kitchen maid for Lord Sommerville. Her name is Matilda. I'd like to know her surname, and also the name of her brother who traveled to Hampstead to identify her body."

"What do you want to know for?"

"I'm interested. Also, any information on a woman called Charlotte Morrison, who disappeared about the same time the girl was killed."

"Oh-ho. You think the two are connected."

"They might be. I have no idea. Have you had any leads regarding Jane Thornton?"

"Not heard a word, but I've got an ear out. I saw your notices. I wouldn't mind ten guineas meself.

You giving out rewards for information on the other two?"

"Not as yet. When you hear anything at all, send word to me." I started to walk away.

"I ain't your sergeant anymore, Captain. I don't take orders from you, you know."

I swung around. "But I'm mad, remember? You never know what I might take into my head to do."

I left him then, muttering not quite under his breath about right-bastard officers who liked to make a hell of everyone's lives.

*** *** ***

I went back to the Thorntons' house in the Strand. The one person who had been present for Horne's murder was Aimee. I'd wanted to leave her alone, to let her turn her back on Horne and his house, but Bremer's fate might depend on her answers to my questions.

Alice greeted me and informed me that Mr. Thornton was still alive. He had come 'round the day before, but now lay asleep again, dosed with laudanum. I was encouraged, but did not give in to hope. He still could so easily slip away.

I asked to see Aimee. Alice looked surprised, then told me that she'd gone to stay with her aunt, a woman called Josette Martin. She gave me the direction, and I headed east in a hackney through the Strand and Fleet Street and into the City, to a small boardinghouse near St. Paul's Churchyard.

"Captain." Josette Martin met me in the middle of a neat, though shabby drawing room and shook my hand. Threads of gray laced her brown hair, which was braided and looped in neat coils. Her face was square and her nose snub, but her eyes were large and wide, framed with long black lashes.

"Mrs. Martin."

"You are the gentleman who brought Aimee home?" She spoke flawless English, but with a fluid French accent.

I acknowledged that I was.

She motioned to me to sit in an armchair then perched on a sofa a little way from me. "It was very good of you to help her. How did you come to find her? She remembers very little."

Even as she expressed gratitude, her look was wary. She must have wondered what I'd been doing in the house where her niece had been held captive.

"Will she live with you now?" I asked.

She nodded, candlelight catching in the gloss of her hair. "I raised Aimee after her parents died in France. I trained her to be a lady's maid, as I was. But I believe we will not stay in England. We will return to France when she is well."

"How is she?"

"You are kind to ask. Aimee will recover, in body at least. He was very cruel to her. The man is dead?"

"Most definitely dead."

Josette's eyes hardened. "Good. Then God has taken his vengeance. Do you think that wicked of me?"

"To be happy that the monster who hurt your niece is dead? I feel the same."

That seemed to satisfy her. "I thought at first you'd come from the magistrate. To question her."

I kept my voice gentle, though impatience pricked me. "I do want to ask her a few questions if she is well enough to speak to me. I am trying to find what became of her mistress."

"Miss Thornton? I am worried for her as well. The Thorntons are poor. Aimee did the duties of upstairs maid and looked after both Miss Thornton and her mother, but they were all kind to her. It was a good place."

"May I speak to her?"

"I am not certain. She was in low spirits this morning, but she may agree to see you. She is grateful for what you did."

Josette rose. I got up politely and crossed to the door to hold it open for her. She flashed me a small smile as she went by, with even, white teeth.

I waited for nearly a quarter of an hour for her return. I tried to keep my patience, but I was annoyed with myself that I had not questioned Aimee from the start. I might have prevented Bremer's arrest—not only did I not believe the butler had killed his master, I also wanted to get Bremer into my clutches to find out what had happened to Jane. Pity had moved me to leave Aimee alone, but I might have cost Jane her safety.

Josette at last returned to tell me that Aimee would see me, but she was very tired. I promised I would ask Aimee only a few questions, and Josette led me down a hall to a small bedroom in the rear of the house.

The room was dark, the curtains closed. Aimee lay on a chaise, wrapped in a shawl, her feet covered with a rug. She looked at me with enormous dark eyes in a pinched face.

Josette went to the window and rearranged the curtains to let in more light. Then she drew a stool next to the fire, fished mending out of a basket next to it, and began stitching. I pulled a straight-backed chair from the wall and seated myself next to the bed and Aimee.

During the war, I'd seen women, and also men, who had been brutalized by soldiers, wear the same look of blank fear that Aimee wore now. Their trust had been broken, their peace destroyed.

I kept my voice quiet. "Aimee, do you remember me?"

Aimee nodded, her yellow hair limply brushing the pillows. "From the house."

"How are you?" I asked.

Aimee turned her head and looked at the window, where weak sunlight tried to filter through clouds. "Alice and the mistress were kind to me. And Mrs. Brandon."

She spoke woodenly, and I noted she did not answer my question.

"I've come to talk to you because I want to find Jane Thornton. Anything you can tell me, anything about how you came to Mr. Horne's house and how she left it, will help."

Aimee had closed her eyes during my speech. Now she opened them and plucked at the fringe of the shawl. "I do not remember very much."

"Anything you can," I said. "I want to find Jane and bring her home."

Her gaze flicked to me briefly then away. "Alice told me how kind you've been. But I don't know how much I can help. They gave me opium to make me sleep and would not let me stay with Miss Jane. I want the opium all the time now, and it hurts when I cannot have it. Isn't that funny?"

I didn't find it in the least amusing. "Do you know how you came to be in Mr. Horne's house at all?"

"Not very well." Her voice died to a whisper. "I remember my young lady and I had gone to the Strand to wait for the carriage. It was so crowded that day, I did not know how it was going to find us. A woman, she came to us and asked Miss Jane to help her. She was dressed in rags and crying and begged for Miss Jane to come with her."

"And Miss Thornton went?"

"Miss Jane had a kind heart. She was afraid the woman was sick or in trouble, and so she went. The beggar woman took us into a tiny court a little way down the street, and then I remember nothing. Perhaps someone hit me, I do not know. I awoke in an attic and I was very frightened, but Miss Jane was there, and she comforted me."

"Was this attic in Mr. Horne's house?"

"No. I do not know where we were. We were bound hand and foot in the middle of the floor and could not get loose. When it was very dark, people came and gave us something to drink. I knew it was opium, but they made us drink it. When I awoke again, I was in another attic, but in a bed, and Miss Jane was there, with him."

"With Mr. Horne?"

She nodded, her eyes filling. "He told Miss Jane he'd hurt me if she did not do what he said. I begged her to not listen, to run away, but she went with him. She always did what he said."

"She did not try to run away, or find a constable, or go home?"

Aimee shook her head against the pillows. "He did not have to hold her with a lock or a door. She was so ashamed of what she'd become, even though it was not her fault. I told her to go, and it made no difference about me, but she would not. And then he sent her away. All alone, with nothing. He broke her spirit, then he tossed her out like rubbish."

For the first time since I'd entered the room, Aimee looked directly at me. Her wide brown eyes held deep and unwavering pain and unmasked fury.

"Did he send her somewhere?"

"I do not know. One morning, she was gone, and he would not tell me where, though I asked and asked. I know he must have thrown her out."

"Was she going to have a child?"

"I do not know. She would not tell me. But I think so. *He* thought so."

I hesitated a long time, trying to put my questions in a way that would not hurt her. "You were in the wardrobe in his study the day he died," I said. "He put you there."

"Yes."

"When?"

Her fair brows drew together. "What do you mean?"

"Did he put you in that morning, or later, after his visitor had departed?"

Aimee's body drooped. "I do not know. I have been trying to remember. But I hurt so much, and I was so tired."

"Do you remember the visitor?"

"I remember Mr. Bremer coming to the study and telling him someone had come to call. Mr. Horne was angry at him. But then he told Mr. Bremer to let the guest upstairs. I do not know who it was; Mr. Bremer spoke so softly. After Mr. Bremer left, Mr. Horne carried me to the wardrobe. I cried and begged him to let me go back to the attics so I could rest, but he pushed me in and locked the door."

"Could you hear through the door what the two gentlemen spoke about?"

"I cannot remember if I heard them or not. The doors were thick, and I was sleepy."

I decided to try another tack. "After the other gentleman left, did Mr. Horne open the wardrobe again?"

She went silent a moment, her eyes reflecting pain. "I do not believe he did, sir. I was well and truly asleep after that, and I remember nothing."

I sat back. If Horne had not opened the wardrobe again, that might mean he'd been dead when his visitor, Denis, had left him. But Horne may have simply decided to leave Aimee there, and someone else could have come to the study and killed him while she slept.

"The butler, Bremer, has been arrested for Mr. Horne's murder," I said.

Aimee's eyes widened. "Mr. Bremer, sir? He did not. He could not have."

"It is possible that he did. After Mr. Denis—Horne's visitor, that is—departed, Bremer could have come in and stabbed Mr. Horne, not realizing you were in the wardrobe."

"Oh, no, sir, not Mr. Bremer."

"Why not? You said you heard nothing."

She shook her head, alert now. Josette looked up from her stitching.

"Mr. Bremer is a foolish and weak old man," Aimee said. "He was terrified of *him*. He never could have done such a thing."

"You do not think that even an elderly man, cowed and frightened, could have killed him in a fit of terror?"

Her lips whitened. "I do not know."

"What about the other staff? Could any of them have killed him?"

"I never saw the others. Except Grace."

"What about Grace?"

Aimee's brow puckered. "I think—I don't remember. I never saw her that day, I do not think." Her eyes lost their glitter, and she touched her hand to her throat. "I am sorry, sir. I'm very tired."

Josette put aside her stitching and rose. "Aimee should rest now, sir."

Disappointment touched me, but I got to my feet. I'd hoped Aimee would tell me everything I needed to know, but I could not expect a tormented and ill woman to have all my answers for me.

I wanted to give Aimee words of comfort, to help her with pretty phrases, but I had nothing to give. She had been broken, body and soul, and it would take a long time for her to heal. Perhaps she never would, completely.

Josette accompanied me to the front room, her gait rigid with disapproval.

"Forgive me," I said. "I did not mean to upset her."

Josette looked up at me in sympathy. She truly did have beautiful eyes. "It is not your fault, sir. You had to know."

"I will look for Jane. I will find her."

"Yes, sir. I know you will. Thank you for being good to Aimee."

I took Josette's hand in farewell. Something sparked in her eyes, something behind the gratitude, and the anger, and the sorrow, something I did not understand. She looked back at me, bemused, and I released her hand and took my leave.

*** *** ***

That evening, I began looking in the brothels for Jane Thornton. I began with those known near Hanover Square and fanned out my search from there.

The witty called such houses nunneries or schools of Venus, and coined the madams who ran them, abbesses. But they were nothing more than bawdy houses in which a gentleman could purchase the company of a lady for an hour or a night. Many houses nearer Mayfair housed fine ladies, who might have begun their lives as gentlemen's daughters. The fashionable thronged to these high-flyers for clever conversation as well as for baser pleasures.

The farther east I traveled, the coarser the houses became and the less clean the girls. In each I asked about a young woman called Jane or Lily.

What I got for my trouble were threats, being shoved from doorsteps, and nearly being pummeled by the bullies who guarded the doors. After the abbesses discovered I had no money, they considered me a nuisance and wanted to be rid of me. I had to show the length of steel in my swordstick a time or two before their bullies would let me go. They must have sent word 'round to each other, because some were ready for me before I even arrived.

I visited the nunneries near my rooms later, after dark, just to be thorough. None were any more pleased to see me than those in Mayfair had been.

As I tramped down Long Acre, Black Nancy sidled up to me and slipped her hand through the crook of my arm.

"If you want a game girl so bad, Captain, yer can just come to me."

I glanced sharply down at her, not really in the mood for her banter. "I am looking for a girl who shouldn't be in the nunneries. Not one who should."

"You're that baffling, Captain. What are you on about?"

"A young lady's family is looking for her. I want to find her and send her home."

Nancy made a face. "Well, what if she don't want ter go? Reformers try to send me home all the time. Stupid sods. Me dad's worse than any flat I ever had."

Nancy had once told me that her father beat her, and I'd seen the bruises on her face that she tried to hide with paint and powder. "I think I do not much like your father," I said.

She chuckled. "Suits me. I don't like him either."

I strolled back toward Covent Garden, and she stuck to me like a dog following its master. "What's this girl's name? Maybe I know her."

"I'm not certain what she's calling herself. Maybe Jane. Or Lily."

She pursed her lips. "I know lots of Janes. No Lilies."

I looked down at her. "Are there any new girls on the streets of late? One who doesn't seem to fit in?"

"There's new girls all the time. They don't last. Would she work Covent Garden?"

I shook my head, depressed. "You don't know anyone called Charlotte, do you?" I hazarded.

"How many ladies do you want, Captain? No, I don't know no Charlottes. Why don't you want a Nancy?"

I studied the white-painted face beside me. "I have one more than I can endure now."

She grinned, her scarlet mouth wide. "Ain't you lucky I like you? 'Cause I'll tell ya something, Captain. I found your coachman."

Chapter Thirteen

I stopped short and looked down at her in astonishment. A squat man stumbled into me, then pushed past me with a curse.

"Why didn't you say so?" I demanded.

"You never asked. You were pleased to go on about your Janes and Lilies and Charlottes."

"Where is he?"

"Keep your trousers on, Captain. Or rather, no. I bet you're handsome in your skin."

"If you are only going to babble nonsense, I'll go home and keep my shillings."

Nancy clung to my arm. "Wait a minute. I'm only teasing yer. I did it just like yer said. I hung about watching the nobs come to the theatre. I asked and asked about people called Carstairs until I found their coach. But the coachman was new. Only been coachin' for the Carstairs for a couple weeks. Last coachman gave notice, you see, and went off."

"Damn."

She laughed and squeezed my arm. "Don't fret, Captain. I kept plaguing him until he told me where the last coachman had gone. He drives for some cove called Barnstable or some such name. But I found him. This Barnstable goes to the opera, too. We're fine pals now, Jemmy and me."

"Jemmy is the coachman?"

"Well, it ain't Mr. Barnstable, is it?" She snorted a laugh. "So I found him for ya. Where's my two shillings?"

"I wanted him to pay a call on me."

"Well, Jemmy don't want to. Why would the likes of him be going to a gentleman's rooms? No, I got him tucked away in a public 'ouse. Said I'd come and fetch you."

"All right, then. I'll give you your money when I've spoken to him."

"You're a mean one. Come on, then. It ain't far."

She led me back toward Covent Garden market, closed now, through the square and to another narrow street. A pub with the sign of a rearing stallion stood halfway down the curved and aged lane, and Nancy took me inside.

The pub was crowded, with a stream of people coming and going. Burly lads in household livery were obviously footmen who'd stepped in for a pint while their masters and mistresses sat in the theatre watching plays or operas. They risked their places doing so—the master or mistress might want them at a moment's notice—but they seemed content to take the chance.

Men and women of the working and servant classes lingered contentedly, talking loudly with friends, laughing at anecdotes. In the snug, a barmaid led a rousing song. Nance took me to a highbacked settle with a table drawn up to it. She smiled at the man sitting there before snuggling in beside him and plopping a kiss to his cheek.

"This is Jemmy. I brought the captain to yer."

I slid onto the bench across from them. Jemmy was not a big man; he'd be perhaps a half-head taller than Nance when standing, but his black coat, shiny with wear, stretched over wide shoulders and tight muscles. His brown hair was greasy and fell lankly over his forehead. His wide face split into a grin at Nancy, showing canine teeth filed to points.

Jemmy raised a hand, washing the smell of sweat and ale over me. "Well, here I am, Cap'n. What do you want of me?"

A plump barmaid plopped a warm tankard of beer in front of me. She smiled at me, revealing two missing teeth, ignored the coachman and Nance, and sailed away.

"Bitch," Jemmy muttered.

"Aw, Jemmy, you don't need her. You got me." Nance wriggled herself under his arm. He encircled her shoulders with it, letting his fingers rest an inch from her bosom.

I had planned to question Jemmy subtly, but I was very bad at anything but blatant truths. Plus, the way he touched Nance sent flickers of irritation through me.

"You used to coach for the Carstairs family," I said without preliminary.

"Yeah. What of it?"

"You once drove to the Strand and retrieved Miss Jane Thornton and her maid for an afternoon of shopping with young Miss Carstairs."

He hesitated for a long moment. "Who told you that?"

"I know it. Many people know it."

Alarm flickered in his eyes. "They sent me on all kinds of errands for the spoiled little chit. Don't remember all of them. I'd give her the back of me 'and, she was mine."

I went on ruthlessly. "On that particular day you went to fetch Miss Thornton and her maid, but when you reached the Carstairs' house, they were gone."

His eyes went wary. "I know that. They got in, but there wasn't a sign of 'em when I opened the door at the house in Henrietta Street. Could have knocked me down with a feather."

"You never saw her get out of the carriage."

"Saw who?" The corners of his mouth had gone white.

"Miss Thornton."

"Oh, her. You ever driven a coach, Cap'n? You got to drive the team and watch out for other coaches and wagons who have no business being on the streets. They lock your wheels, you're done for. I don't got time to look out what my passengers do."

"Or perhaps the passengers never got into the coach in the first place."

His mouth hardened. "Who's been telling you things? It's a pack of lies."

I leaned toward him, the stale steam from my beer engulfing me. I was making guesses, pieced together from what Aimee and the orange girl in the Strand had told me, but I had to try. "Someone paid you to look the other way that day. To drive to the Strand, wait a few minutes, then drive away again. You were to go back to Henrietta Street and claim you didn't know what happened. Perhaps later that night you were paid to return, to fetch the young ladies in earnest this time and drive them to Hanover Square."

"I never. It's lies, that is."

"If it is not the truth, it is very close to it."

Jemmy shoved his glass away from him. Ale slopped onto the pitted and stained tabletop. "Who says it is? You going to take me to the beaks? And tell them what? No one is left to prove it."

"No," I mused. "Horne is dead; Miss Thornton is gone. Did Mr. Carstairs ask you to go? I wager he did not like the questions people asked when Miss Thornton disappeared. Or perhaps your real employer decided you should quit the house before anyone became suspicious."

"Don't know what you're talking about. I'm a coachman. I drive coaches for gentry."

"It must be lucrative," I said steadily, "but difficult, to work for Mr. Denis."

Jemmy flushed a sudden, sharp red, and his eyes held fear and hate. "Is that why you came, to throw lies in my face? Is that why you got your whore to chum to me?" He shoved Nance from him. "Get out. I don't want you."

"Aw, Jemmy —"

"Get out. I don't want to see you, understand?"

Nance's lip trembled. "Jemmy, I didn't know."

"Go on. And take your flat with you."

Nance stared at him in hurt dismay. I rose and took her arm, gently getting her to her feet and leading her away. The red-faced barmaid grinned at me, and I tossed her coins for the ale. She winked and tucked the money into her bodice.

I led the dejected Nance out of the pub and into the dark streets.

"Don't mourn him, Nance. I am just as glad you're away from him. I don't like the way he put his hands on you."

She brightened, though tears glittered on her face. "Are you jealous?"

"Disgusted, rather."

She stopped. "You think I am disgusting?"

"I did not say that."

"You do think so. That's why you always put me off." Another tear rolled down her nose.

I took her arm and pulled her to the brick wall of a house, out of the way of traffic. "I'll thank you not to put words in my mouth. I found your coachman disgusting. I do not find you so, and I am happy that you are away from him."

"Oh." She gave me a long look from under her lashes. "I took a bath. Washed meself all over."

"Did you?" I asked, bemused.

"Because you likes girls as bathe themselves. It wasn't fancy soap, but I smell clean. Don't I?"

She shoved her hand under my nose. I moved it away. "Nance."

"You don't have to give me money for it. Or for finding Jemmy, because he turned out a bad 'un." She drew her finger down my lapel. "I fancies ya, yer know. That's why I'm always teasing yer."

I would never make her understand. Her world was not my world, even if the edges collided from time to time. "We had a bargain. Two shillings when you found the coachman for me. Here." I pressed coins into her hand. "Take yourself home for the rest of the night."

"And get knocked about by me dad for coming back too early? But you don't care tuppence for that."

"I do."

"If you did, you'd take me as your own."

Her brown gaze measured mine. I held it, wishing I could help her—not in the way she wanted, but in a way that would keep her from harm. But a man without money in London is powerless. I looked away.

"Not tuppence," she said. "I don't care *that* for your airs. Yer no better than the rest of them. And you lost me Jemmy, too." She squirmed from my grasp and ran off.

"Wait."

I could take Nancy to Louisa. Louisa was no fainting flower. She could do something for her, train her, give her a character, find her employment.

Nance ignored me and kept running. I started after her. A rumbling cart, driven by a madman, swept between us. By the time it had gone, Nance was far from me, darting in and out of clumps of hurrying people. I would never catch her. With my lame leg, I was no match for a young, healthy girl.

I went home. I'd see her again. Nance's regular haunts were Covent Garden market and the streets around it; our paths would cross soon.

If I had known then under what circumstance we'd meet again, I'd have gone after her then and there, damn my leg and the London streets. But one does not expect life to be so capricious.

Chapter Fourteen

The next morning I returned to Hanover Square. Number 22 looked shut up: curtains drawn, the doorstep unswept. The handsome houses to either side of it radiated disapproval. A murder, and such a murder, occurring between them was not to be borne.

I had written Grenville to ask who Horne's heir was, and had read the answer in both his letter and the newspaper. Horne's cousin, a man called Mulverton, had arrived in town to bury Horne. I wondered if he would hasten to sell the house, and if he had any knowledge of his cousin's death. I wondered if he was a poor man who would happily send Horne out of the way in order to inherit a fine house in Mayfair and any income that went with it.

I knocked at the door. No one came. The neighboring houses regarded me in icy silence. I leaned over the railings and peered down at the scullery door. In the darkness, I sensed a movement, although it might only have been a cat.

I made my way down the stairs, which were slippery with drizzle. I saw no one, but I heard a faint snick, as if a latch had been closed.

I rapped on the thick scullery door. Here, beneath the street, the odor of fish and slops hung heavily in the damp air.

The door opened a crack and the frightened eyes of the young footman, John, peered out.

He released his breath. "Oh, it's you, sir. I thought it were the constables coming back for me."

"Why should they?"

John opened the door, and I removed my hat and stepped into the chill kitchen.

"They might arrest me, too. Maybe Mr. Bremer told them I killed the master."

"And did you?"

His eyes rounded. "No!"

"I do not think Bremer did, either."

The kitchen table was cluttered with boxes and sacks, bowls and copper spoons, all resting on the grimy flour left behind in the cook's hasty departure.

"Then why did they arrest him?" John asked, closing the door.

"Because they had no one else to arrest. Where are the rest of the servants? Why are you still here?"

He blinked at me, and I realized I'd asked him too many questions at once.

"The new owner, the master's cousin, came to take possession today. He told me to pack up all the things and have them carted off so he could sell the house. He didn't like Mr. Horne's things."

I couldn't blame him. The dreary furniture, the bad paintings, and the Egyptian friezes would have grated on me as well.

I leaned my hip against the kitchen dresser and watched him resume activity at the table. "When did the cousin arrive?"

"Yesterday, sir."

"Is he here?"

"No, sir. He's been and gone."

"Gone where? Back home? Or does he stay in town?"

John clanked copper spoons into one of the crates and tossed a platter on top. "He never said. No, a moment, I lie. He said he was taking rooms. In St. James's." He heaved a long sigh. "He wants to sell the house right away. As soon as I'm finished here, I'm out a position. A good one, too."

I folded my arms. "What about the other maids, Grace and Hetty? Where have they gone?"

"Dunno, sir. Hetty marched out the morning after the murder was done. Went to stay with her ma, she said. Gracie, I ain't seen."

"Does Grace have family, or friends she might have gone to?"

"There's her sister."

I checked my rising impatience. "Do you know where she lives?"

"Place near Covent Garden. I took her home once. Street called Rose Lane."

I felt a dart of irritation. Rose Lane was one over from Grimpen Lane. The girl had been under my nose for days.

"What about the valet?" I asked.

John snorted. "Marcel? Gent next door snatched him up, didn't he? Had his eye on Marcel ever since Marcel came here, oh, three months ago. Soon as he heard the master was dead, Marcel lit out and took his new position that very night."

The gent next door must have made Marcel an unrefusable offer. I wondered, had the valet made all haste to dissociate himself from the crime, or had he simply jumped at the offer of a lucrative position? John was right, good places were hard for servants to find. But if Marcel had anything to do with Horne's death, why would he have gone only as far as next door?

"What is the name of this gent?" I asked.

"He's a lordship. Lord Berring. A viscount or some such."

"Right- or left-hand?"

"Sir?"

"Which house? The right- or left-hand house as you face them?"

John blinked a moment then pointed toward the south wall. Left-hand it was.

"And who is in the right-hand house?"

John stared a moment, then to my surprise, he broke into a grin. "Gent called Preston. Never home. Son is, though."

I remembered the very first time I'd stood before number 22, when Thornton had been throwing bricks at it and screaming his grief. The curtain in the window above number 23 had shifted, the person behind it far more interested in what was happening outside than in protecting himself.

"Who is this son?" I asked.

John chuckled. "Young Master Philip. He likes a chat, sir, whenever I goes by. Hasn't got many who'll talk to him, poor lad."

I stored that information away, reflecting that a lad who liked looking out the windows might prove useful.

"Thank you," I said, and turned to depart.

"You wouldn't happen to be looking for a footman, would you?" John asked wistfully. "Only I can do all kinds of work. Except garden."

I shook my head. "If I hear of anything, how may I send you word?"

"Oh, I'm going back to my ma too. In the Haymarket. She so wanted me to go into service. She thinks I'm a useless lout. Maybe she's right." He stopped a moment. "What happened to the girl, sir? The one called Aimee."

I raised my brows. "Aimee has gone to live with her aunt."

John sighed and dropped a bulging sack into the crate. "I told her, if she ever wanted me, all she had to do was send word. She never did."

I could not feel surprised by this. Likely Aimee wanted to put anything associated with Horne's household far behind her.

"She needs time to heal," I offered. "When she has rested and mended, perhaps she will remember you."

I very much doubted it, but he so wanted the crumbs I tossed him.

John brightened. "That may be, sir. I can wait."

I wondered for a moment if John had murdered his master in jealousy and anger over Aimee. He was a large and strong young man who could easily have overpowered the smaller Horne and stabbed him in one quick blow.

My speculation ended there. I could not imagine John calmly waiting for the body to be discovered, and still longer for Aimee to be found. He would have smashed open the wardrobe door and carried her off into the night.

I said good night and left the kitchen through the scullery. As I closed the door, John tipped an armload of cups into a crate, where they landed with a smash of porcelain. He tossed in a copper pot on top of the lot.

I climbed back to the street. The rain came down harder, and the low clouds darkened the day. I walked to the left-hand house, my shoulders hunched against the wet.

I did not know Viscount Berring, and calling on him without introduction or appointment, especially with his lofty station, would be extremely bad manners. He'd think me an uncouth lout, but I had to waive etiquette in pursuit of my quest.

The footman, who looked as though he had a few more thoughts between his ears than did John, took my card, ushered me silently into a reception room, and disappeared.

This house matched Horne's in layout—a fine staircase on one side of the house, and two grand rooms on the other—but there the similarity ended. Berring had decorated his house with paintings of taste and furnishings of comfort and elegance. I sensed a woman's touch, evident in the embroidered cushions, soft colors, and overall feeling of warmth.

The footman reappeared and, to my surprise, told me to follow him upstairs.

High above, on the landing that encircled the very top of the house, a little girl, a slightly older girl, and a woman, clearly their mother, watched me with undisguised curiosity. I saluted them, and the two little girls giggled. The woman gave me a gentle smile.

An unlooked-for and nearly overwhelming wave of loneliness swept over me. The image of a very small girl, very long ago, filled my vision, and in an instant I was carried back in time. I felt warm sun on my face, saw the flash of gold on my daughter's hair, saw her smile at me, reaching her small hands to mine.

The chill dark of London rushed back at me. It mocked me, that chill, reminding me of all I'd lost. I quickly looked away and followed the footman to the first-floor hall.

Viscount Berring received me in a bright room facing the square. He was a middle-aged man, slim and upright, with a full head of gray hair. He held out his hand.

"Captain Lacey? I have heard of you."

I grasped his hand politely. "I apologize for the intrusion," I said. "It is actually your valet, Marcel, that I have come to see."

Berring gave me a look of surprise and alarm. "Don't tell me Mr. Grenville sent you to lure him away. I pay the fellow well—he's a topping valet—but I could never offer him the distinguishment he'd get valeting for Mr. Grenville."

"Grenville is in no need of a valet that I know of. I wished to ask Marcel about his former master, Mr. Horne."

Berring made a face. "Nasty business, that. My footmen had to bodily evict the newspapermen all that night. Impudent fellows. What have you to do with it?"

"I am trying to discover who killed him."

He raised his brows. "Why the devil? Isn't that what the constables and Bow Street are for? Oh, do sit down, there's a good fellow. But you must already know Horne's butler has been arrested. Marcel told me all about it. Nothing more to discover."

"But I believe Bremer did not kill him. That the murderer has not been found."

"Good Lord." Berring looked at his sofa cushions as though the murderer might be hiding beneath them. "Are you certain?"

"Fairly certain," I said. "If I can find another culprit, I can make the magistrates certain."

"But see here, surely you have no need to muck about in it yourself?"

I knew what he meant. A gentleman didn't soil his hands chasing criminals or investigating crimes.

"I'm afraid there is no one else to muck about in it. On the day Horne died, did you happen to note anyone going or coming from his house?"

He shook his head. "We weren't home that day at all, which is a mercy. We'd journeyed to Windsor to visit my wife's family. Her father has an excellent wine cellar."

"But you returned that night."

"Very late. Such a ruckus there was next door. My footman came running back to tell of the murder, and I locked my wife and daughters and myself up tight in this house, I must say."

"After you sent for Horne's valet."

Two spots of red stained his cheeks. "Had my eye on the fellow since my own man departed to get married. Marcel's talents were wasted on a man like Horne. I saw no reason not to set him up here at once."

"But he might have murdered Horne."

"No, no, no. No question of that. He was away all that day, he told me. Only arrived home an hour after we did—and found his master dead. Took my offer there and then."

For a moment I contemplated that Lord Berring murdered Horne for his valet, then I dismissed the thought. "I wonder if you'd allow me to speak to Marcel myself."

Berring looked surprised. "Speak to him? He can't tell you more than I have already."

"Even so, I'd like to ask him a question or two."

"Very well, I suppose it would do no harm." He rose and tugged the bell pull, his expression bewildered. "Have a drop of port while we wait?"

Marcel was a tall and slim young Frenchman with a long, thin nose and wide-set brown eyes. He regarded me with an air of rigid politeness, his correct bearing betraying only the faintest hint of curiosity.

"Yes, sir?"

Berring waved a hand at me. "This is Captain Lacey. He wants to ask you questions."

Marcel turned forty-five degrees and faced me. "Yes, sir?"

I had hoped to speak to Marcel alone, but Berring handed me a tumbler of port, then settled into the sofa and looked on with interest. I would have to make the best of it.

"The day your former master died," I began, "you were out."

"Yes, sir." Marcel's accent was faint, his English precisely pronounced. "I was gone all that day. Arrived home at nine o'clock, and found he had been killed. The staff were most upset."

"And what did you do?"

"I went upstairs, packed my bags, and came here. His lordship had kindly offered me a place if I ever left Mr. Horne, and I came here to ask if he still wanted me. He did, and I took up the post immediately."

"You were quick off the mark."

Marcel made a gesture of indifference. "Mr. Horne was dead. What could I do?"

"Did the constables question you?"

"Indeed. The man, the Runner, was quite rude. Asked me a dozen questions about where I had been and what I had been doing."

"And what did you tell him?"

"That my business was my own on my days out. But I had not ever returned to the house, so how could I know what had happened?"

"You did not return at all that day?"

"No, sir. I had gone to Hampstead. I was very late returning. I was afraid Mr. Horne would be angry."

"Was he often angry at you?"

"No, sir. He was seldom angry at all. But he liked his routines and did not like to vary them. At ten he liked a glass of port and for me to help him undress."

"Every night? Did he not go out?"

"Not often, sir. He liked to stay at home."

"You knew, then, about Lily and Aimee."

Marcel looked blank a moment, then his cheeks reddened, though his countenance remained fixed. "Yes, I knew about them."

My temper mounted. Like the rest of the staff, Marcel had known and had silently condoned. "And yet, you said nothing?"

Marcel gave me a direct look. "If you want frankness, sir, I will give it to you. I found Mr. Horne disgusting. I much prefer valeting for his lordship. But Mr. Horne paid me to look the other way, and so I looked the other way."

I tapped my fingertips together. "Did it surprise you that someone had killed Mr. Horne?"

"It did very much, sir. He was not the most refined of gentlemen, but many men are not. I saw no reason to kill him for this. To murder must take great anger or hatred. To have enough of either, to be able to kill, one must be a madman."

"You believe whoever killed him was a madman?"

"He must have been, sir."

Berring looked up with a pained expression. "Is that all, Captain? This talk of murder is making me quite ill."

"One more question, Marcel. Did Mr. Denis call often?"

Marcel blinked a moment. "Mr. Denis? No, sir, he never called at all. He sent someone when he wanted to communicate with Mr. Horne. I believe Mr. Horne owed him a great deal of money."

"He came to the house that morning. Before Mr. Horne was killed."

Marcel raised his brows. "Indeed, sir? That is very surprising."

I regarded him in silence for a moment. Marcel kept his emotions below the surface, but he did not disguise them. I was certain Pomeroy would have checked in Hampstead regarding Marcel's whereabouts, making sure the man had truly been where he said.

"Thank you for speaking with me," I finished.

Lord Berring nodded at Marcel, who bowed and made his way out.

I deflated, as I realized that Marcel knew little more than I did. A pity Lord Berring's family had been in Windsor that day. The curious females I'd seen upstairs would no doubt have known every coming and going next door. But I doubted that Lord Berring would have let me question his wife and daughters whether they'd been home at the time of the murder or not.

"Thank you," I told Berring. "I'll take no more of your time."

Lord Berring waved me back down. "Nonsense, my good fellow. It's a dreary day. Have some more port and stay for a chat. Only, let us turn the topic from murder, shall we? Aggravates my dyspepsia something horrible."

Chapter Fifteen

After spending another three-quarters of an hour in unenlightening conversation with Lord Berring, I departed. I had tried to pry from him any information regarding Jane Thornton and Aimee, but he gave me a puzzled look and said he knew nothing about such goings-on. He could have been a master actor, but I didn't think so.

Before leaving Hanover Square, I took a chance and knocked on the door of number 23. A footman answered.

"Mr. Preston is not at home, sir."

"I've come to see Master Philip," I answered. I handed him my card.

The footman studied it curiously, then me. "Master Philip is not here either, sir. He's gone out in the carriage to take the air."

I suppressed a dart of impatience, but there was little I could do. I did not know the family and I could hardly force myself inside to wait. I made myself nod. "Please tell Master Philip that I called and that I will write to him for an appointment."

The footman regarded me dubiously, but nodded. "Yes, sir."

I made my way home then, intending to begin my search for Jane again, and to plan how to go about finding and getting myself introduced to Horne's cousin, Mulverton. Then there was the matter of Charlotte Morrison to look into. But Grenville's carriage stood in Russel Street, at the top of Grimpen Lane, and his footman politely informed me that Grenville was waiting for me at his club.

I was becoming irritated at Grenville's arbitrary summonses, but he might provide me some information on Mulverton. I let the footman help me into the coach. The conveyance was truly luxurious, with plush and tufted walls and deep cushions, and it was so well sprung that the hard cobbles of London jolted me far less than they did in any hackney. I rested my foot on the cushioned stool and resigned myself to the comfortable journey.

I descended into St. James's Street and made my way through the rain and lowering fog to Brooks's club. This early in the afternoon not many gentlemen were about. The club would fill to the brim later in the night when men would risk their fortunes, estates, and family reputations on the turn of a card. Even now, the more hardened players sat in the games room, hunched over green baize tables taking chances on macao or whist.

I asked for Grenville and was shown to one of the parlors. Three gentlemen, necks swathed in starched white, stood at the window, discussing everyone who passed below. Grenville was enthroned in a wing chair near the fire, facing an avid audience of two young dandies, a young lord, and Mr. Gossington, a prime gossip who cared only for his clothes and for sport.

". . . lime green waistcoat," I heard Gossington say as I approached. "*And* his trousers so puffed out he had to turn sideways to enter the room. I ask you."

Grenville saw me and lifted his hand to interrupt. "You must excuse me, gentleman. I have business with Captain Lacey."

His audience turned glassy stares on me. Gossington raised his quizzing glass and surveyed me through it from head to toe.

Grenville rose, greeted me, and led me to an empty sitting room beyond the parlor. He closed the door. "Gossington fancies himself the arbiter of fashion when Brummell is out of earshot, but he comes nowhere near. Though Brummell is getting perilously close to landing himself in the Fleet."

I had no interest at the moment in the famous debt-ridden dandy, though I could not know that a scarce month later George Brummell would quietly flee England and his creditors and never be seen in London again.

Grenville faced me. "You haven't been keeping me apprised of what you are doing. What is our plan of action?"

I hadn't realized we'd decided on one. I told him I had begun scouring the brothels for any sign of Jane Thornton, what I'd learned from the valet and John, and my plan to speak to Mulverton.

Grenville shook his head. "Mulverton might have killed him for the inheritance, but he probably knows nothing of Miss Thornton. No, we'll have to rely on the reward there, I'll wager."

I silently agreed. "Have we received any more replies to our advertisement?"

"A good many. All with no idea of Jane's whereabouts. They smell the reward, that's all."

"So it was a waste of time," I said flatly.

"Not necessarily. I hold out hope. We did discover the parallel disappearance of Charlotte Morrison. What shall we do about that?"

I thought over again what Charlotte's letters contained. We had discussed them a little on the way home from Hampstead but had drawn no conclusions. "It might be worth contacting this Geraldine Frazier in Somerset," I said. "Charlotte might have revealed something important in the letters she did not copy out."

Grenville tapped his fingers together. "One of us could travel to Somerset and speak with her personally. I could take on the task, while you remain in London and continue to search for Miss Thornton."

"It might be all a mare's nest, a false trail. You would journey all the way to Somerset for nothing."

Grenville shrugged, spreading his hands. "Perhaps Charlotte has gone there herself. Or the people who knew her—friends, villagers—might have an idea where she would go if she did run away."

"And if she did not?"

"Then we continue searching."

I sat back, frowning. "You seem eager to dash across England on only a slight possibility."

"I am restless. London has palled."

I raised my brows. "You have been in Town only since January. That has been, what, four months?"

"Laugh at me if you wish. I told you why I wanted to help you."

"Yes, your great fatigue with life."

Grenville jumped to his feet. "Damn it, Lacey. I might actually discover something useful. Perhaps I'll redeem myself in your eyes if I do."

I blinked. "What the devil do you mean by that?"

"I mean that you disapprove of me. I am frivolous and too rich and the people of London give me too much adulation. I agree with you. I want to prove you wrong."

I watched him, surprised. "I have never said such a thing."

"You do not have to. It's in your face every time you look at me."

"Perhaps I am thinking of the woman who lives upstairs from me, who has to shave every penny and even resorts to pinching coal and candles from me."

"While I pay fifty pounds for a pair of boots."

"Something like that."

Grenville was silent for a long time. When he looked at me, I saw a new expression in his eyes, but I was not sure what it meant. "If I offered her fifty pounds," he asked, "would she take it?"

I thought about Marianne and her pretty smiles and hungry eyes. "She's greedy and grasping, but life has made her so. I would be careful. She might believe you want to become her protector."

Grenville looked pained. "Perhaps I will make an anonymous donation and style myself a secret philanthropist. But there is another reason I am eager to help you."

"What is that?"

He smiled, his mouth drooping into its usual ironic lines. "I made a rather large wager that you'd clear up the mystery of Horne's murder and find the missing Jane. If I lose it, I will not be able to make donations to your upstairs neighbor. So it's in my own interest to help you as much as I can."

*** *** ***

I left Brooks's and went back out into the rain. I had to admit that Grenville's journey would be a great help. I longed to question Charlotte's friends myself, but I could ill afford to travel across England simply to talk to someone. If Grenville wanted to spend the time and money, I would not stop him. Also, his leaving would coincide with my appointment tomorrow with Denis. I hadn't bothered to tell Grenville about it. He'd only postpone the journey, and I wanted to face Denis without him.

On St. James's Street stood the Guards' club, founded for members of the Foot Guards. The cavalrymen, not to be outdone, had taken to meeting in a coffeehouse 'round the corner. I found myself in front of the coffeehouse before I'd decided what to do next, and ducked into its dark interior.

I scanned the rooms. Lieutenant Gale or his commander might well have stopped for a warm ale or coffee, and I wanted to ask again who had given Gale the order to halt the disturbance in Hanover Square. Perhaps I could shake it out of one of them.

My anger over Thornton's shooting and the abduction of Jane still had not abated. The helplessness of that family and the real grief of Alice, their maid, haunted my dreams. They were crushed and forgotten. Although the magistrates were very interested in the murder of the despicable Josiah Horne, no one gave a damn that a poor clerk's daughter had been ruined and violated by the same Josiah Horne. Gale and young cornet Weddington, after piling more grief onto the Thornton family, had dusted off their hands and walked away. If I ever saw Cornet Weddington again, I might be moved to violence.

Fortunately for Gale, Weddington, and my temper, I did not find either of them within. I found Aloysius Brandon instead.

Louisa Brandon's husband was five years my senior, and had been my commanding officer since I'd been a green and youthful lad. His dark hair was just going to gray, but his ice blue eyes still held the fire that had inspired me to follow him that long ago day when he'd convinced me to leave my fruitless life and venture with him into the unknown.

These days he wore a fretful look that came from the incidents between us, his boredom with civilian life, and the fact that he had no children, which meant that his wealth and tidy estate in Kent would be handed to a dissipated cousin he despised.

His trim body and handsome face had barmaids all over London vying for his favors, but he remained oblivious of them. Brandon showed no overt devotion to his wife, but it was inside him, burning and deep. I'd discovered how deep one day in Spain, and I believe he himself had realized the extent of his devotion that very same day.

Before that fateful moment, we had shared campaigns and wearying marches, happiness and grief, and we'd once been as close as brothers. Now we were bitter enemies, pretending, in public, to still be friends.

We regarded one another in tight silence. Brandon's eyes held apprehension, anger, and impatience.

"Lacey."

"Sir."

Three men of our acquaintance stopped at that moment to wish us a good afternoon. Brandon's relief was palpable as he turned to speak to them. When they bade us good-bye and moved on, the silence pressed us again.

Brandon gestured to the chair next to him. "Stay and have some port with me." His hand trembled, then stilled. He wanted me to refuse, walk away, return to the gray street.

I decided to punish him. I sat. "Thank you. I will."

Brandon moved away from me a fraction, then barked an order for port and water. We sat without speaking until the waiter brought a decanter, a small bowl, and a caster filled with sugar. I took my wine straight, with only a little water, but Brandon sifted a large amount of sugar into his glass and poured the dark liquid over it.

He took a sip of the concoction and regarded me with disapproval. "So you have mixed yourself up with the murder in Hanover Square. Sergeant Pomeroy told me. He said you had asked him any number of questions about this Horne fellow, then turned up to discover his murder."

I ran my finger around the rim of my glass. "I am taking an interest, yes."

"Why? Did you know the fellow?"

"No."

Brandon gave me a cold stare. "Then I don't understand why you've involved yourself."

"I happened to be there. Of course I am interested."

"Louisa told me about the girl he abducted. Did you murder him yourself?"

A passing gentleman heard the question and stared in astonishment. Brandon glowered at him until he hastily walked on.

"Believe me, sir," I said quietly, "I had thought of it."

"Disgusted me, what Louisa told me. I cannot really blame you for your anger this time. But wasn't someone arrested for the murder?"

"The butler. But I don't believe he killed him."

"Why the devil not?"

I shrugged, pretending that sitting next to him didn't make me tense as a violin string. "A feeling, an instinct, I am uncertain what. It also irritates me that everyone is happy to let him swing for it, mystery solved."

"Simple explanations are best, Lacey. You always want things to be complex."

I sipped my port. "The simple explanation is not always the right one."

"But it usually is, isn't it?"

I knew Brandon had stopped talking about Bremer the butler. He'd always believed I'd lied to him about Louisa, which had made me realize that for all his bleating about honor, he did not really understand it.

I did not bother to answer. What happened was over and done with, flogged to death long ago.

Brandon held my gaze for a long time then finally turned away and studied his sweetened wine. "I admit, your taste for trouble has proved beneficial before. You did find that would-be assassin while the rest of us were looking in the wrong place."

It was true that I had stopped an assassination plot against Wellington, based on a chance remark overheard around a barrel of brandy purloined from a French officer. Some had admired me for it; others accused me of currying favor. The deed did not garner me a promotion, and the accusations eventually stopped.

But although Brandon's nearness irritated me until my teeth ached, I could not let pass the opportunity to use him as a source of information. "Do you know Lieutenant Gale's commanding officer?" I asked him.

"Yes. Colonel Franklin. What about him?"

I studied the ruby red port in my glass. "I wondered why five cavalrymen were sent to put down the riot in Hanover Square the other day. Usually the military isn't called unless things are far out of hand. This was simply a handful of people throwing stones at one house."

"Perhaps they were taking precaution."

I raised my brows skeptically.

"Ask him yourself," Brandon grunted.

"I am not well enough acquainted with him to engage him in idle conversation."

Something glinted in Brandon's eyes. "He knows you lambasted Gale for it. He likely won't speak to me either."

I slanted him an annoyed look. "If he happens to mention it . . ."

"I'll write you."

We regarded another in silence. I noticed that Brandon had carefully not asked me why I had been seen at the opera with Louisa several nights before. But his eyes held winter chill, and his neck was red.

Once, when I'd first come to London, Brandon had tried to apologize. I had not let him. He'd never tried again. He wanted my forgiveness, but he didn't want to extend the same forgiveness to me, and I knew it.

So it went. We finished our port. Brandon feigned interest in billiards, and I declined, as he'd known I would. I felt his eyes on my back as I departed. I never would have dreamed, as a lad of twenty, how viciously, and how completely, love could turn to hatred.

*** *** ***

I took a hackney home. I descended at Grimpen Lane and stumped to Rose Lane, wondering where to begin looking for Grace, Horne's former maid. John hadn't been precise about where she was living.

I simply began inquiring at houses. The third door I knocked on produced a mobcapped maid who seemed to know all the goings-on on the street. She directed me to Grace's sister's house, informing me that Grace had recently been employed at a house in which the master had gotten himself murdered, just imagine.

I thanked the profuse woman, walked three houses down, and knocked at the door.

Grace herself answered it, and her eyes widened in astonishment. "It's you, is it? You'd better come in, sir."

Chapter Sixteen

She opened the door and allowed me into a narrow hall that smelled of boiled vegetables. "You were Mr. Horne's friend. I know you were. It's a terrible thing."

Her large eyes filled, and she drew a handkerchief from her pocket.

I followed her to a tiny, dark parlor in the front of the house, and we sat down facing each other. "I am trying to discover who murdered him," I said.

She sniffled into the cloth. "Mr. Bremer did, sir. They arrested him."

"But I do not believe he killed him."

The handkerchief came down. "To be truthful, sir, nor do I. The master was stabbed something hard, and Bremer couldn't have done that with such force. He had to have John carry trays up the stairs for him."

"Then who do you believe could have?"

Her eyes were large in her tearstained face. "I don't know. John would be strong enough. Or Cook."

"Did you find him?"

She started. "What?"

"Mr. Horne. When I came upstairs that day, you were in the doorway to your master's study. You were crying. Do you remember?"

"Yes, sir. I couldn't believe my eyes. There he was, the poor master."

"Did you find him? Did you open the door and find him there?"

She shook her head vehemently. "I would never have gone in without his permission. I would have knocked first. No, Bremer opened the door, and I looked inside."

"Why were you upstairs at all?"

The hand holding the handkerchief whitened. Her eyes moved past me, then back to my face, and she wet her lips.

The obvious explanation would have been that she was going about her duties. But she brushed her lips again with her pale tongue and replied woodenly, "I was fetching something. For Bremer. When he came to open the door, I looked into the room."

I pretended to believe her. "Were you fond of your master?"

She relaxed. "Oh, yes, indeed, sir. A kind gentleman he was, always giving presents and the like, and letting us have more days out than most. I'd have done anything for him."

"Including locking a girl in an attic and giving her opium to keep her quiet?"

Her handkerchief came down. "Aimee would whine and fuss so, just because the master liked to play a little. Lily were much more of a lady. She always did what she was told."

A hard edge entered my voice. "Do you know what happened to Lily?"

"The master sent her away, didn't he? Not surprising, really. He had set her up nice and proper, but she didn't like it one bit. Ungrateful cow."

"You said she always did what she was told."

"Oh, indeed. But with such airs, she did. Like she was being put upon, instead of the master favoring her. I'd have given anything to have the master's favor."

I tasted bile. At least Bremer had been ashamed. "The day Mr. Horne died, how long were you upstairs?"

"Why do you want to know that, sir?" she asked around the handkerchief.

"Were you there when Mr. Denis left?"

Her eyes went round. "Mr. Denis was there?"

"Yes. He visited for a time."

"Oh. I didn't know that. I was out shopping for cook until . . . Why did he want to come there? Bothering the master for money, I'll warrant. He was always writing the master letters, and the master would get fair put out when he got them. But it was so much safer for him not to come. You know that."

"I don't work for Mr. Denis, Grace."

She regarded me in astonishment. "You don't? But I thought . . ."

"You thought I was a go-between. Why did you think that?"

"Who do you work for, then? The magistrates?"

"No. I am working for Aimee, and Lily, who was really a young lady called Jane Thornton."

She gave me a puzzled look that wondered why I'd want to do anything for them. "I thought you were with Mr. Denis. He always sent someone different. Safer, wasn't it? Mean of you to let me think you came from him."

"What time did you return from your shopping that day?"

"I don't know, do I? Maybe about three."

Denis would have been gone by then, if John had told me the truth that he'd let the man out at half past two. "And you went upstairs?"

"I gave Cook her things and listened to her snarl about them. I slipped upstairs to get away from her."

"What were you to fetch for Bremer?"

Grace jumped. "What?"

She'd already forgotten her lie. I leaned forward. "What did Bremer tell you to fetch for him?"

Her face reddened. "Oh. I don't remember."

"You went upstairs on your own. Bremer had nothing to do with it. Why?"

She gave me a confused look. "Why do you say so?"

"Because you had plenty of time to dash upstairs, go to your master's study, stab him through the heart, and then pretend to be about your duties when Bremer came and found him."

Grace looked outraged. "I would never. I would never have hurt Mr. Horne. Never, ever."

"Then why were you upstairs?"

"That isn't your business, is it, sir?"

"You tell me the truth or I'll drag you off to the magistrate and you can answer his questions. I'll take you by the ear if necessary."

"But I didn't kill him."

"I don't care whether you did or not. I can make a magistrate believe it, and then you'll go to Newgate and Bremer will go home. So will you tell me? Or shall we go to the magistrate?"

Whatever Grace read in my eyes made her whiten. She glanced about as if looking for help but found none.

"All right, I'll tell you. I was listening at the door."

"Why?"

She twisted the handkerchief. "Always did, didn't I? When he was with her. In case he needed my help."

"Help with what?"

A shrug. "Anything. Sometimes she'd fight him, and I'd help him quiet her. Stupid girl. I wouldn't have fought him. Ever."

"So you were listening at your post that day, hoping Horne would call for you. What did you hear?"

"Nothing."

"Nothing at all?"

Grace shook her head, looking disappointed. "Nothing. But sometimes I can't hear nothing, no matter how hard I listen. The door is a bit thick."

"How long did you stay there?"

"Until I heard Bremer coming upstairs. Then I hid until he opened the door."

I fell silent. Would she have heard the murder take place through the heavy wooden door? Could the murderer have escaped between the time she fled and the time Bremer reached the door? Or had Denis left him dead, annoyed with the man for not paying him for Aimee and Jane? Or perhaps it had nothing to do with money. Perhaps Horne simply could not be discreet.

Anger boiled inside me. None of Horne's people gave a damn about the two abducted young women, except perhaps John, who'd become infatuated with Aimee. They cared only about a good place, high wages, or Horne's foul attentions, willing to look the other way at whatever the monster did.

I leaned to Grace again. "Where is Jane Thornton?"

Her brow wrinkled. "Who?"

"I just told you. The girl called Lily. Where is she? What did Horne do with her?"

"How do I know? She was there one day, gone the next. Good riddance, I say."

"Did he take her somewhere?"

"I don't know," Grace repeated in a hard voice. "I never asked. Most like she ran off."

"She disappeared, and it did not occur to you to inquire?"

"Why the devil should I? I didn't like her. Why the master liked her, I'll never understand. Such a milk-and-water miss. No wonder she was chucked out in the end."

I held my temper barely in check. "She was a respectable girl from a respectable family."

"Why didn't she go home, then? I wager it was she who done the master. She crept into the house and killed him. You should be trying to arrest *her*. "

I rose. "I have not ruled out the possibility that *you* murdered him, Grace. You had plenty of time and plenty of opportunity. And you were jealous."

She sprang to her feet, her eyes blazing. "How dare you say that to me. As if I'd ever have hurt him. They arrested Mr. Bremer, didn't they? Not me."

"But you were alone upstairs, listening at the door, and you disliked him giving his attentions to Aimee and Jane."

Grace's eyes widened, her voice rising with hysteria. "You can't prove that. A magistrate would never believe you."

But a magistrate most likely could and would. From the fear in her eyes, she knew that.

"I never killed him," she repeated breathlessly. "I never would."

I left her standing in the middle of the dingy sitting room, her mouth open in fear and outrage. I opened the door to the dark rain and let myself out.

*** *** ***

My rooms in Grimpen Lane gave me a cold and cheerless greeting. The fire had died and flakes of plaster floated down as I slammed the door. I limped to the fireplace, shivering, knelt, and began the tedious process of striking a spark to ignite the coal.

As the tiny flame licked over the dead black coals, I remained kneeling, staring into the fireplace. London was so damn cold and dank and dreary after the bright heat of India and Portugal and Spain. In Wellington's army, I had fought for my life and watched men die, endured disease and heat and the near madness of grief.

But I had lived. Every day, I had lived, as Grenville said I had. He envied me for it. Here, I simply existed. I did not fit in to London, and it did not know what to do with me. A career required money, connections, and influence, and I had none of those. Marriage required the same. Many a man without wealth or the right family might ship himself to the colonies of Jamaica or Antigua, but plantations there were built on the backs of slaves, and I could not be a part of that vileness.

I rested my face in my hands and thought of Spain, of the long days and weeks as we slowly, slowly pushed Bonaparte back to France. Summer nights had been warm there, balmy. I had known a Spanish woman, a farmer's young wife. She had not been beautiful, but her cup of water, delivered to me with gentle hands, had brought me back from death.

She and her two small children had nursed me in a tiny farmhouse miles from anywhere. Her husband had been killed by French soldiers, and she lived off the remains of the farm, hidden far from the lines of battle.

Upon reflection, I ought to have remained there. The army and Brandon and Wellington had thought me dead. Easy to have let them believe it and finished my life on that Spanish farm with Olietta and her two little boys. But I had been fevered to get back to my regiment, to reassure everyone that I was still alive.

I wondered whether Olietta would welcome me back if I journeyed to Spain to find her again. More than likely she'd found a Spanish man returning from the wars, happy to share the farm and her life with her.

I sent a silent greeting to her while the flame danced higher.

Someone knocked on the door. A fleck of bight yellow plaster, the color of the Spanish sun, landed on my finger.

"Come," I said.

The door opened and shut behind me, but I remained staring at the fire. Melancholia took me that way sometimes, suddenly, rendering me unable to move.

A swish of silk and the scent of Janet's perfume, and she knelt beside me and smoothed my brow.

"Hello, my lad. Are you blue-deviled again?"

I turned my head and pressed a kiss to her palm. "As ever."

"Remember how I used to drive the blue-devils away?"

I remembered. She kissed me. I slid my hands around her waist. A wisp of heat floated to me from the igniting coals, resuming the battle against the chill.

I laid Janet down on the hearthrug and we loved each other on the hard and soot-stained floor. Not elegant, but we'd shared less comfortable bed spaces in the past. The coal flamed yellow, then settled into a steady red glow, prickling our skin with heat.

We took each other fiercely, hunger in our mouths and in our hands. As I loved her, I remembered everything, the laughter, the foolishness, the unbearable summer heat, the brief, intense time when she had meant everything to me.

When we'd finished, I drew her close. "I had just been thinking of Spain."

"I was thinking of Portugal." Her eyes glinted. "How I told you that first night that I may as well sleep in your tent, as I had nowhere else to go."

"And in my bed, as there was only the one."

"Exactly." She snuggled into my shoulder, her auburn hair snaking across my chest. "I never thought I would miss following the drum."

"We did not know what the world was like."

"And what one had to do to survive."

"No," I answered, heartfelt.

We lay there in silence for a while as the fire warmed our bodies. I breathed the scent of her, trying to forget the grim world outside, the cold beyond our circle of warmth.

Half an hour passed. She sat up and reached for her clothes.

I caught her around the waist and pressed a kiss to her belly. "Stay."

"I can't, my old lad."

"My bed is not very comfortable, but I offer it to you anyway."

She pressed her fingers to my lips. "I truly can't, Gabriel. I'm sorry."

I licked her fingers.

She withdrew them, her face reddening. "I ought to have told you right away. Sergeant-major Foster has found a house in Surrey. He wants me to go and live with him there. I came here today intending to say good-bye."

Chapter Seventeen

"You are quick to dash a man's hopes," I said, trying to keep my voice light.

We stood in the chill staircase hall, both of us dressed, Janet tying on a yellow straw bonnet with a blue feather.

"I meant to tell you at once. Truly I did."

I folded my arms and leaned against the doorframe, my pulse beating fast and hard. "So you should have. Before you took pity on a fellow in his melancholia."

She flushed. "Please don't be angry with me, Gabriel. I came here on purpose to tell you I could not see you again. But I found I couldn't. Not so abruptly as that."

I regarded her steadily. "You could not before either, remember? When you left me for England? No promises, you said, no hopes."

"It is better that way, is it not?"

"I don't find it so."

She studied me, her eyes still. "I thought you would understand."

"That you would rather live with a man who's come into money? Did you decide that after you saw the state of my rooms, my poverty —"

"He'd invited me to live with him months ago. He said that when he found a house he wanted, I'd come live with him. He might even marry me."

My lips tightened. "Then why were you so anxious to see me again? If you knew you already had better prospects?"

"Because when I saw you . . ." Janet broke off, her eyes filling. "How can you ask me that? When you looked at me, and I knew you hadn't forgotten me, I realized how much I'd truly missed you."

I nodded, my throat tight. "And you assured me that Foster was a mere acquaintance."

"I didn't lie. I truly do only see him in the pub. I never thought he would find his house. I thought he was just talking. But today, he asked me."

"You ought to have told me you were waiting for such an offer. I might have beaten him to it."

She shook her head until her feather twitched from side to side. "I never expected anything from you. I would not demand anything. I thought we would simply come together and talk over old times, that is all."

I traced patterns on the doorframe. "Perhaps I wish you to demand something of me."

She looked down and away. "Mrs. Brandon told me what you have become. I can't be a burden around your neck, Gabriel. I won't. You have burdens enough of your own."

I stilled, anger filling me. "*What I have become?* Dear God, what the devil did she say to you?"

"That you are hurt. That you were broken."

"So you came to pity me, did you? Damn you. Why didn't you simply stay away?"

Her eyes flashed, answering my anger. "I didn't come to you out of pity. I promise you that. I came to find the man I'd left on the Peninsula."

"That man is gone, Janet. I see on your face that you realize that. And the man I am now is not the one you want, is it?"

"Gabriel, please don't."

I caught her chin, twisting her face up to mine. "You don't understand, do you?"

Her eyes told me she didn't. I leaned down and gave her a fierce kiss, and tears beaded on her lashes.

"I'm sorry," she whispered.

I lingered there, drinking her in, wishing to God I could buy her with houses in Surrey and that I could still dash through a rain-drenched camp just to bring her coffee.

I released her. "Don't worry, Janet. I know when I've lost."

"There are reasons. I promise you, someday, I will tell you my life story, and we will have a good laugh."

"A good laugh. Is that what we are sharing now?"

Janet's gaze flicked to mine. "You always did know how to hurt, Gabriel. You have a cruelty in you that frightens me."

"Perhaps it keeps me from being pitied."

"God help whoever pities you."

I let out a breath. When I spoke, I forced my voice to soften, though the anger did not leave me. "To lose you again so soon after finding you is difficult to bear, Janet."

She touched my cheek. "You will never lose me. You can't imagine how fond I am of you, my old lad."

I seized her wrist and pressed a kiss to it.

And then, despite my pride and my temper, I let her go. She gave me a crooked smile, Janet's warm smile, and she turned away and went down the stairs. Her footsteps echoed in the cold staircase and then were gone.

I leaned back against a painted shepherdess and closed my eyes. I'd had nothing to offer her, no reasons to expect Janet to stay. I had known when she'd left me in Spain that we would drift together and then apart again, without bond, without promise. But I no longer wanted that. I wanted something more.

My wounded spirit told me to go after her and beg her to stay. My pride and anger forbade it. As I leaned there, I remembered another loss, years and years ago, that had torn me apart until I'd gone nearly mad with grief. Only Louisa's quiet voice and her hand in mine had saved my life that time. I reflected with ironic mirth that this loss was comparatively easy to bear.

Footsteps clattered above me. I opened my eyes to see Marianne Simmons tramping down the steps, a folded newspaper in her hand. She peered at me in the gloom, her yellow ringlets a golden halo around her sweetly rounded face.

"Devil a bit, Lacey, I thought she'd never go. Who was she?"

I straightened up. "Someone I knew long ago."

Marianne gave me a cynical look. "So I concluded from your argument. In my opinion, you are better rid of her. That kind of woman wants to be sheltered, is afraid of being alone. She truly would be a burden around your neck. You need a girl with more pluck. One who does not need you."

I smoothed my hair back from my brow, trying to cool my temper. "My private affairs are my own business, Marianne."

She shrugged. "Then best not discuss them in an open stairwell. But that isn't why I came down. Did you put this advertisement in the newspapers?" She held up a copy of the *Times*. "Wherever did you find ten guineas?"

"Grenville is paying it."

"Ah, the famous Mr. Grenville. But I may be able to help you."

"Help me how? What do you mean?"

"I might know where this girl went. Was she belly-full?"

I nodded, trying to suppress my twinge of hope. I knew enough about Marianne not to take her words for absolute verity, especially not where money was involved. "Very likely."

"All right then. I know a place she might have gone."

"Where?"

"Show me the ten guineas."

I made an impatient noise. "Grenville will pay it."

"Let us pay a call on Mr. Grenville, then."

"He's gone to Somerset," I said.

"Then I'll wait."

I took a swift step toward her. Marianne backed away, clutching the newspaper. "If you beat me, Lacey, I won't tell you a thing."

"I am not going to beat you. The girl's father is dying. Each day I delay finding her might mean the end of him. If you know where she is, I swear to you on my honor you will get your ten guineas when Grenville returns."

Marianne pursed her childlike lips and tilted her head to one side. I imagined that when she regarded her rich dandies thusly, they fell all over themselves to please her. "I suppose if I have your word. You usually keep it."

"A gentleman's word is his honor."

She gave me a pitying look. "You have not met some of the gentlemen I know. Very well. Shall we go?"

*** *** ***

I rented a hackney at a stand and made Marianne accompany me to the Strand first, where I asked Alice to come with us. I did not know what Jane Thornton looked like, and I didn't trust Marianne not to play a trick on me for the dazzling prospect of ten guineas.

Marianne directed us to Long Acre then along Drury Lane toward High Holborn. After traveling this thoroughfare for a few minutes, we turned to a narrow lane and a little house that looked no different from the somber brick houses surrounding it. I raised a hand to ply the knocker, but Marianne stepped square in front of me and seized the knocker herself.

The door was open by a sullen maid with greasy hair and clean apron. "What'ya want?" was her greeting.

Marianne walked right in. "I'm looking for my sister."

The maid glared at me and Alice. "Who're they?"

"My brother and my maid."

The woman's look told me she no more believed her than if she'd said it had suddenly become July. But she stood aside and let us in.

The house had seemed quiet on the outside, but noise filled the inside. Voices poured down the stairs, women's voices: laughing, weeping, shouting, cursing, singing. An angry tirade rose in the upstairs hall.

"Give that back, ye thieving bitch!" A door slammed, cutting off the rest of the argument.

This was no brothel. The house had no comfortable front parlor for gentlemen to gather for cards or to talk sport before seeking a different sort of sport upstairs. No madam or abbess met us to rub her hands and offer me her finest—or call her bully-boys when she realized she'd not get any money out of me. But this was not a boardinghouse either. It resembled a boardinghouse, but the atmosphere was wrong.

"What is this place?" I asked Marianne. The maid had tramped away down the back stairs.

"It's a house where girls can come who need a rest. Or to lie low. Or for a lying in. Mostly for that."

I craned my head and looked up the dark, dusty stairs. "Who is the benefactor who lets them stay?"

"There is no benefactor. They pay to stay here, same as any boardinghouse. Nine pence a week, bed and board."

"You think Jane might have found her way here?"

"Could be. A girl at the theatre told me yesterday that there's a lady here that's stayed a long time. She came in same as the other street girls, but she's not a street girl. She talks genteel and is obviously well born and bred. But she's ruined like the rest of them. She helps the other girls through their lying-in and talks to them when they're blue-deviled. They call her Lady, but no other name."

My heart beat faster. "May I see her?"

"Cool your heels in the sitting room, Lacey. I'll find her."

Alice and I went to the small and dusty sitting room, while Marianne skimmed her way up the stairs.

"Do you think it's her, sir?" Alice asked. "It's just what my lady would do—never mind her own troubles to help others."

"We'll know soon enough," I said, though my characteristic impatience trickled through me and wouldn't let me sit. I paced while Alice watched me, not daring to hope.

After what seemed a long time, I heard Marianne returning. Another pair of footsteps overlapped hers. I turned, and Alice jumped to her feet beside me.

Marianne entered the room with a small young woman whose back was straight, her eyes large and brown, like a doe's, but holding a calm serenity. A white cotton fichu crossed her shoulders and tied at her sash, and she lightly touched it, as though it gave her comfort.

Alice's dark eyes filled with tears. "It ain't her. It's not Miss Jane."

"You are looking for someone?" The young woman's voice was polite, but her tone held caution.

"A girl called Jane Thornton," I said. "Or she might have used the name Lily."

"You are her brother?"

I shook my head. "Her family is looking for her. I'm helping them."

The woman assessed me a moment then relaxed a fraction, as though I'd passed some test. "If she came here, sir, then she is truly lost."

Alice sat down abruptly. "You've not seen her?" I asked the woman.

She shook her head. "I've lived here since Epiphany and have met no one by those names. She may have used another name, of course."

"You help the girls here?"

Lady inclined her head. "I'm one of them. I help as I can. I like to be useful. I, too, am lost, as they are."

My curiosity grew despite my disappointment. "You came here for sanctuary?"

"I came here for my-lying in. I decided to stay, as I had nowhere else to go."

Lady met my gaze with eyes calm and strong, but I saw grief in them. There were no signs or sounds of children here. If her child had not died at birth, she'd have given it up to someone else's care. I read in her that the decision had been a painful one.

Her acceptance made my anger flare. "And the name of the blackguard who made it necessary for you to come to this place?"

To my surprise, Lady smiled. "I will keep that to myself, sir. The sin was not all on his side, and I have been punished."

Had *he* been punished? I wished with all my heart she'd tell me his name so I could break his neck. I needed to put at least one person's wrongs right.

I handed her one of my cards. "If you hear of a girl called Jane Thornton, or Lily, or if she comes here, please send for me. Her family are worried."

She took my card, read it, and looked as though something amused her. "I will send word, of course, Captain."

I thanked her, and we departed. Another argument began above stairs as we left that house, disappointed and dejected. I looked back once before ascending the hackney, and saw Lady framed in the sitting room window, her white fichu bright against the dark panes. She looked back at me, but did not raise her hand or nod in farewell.

We traveled back down Drury Lane toward the Strand. Carriages from Mayfair were just making their way toward the Theatre Royal, the glittering coaches and glittering people emerging a sharp contrast to the wretches who scrambled to get out of their way. Beggars thrust hands at the fine ladies with diamonds in their hair until liveried footmen drove the beggars away. Across the road, street girls sashayed back and forth and called to the men. Two well-dressed gentlemen broke away to speak to them, never mind the respectable ladies who stood not a yard from them.

I didn't see the Brandon carriage anywhere around the theatre, and Grenville was out of town. Lady Aline Carrington, however, was there in full force, I saw as we passed, the gossipy Mr. Gossington with her.

Our one-seated hackney was crowded with the three of us. Alice, stuffed between myself and Marianne, sniffled into a handkerchief, and Marianne crossed her arms and glared out the window, not bothering to hide her disappointment. We reached the Strand, and I stood down to help Alice out at the end of the lane to the Thorntons' lodgings.

Marianne did not speak to me as we rolled up Southampton Street and through Covent Garden to Russel Street and Grimpen Lane. I paid my shillings and caught up to Marianne waiting upstairs outside my door. She swung around as I stepped off the landing. "What about my ten guineas?"

My mood had soured considerably. "We did not find Miss Thornton."

"I know, but I led you to a good place. If she's belly-full, it's likely she'll go there. I can use the blunt."

"God damn your ten guineas, Marianne."

She reddened. "I like that! I go out of my way to do you a bit of good, and you throw curses at me."

I strode into my sitting room and crossed to the writing table. I scribbled Grenville's address on the back of one of my cards, returned to the hall, and thrust the card at her. "Give Grenville time to return from Somerset, then go ask for your bloody ten guineas. Tell him I sent you."

I closed the door on her startled face. The image of Grenville's expression when she turned up on his doorstep filtered through my melancholia, and just for a moment, I let myself feel amused.

*** *** ***

The next afternoon, I took a hackney to Curzon Street, the heart of Mayfair, pulling up, just at the stroke of three, in front of the house James Denis had directed me to.

The house reminded me strongly of Grenville's. The outside was plain, without ostentation; the inside was elegant, tasteful, quiet, and expensive. I paused before a painting on the landing, which depicted a young girl standing by a window, pouring water from a jug. The bright yellows and blues and greens were astonishing. I recognized the painter, one of the Dutch school of the late seventeenth century. The painting was exquisite, rare, genuine.

The footman's dry cough tugged me away, and I followed him up the polished staircase. A sharper contrast to Horne's household could not be imagined. Everything here spoke of refinement, of a person who knew the value of things and what made them precious.

The footman opened two double doors of rich walnut and ushered me into a library. The room smelled of books and wood and of a fragrant fire on the hearth. My boots sank into a red and black oriental carpet without sound.

Mr. Denis sat behind a large desk devoid of everything but one small stack of clean paper, a bottle of ink, and a pen. He was much younger than I'd expected; I put him to be in his late twenties at most. His hair was brown, close-cropped, and curled naturally, and his eyes were small under black brows. His mouth was straight and long, his face square. He rose while the doors closed behind me and motioned for me to advance.

As I limped forward, I noticed the large man standing still as a statue near the window. His arms were folded across his large chest, and he watched me from heavy-lidded eyes, as though he were half-asleep.

Denis came around the desk and shook my hand. He was of a height with me. His face might be described as handsome, but when I looked into his dark blue eyes, I saw nothing. No emotion, no speculation, no thoughtfulness. Nothing. If eyes were windows to the soul, the shutters of James Denis were firmly closed.

"Please sit down, Captain." Denis returned to his desk and rested his hands on the bare surface before him, as if fully expecting to be obeyed.

A pair of damask chairs waited in the middle of the carpet. I moved to one of them and sat.

Denis studied me a moment with his emotionless eyes. "Please clarify something for me. Are you an acquaintance of Mr. Grenville or of Mr. Horne? It is most unlikely for a gentleman to be both."

"Grenville is the acquaintance," I answered. "I met Horne by chance."

"And you prevailed upon Horne to write to me for an appointment. Why?"

"He told me that you obtained things for gentlemen."

Denis inclined his head a fraction. "I have, in the past, provided certain assistance to people I know. I do not know you. What is it that you hoped me to find for you?"

I made an uncomfortable movement, but I was determined to brazen it out. "A young lady."

"I see. For what purpose?"

"What do you mean, for what purpose? For what purpose do you suppose?"

"You might have a benevolent streak and wish to adopt an orphaned young woman to raise as your own. Or you might want a companion to share the rest of your hopefully long life. Or you simply might want someone upon whom you can relieve your base lusts."

A trickle of perspiration slid down my back. "It is the latter, I am afraid."

Denis regarded me for a long moment. When he spoke, his voice was even more colorless, as though he regarded me with distaste. "You could obtain such a thing for yourself. London has an unfortunately large commodity of women for just that purpose."

"I do not want a girl from the streets. I want—a young lady." I had difficulty making my mouth form the words.

"And you believe I can find one for you."

"As you did for Mr. Horne."

In the silence, a green log popped and a smattering of sparks hissed back into the fire. "He told you this?"

"Not in so many words. I drew the conclusion."

Denis studied me for a long time, his expression still neutral. Finally he spoke, as though ending an internal debate. "What I obtained for Mr. Horne cost him a large sum of money. A very large sum. Such a thing was difficult, dangerous, and I must admit, distasteful. You, Captain, cannot afford it."

"No," I said. "But Mr. Grenville can."

His lids lowered briefly. "Mr. Grenville would hardly lend you money so that you could satisfy yourself on a respectable virgin. He is careful of his acquaintance and unlikely to cultivate a friendship with a man of such disgusting tastes."

I made a conspiratorial gesture. "He does not need to know."

"He knows everything about you," Denis said. His blue eyes bored into mine. "As do I. I suggest, Captain, that you drop the pose."

Chapter Eighteen

I said calmly, "I have always been bad at lying."

Denis sat back and rested his hands, palms down, on the desk. "Yes, your skills are remarkably ill developed. What is it you truly came here to discuss?"

I looked him straight in the eye. "Miss Jane Thornton. And her maid."

Nothing, not even a flicker of recognition. "Who are they and what have they to do with me?"

My pulse beat faster. "You procured them for Mr. Horne. The late Mr. Horne."

"I did read in the newspaper of Mr. Horne's unfortunate death. London is a dark and violent city, Captain."

"You destroyed an entire family, damn you. For his paltry fee."

Denis's smooth fingers tightened the barest bit. "If I had done what you accuse me of, the fee would not have been paltry, I assure you."

I no longer tried to rein in my temper. I'd had enough of people caring nothing for the missing Jane, and for Aimee, frightened and destroyed. I rose. "You procured her, and you sold her, just as you sold the painting to Grenville and his friend."

I sensed a movement beyond my right shoulder. The man at the window, no longer looking half-asleep, had come alert.

Denis gave him a small, subduing gesture. "Gentlemen sometimes ask me to obtain for them things that others cannot. It is expensive. One needs planning, the right contacts. I can do what they can't. That is all."

"You cloak it in vague words, but you sold her the same as you would a prostitute to a nunnery."

Faint color touched his cheeks. "If you have come here to crusade, I suggest you rethink your position. I know you've questioned my coachman, and you questioned Horne and Grenville. But I warn you, Captain. Do not interfere in my business. You do not have the power or wealth to do so with impunity. And do not think to hide behind your friend Grenville. His greatest quality is his discretion. He will not help you."

"Do you expect me to turn my back as you ruin young women and their families?"

"You must do as you please, of course."

I rested my fists on his desk. "Horne didn't pay you for it either, did he? That's why you went to see him the day he died."

Denis steepled his fingers and regarded me quietly over them. "My financial arrangements are my own affair."

"I know Horne owed you money. That fact has not been hidden. Did you murder him, then? Because he would not pay?"

"How foolish for me to kill a man who owed me money. I prefer to have money in my coffers than blood on my hands."

"And you wouldn't be able to pursue his heir for it, because you would have to explain the business transaction," I said. "I doubt you keep any records. I suppose I will have to satisfy myself with the fact that you will never see tuppence for Jane Thornton's ruin."

Denis regarded me through another long silence before he unclasped his hands. "I admire your bravery, Captain. Very few men would think to enter my house and make such accusations to my face. Or perhaps you simply do not know your danger."

"I was warned." Grenville had told me not to come here alone. Pomeroy had told me I was insane. I was beginning to think they were both right.

"And you came anyway?" Denis asked. "I must say, you have astonished me." He rose. "I bid you good day, Captain."

My breath came fast, and I did not take his outstretched hand. "I can't say I wish you good health."

The corners of his mouth twitched the slightest bit. "You are refreshingly blunt, Captain. But have a care. Do nothing more to inquire into my business. It is not worth it."

His eyes, again, held no menace, but I sensed a cold ruthlessness behind them. That coldness no doubt inspired fear in those who became acquainted with him.

I had lost my fear long ago.

I did not say good-bye. I simply turned and left him.

*** *** ***

I returned to my rooms, enraged and no further forward. Yesterday, I had believed that Denis murdered Horne, but after meeting him, I changed my conclusion. I believed Denis when he said he would have gotten more out of Horne if the man had remained alive. Denis must have been in a fair temper with Horne in order to pay him a personal visit.

I toyed with the idea that Denis had told the brute of a man who'd stood guard in Denis's study to physically frighten Horne, and said brute had accidentally killed him, but I discarded that idea as well. Denis was too careful. The brute would not have made a mistake. And Denis certainly would not have murdered a man when he'd been publicly seen paying a call on him.

But no one else had called on Horne that day. I was back to nothing. Perhaps the wretched Bremer had murdered his master after all. Or the cook had, because Horne hadn't sufficiently appreciated her sweetmeats. Or Hetty had in a fit of zealous righteousness. Or the frail Aimee had, then tied herself up and locked herself in the cupboard from the outside, all the while managing not to get a drop of blood on herself.

I seized my notes from the writing table and flung them into the fire. All my efforts had produced nothing. Grenville was still pursuing the question of Charlotte Morrison in Somerset, while I blundered about London to no avail. My leg ached, I'd spent a fortune on hackney coaches, and I'd done nothing useful.

No, Janet had found me useful. She'd amused herself with me while waiting to run off to Surrey with her new protector.

I realized suddenly that Marianne, of all people, had been right. Janet had always latched herself on to those who could help her most. She'd fixed her hold on me when she'd been reduced to promising her favors to the winner of a card game. She'd fixed on her sister's neighbor, Mr. Clarke, after her sister had died. She had fixed on Foster now that he was in a position to make her comfortable once more.

My anger spun around and settled deep inside me. For the first time in my life, I contemplated killing a man in cold blood. James Denis would never be touched by conventional justice. He was too careful, and even the Bow Street Runners were afraid of him. Pomeroy had compared my bearding Denis in his den to charging a hill full of artillery. Perhaps he'd been right.

I'd charged that hill because if I hadn't, the battle would have been lost and many would have died. The French had gambled all on that battery of guns. My sergeants had almost refused to give the order, but I had bullied them down. And I'd been right. The guns were trained to blast the squares of infantrymen and rifles below; they'd not anticipated a cavalry charge on their flank. Straight up that hill we'd gone, and captured the guns before they'd been able to turn them around.

Would not killing James Denis be the same thing? I could make another appointment with him, take a primed pistol in my coat, and shoot him across that empty desk of his. Or I could wait until he was returning home from an outing, open the carriage door, and shoot him then and there. Jane Thornton would be avenged, and London rid of a cold-blooded menace.

I would no doubt lose my own life in the process. I had noted the alertness of Denis's bodyguards and knew they were well paid to stop hotheads like me. But what did I have to lose? The society I lived in viewed any physical blemish with horror, and here I was, a lame man half out of my mind with melancholia, trying to be accepted as a gentleman on that society's terms. I never would or could. I saw for myself days and nights spent in melancholia, or in trying to forget I had no life to speak of. Who would regret my leaving it?

Louisa might.

Louisa. I repeated her name silently, clinging to it to bring me back from black despair. Louisa cared. Her caring had been the only thing that had kept me alive after her husband had done his best to kill me. I needed to see her.

I'd received another letter from her today about her damned supper party with the admonition that I attend. I would have to disappoint her. I was in no mood to make inane small talk at a gathering that would include her husband. I contemplated rushing out and shooting Denis at once, so as to have an excuse to avoid Louisa's dinner.

The joke relieved neither black humor nor my need to speak to her. I left my rooms and walked to Covent Garden theatre on the chance Louisa had attended tonight, but I did not see the Brandon carriage among those milling nearby. I did not see

Nance either. I cringed at the thought of journeying to the Brandon house in Mayfair and refused to dash about town looking for her.

In the end, I paid a visit to the Thorntons, and I found Louisa there.

"I thought you'd be deep in whist at Lady Aline's," I said, sitting down in the Thorntons' bare front parlor. Alice returned to a footstool before Mrs. Thornton, pale and worn, who was nodding off over a skein of wool.

"I wasn't in the mood for cards tonight," Louisa answered.

The red and blue and gold wool she was winding made bright splashes on her brown cotton gown. Her gray eyes and the thin bandeau winding through her hair were her only adornments tonight.

"How is Mr. Thornton?" I asked.

Alice glanced at me. "The same, sir."

I knew then I should not have come. Looking at them only made my heart harder. I caught Louisa's cool hand.

"Talk to me."

She looked up, frowning, but what she saw in my face made her still. She'd known me for a long time, and she knew what I was capable of.

She gently pushed my hand away, and then she began to talk of things small and unimportant. I closed my eyes and let her voice trickle through my anger, dissolving my despair, loosening the knot in my heart. I remained there while she and Alice spoke of the small things that made up everyday life, until I was able to trust myself to return alone to my rooms and so to bed.

*** *** ***

I felt slightly better the next morning. The post brought me a letter from Grenville saying he was starting home at once and that Somerset had proved interesting. He did not elaborate.

I tossed his letter aside and opened my reply from Master Philip Preston of number 23, Hanover Square. I'd written him the previous day before I'd set out for Denis's, asking formally for an appointment. He'd answered:

Dear Captain Lacey: I received your letter and thought it frightfully decent of you to write. I've been laid up since the end of Michaelmas term, and they let me see no one, but if you'd call at one o'clock today, I will ensure that you are admitted. I know you have been investigating the murder next door, because I've watched you out the window. You also faced the cavalrymen who quelled the rioters, by yourself, which I thought very brave. I'd much like to meet you and talk about the murder. Your respectful servant, Philip Preston.

The slanted juvenile handwriting and the scattered ink blots made me smile a little. I tucked the letter into my pocket.

At one, I emerged from a hackney in Hanover Square. The weather had turned, and a hint of May and warmer spring lay on the breeze that broke the clouds. May would also bring the wedding of the Prince Regent's daughter, Charlotte, to her Prince Leopold. The festivities were already the talk of London. After that, June would arrive with its long days of light. I looked forward to summer, though I knew it would be gone all too soon. The dreariness of most of the year did my melancholia little good.

I knocked at number 23, managing to avoid looking at number 22. A butler, who might have been cast from the same mold as that of number 21, answered the door. He began to tell me that Mr. Preston was out, but I handed him my card and told him my appointment was with the young master.

An indulgent look touched his face that made him almost human. "Of course, sir. Please follow me."

Chapter Nineteen

The butler led me through an echoing, elegantly furnished house with many pseudo-Greek pilasters and Doric columns and to the upper floors. At the end of one hall, he stopped, knocked, and opened the door when a young voice bade us enter.

The room behind the double doors was stifling. A fire roared high on the hearth and the windows were shut tight. Books littered the room, as did papers, broken pens, the remains of a microscope, and various other scientific-looking instruments.

Philip Preston himself hopped up from a divan. He was a tall, spindly lad of about fourteen, and his voice had already dropped from childish shrill to pre-manly baritone. I couldn't tell if his thinness came from his illness, or if he simply hadn't grown into the fullness of his body. He moved jerkily, as though someone controlled him with strings, and he executed an awkward bow.

"You aren't wearing your regimentals," he said in a disappointed tone after the butler had gone. "John next door, said you were in the cavalry. The Thirty-Fifth Light."

"I was. I only wear my regimentals on formal occasions."

He seemed to find this reasonable. "You are investigating the murder, aren't you? Like a Runner."

I moved newspapers aside and deposited myself on a chair. "Not precisely like a Runner." Runners got the reward money when a criminal was captured and convicted. I would get nothing for my efforts but the satisfaction of preventing a man from being wrongly hanged.

"I saw you talking to one. Big blond chap."

I inclined my head. "Pomeroy. Yes, he is a Runner. He was one of my sergeants on the Peninsula."

"Really? Bloody marvelous. Who do you think did the murder?"

"I came here to get your opinion on that. I believe you watch out the window a good deal."

Philip plopped himself on the divan. "I must. I'm not well, you see. I came home last Michaelmas with a fever and had it for a month. I'm still too weak to go back to school, Mama's doctor says."

I looked him up and down. Thin, yes, but his eyes moved restlessly, and the mess in the room did not speak of weakness.

"You spend much time alone," I said.

"I do. Mama is not well, either. She stays most days shut up in her rooms and doesn't come down. She will go out with Papa sometimes, but most days she will not. Papa stays out much of the time. He has business. He's in the Cabinet, you know."

Ah. That Preston. Right hand to the Chancellor of the Exchequer. A man like that would not have time to indulge a valetudinarian wife and a bored and lonely son.

"Do you ride at all?" I asked.

Philip's eyes lit up, then dimmed. "I have my own pony. But I don't ride. Mama's doctor said it would tire me."

I suspected Mama's doctor had discovered how to keep his fees rolling in from his wealthy patients. "We'll take you and your pony to Hyde Park and I'll teach to you ride like a cavalryman. That means how to ride long distances without tiring yourself."

His face blossomed a wide grin. "Would you, sir? I'd be free Monday. That is—oh, I see, sir. You are being polite to me. I'm sorry."

I shook my head. "Not at all. Good riding is a skill much admired in all gentlemen. I will show you how even an ill lad can do it."

He nearly danced in his seat, then shot a doubtful look at my walking stick. "Do you still ride?"

"I can," I answered. "I will meet you on Monday for a riding lesson, if you will tell me what happened out of the window the day Mr. Horne next door died."

Philip waved his hand. "I can tell you all that. My tutor was supposed to come that day, but Papa dismissed him because he got into a disgrace—the tutor, I mean—and I didn't have anything to do. I sat at the window and looked out. Really not much happened that day at all. The maid, Grace, went out in the morning, and then John, the footman. He waved to me. He talks to me sometimes."

"What time was this?"

"Oh, very early. About nine o'clock. They regularly go out then. Grace comes back with a basket full of things, and John generally brings back parcels. Grace went out again, around one. She was in a tearing hurry, and kept looking behind her as though afraid someone would see her. She didn't look up at me. She never does."

"Which way did she walk?"

He motioned. "Off that way, toward Oxford Street. She stopped to talk to a bloke at the turning."

"Did she? Did you see what he looked like?"

He flushed. "I'm afraid I didn't."

I waited. A young man who knew the servants next door by name and knew all their routines should be able to describe a stranger to perfection. But he looked at me shamefacedly. "The truth is, Captain, I wasn't looking just then."

"Perhaps you were looking at something else," I suggested.

He stood up and paced, hands behind his back, a perfect imitation of a gentleman owning up to his friends about a flaw in his character. "There's a young lady who lives three houses down. Miss Amanda Osborne. She came out and got into a carriage with her mother."

I hid a smile. "And she is very pretty, I expect."

His flush deepened. "I plan to marry her, you see — when I am much older, of course."

I wondered if he referred to a marriage already arranged between their families, or if he'd simply decided his course of life — and hers — already.

"Young ladies can distract us from our more rational purposes," I said.

He shot me a look that said he was grateful that we, both men of the world, understood. "The next thing that happened is that about a quarter past one, a fine carriage pulled up and stopped in front of number 22. I was supposed to go down to dinner, but I couldn't take my eyes off the carriage. It was polished wood, with gilding on the corners and on the door. The wheels were black with gold spokes. There wasn't a crest on the door, and I'd never seen the carriage before, so I couldn't tell who it belonged to. The horses were finer than my papa's, finer than Lord Berring's—he lives on the other side of Mr. Horne. They were bay horses, and each had one white foot. It must have taken some doing to match them like that."

I leaned forward, my interest heightening. "And who got out of this carriage?"

"A gentleman, sir, and his servant. The servant was large and beefy, and had a red face. The man that got out was tall and had dark hair. I couldn't make out his face well, because he didn't look up, but he was dressed fine. All in black with a white neckcloth and a black cloak with a dark blue lining. He looked like he could step right out to Carleton House. He sent his servant up to the door, then followed. He was angry."

I drummed my fingers on my trousered leg. "How do you know? You said you couldn't see his face."

"Well—by the way he walked. You know, moving quick, and stomping his feet. Impatient and annoyed, like he didn't want to be there."

"How long did he stay?"

Philip stared at the ceiling a moment. "About an hour or so. They made me come down to dinner then, and when I finished and came back upstairs, the gentleman was just leaving. That must have been about half past two."

"Was he still angry?"

Philip tapped his cheek with his forefinger. "I don't know. I only glimpsed him that time. He went to the carriage with his cloak swirling, and climbed inside. But he moved different. I might almost say he seemed satisfied."

Interesting. I went on. "After this gentleman departed, did anyone else come to the house?"

"No one all afternoon. They had deliveries, as usual, but they went down to the kitchen. Two chaps with a cart and a lady with a basket."

"Were these the usual people who delivered?"

He shook his head. "They have different ones off and on. The lady has been delivering for about a month, and I recognized one of the chaps, but not the other chap."

They would have gone to the kitchen, and all of the staff would have seen them. Only Mr. Denis, the fine gentleman with the fine carriage, had stopped to visit Mr. Horne through the front door.

"And no one else?"

"You came just as it was getting dark. And then their boy legged it away fast and came back later with the Runner. I recognized you from the day before, when you stood up to the cavalrymen. Did you know the cavalry chaps?"

"I knew the lieutenant."

"You stopped them from hurting the lady. And then you took the man and lady away. Did you cart them off to gaol?"

"Of course not. I took them home. The man, he'd had much grief. Did he frighten you?"

Philip shrugged. "I'm not certain. I watched him come and start beating on Mr. Horne's door. I could tell he was very angry and very unhappy. He started screaming and pulling at his hair. He certainly stirred the crowd, though. I expected them to start breaking windows and charging into the houses, but they didn't."

He sounded disappointed.

"They hadn't much heart in them," I said. "The horsemen easily frightened them off." I hesitated. "Do you watch out the window at night as well?"

He weighed his answer, as though deciding what he should admit, then at last, he chose to trust me. "I don't sleep much. I watch people go out and then come back from their parties and the theatre. When I grow up, I won't be ill, and I'll go to balls and theatres and clubs all the time."

"Did much ever happen at number 22 at night?"

"No, sir. Mr. Horne hardly went out at all."

I pondered. "Did anything out of the ordinary happen on a particular night, say three or four weeks ago?"

Philip's eyes lit with admiration. "How'd you know, sir? That was the night the dark carriage came. No lights on it at all. I thought it was foolish and dangerous for it to go about like that. It sat in front of Mr. Horne's house for about a quarter of an hour."

"Did anyone get out of this carriage?"

"No. But someone got in. It wasn't Mr. Horne; the man was too tall and bulky for him. And he was carrying something over his shoulder, a carpet it looked like. He got in, and the coach just went away."

A carpet. Or a bundled-up girl, unconscious or dead. Had Horne killed her, or found some other means to rid himself of her?

"Does it have something to do with the murder?" Philip asked eagerly.

I spread my hands. "It may have."

"Do you think the fine gentleman who arrived that afternoon was the murderer, then?"

I pursed my lips. "He certainly was in the right place at the right time." I imagined again Denis flicking his little finger and his large manservant jumping to the task of stabbing Horne to death. I still thought it unlikely. And the mutilation of the body did not fit. I doubted that Denis, with his emotionless eyes, would bother lopping off Horne's genitals. It was almost as though that had been done by a different person entirely.

Alertness streaked through my body as the thought came and went. I reached for it again, turned it over slowly. Two *different* people. Threads wove and matched and fitted together.

"I know Bremer didn't murder him," Philip was saying. "He's too old, and he's frightened of everything. Even a spider frightens him."

"He is frightened," I said slowly. "But fear can be a very powerful motivation."

"Can it, sir?"

I nodded once, then rose and made a military bow. "It can. I thank you for your candor, Mr. Preston. It has helped me immensely."

*** *** ***

I left Philip then, reassuring him that I would not forget my promise to give him a riding lesson on Monday.

I stopped at the newspaper office to inquire about further answers to Jane's whereabouts and found nothing. I returned home, ate one of Mrs. Beltan's buns without currants, and went upstairs. Later that day, I went to Bow Street and asked Pomeroy if he knew of any new developments. Pomeroy replied in the negative and seemed surprised that I wasn't satisfied with letting Bremer hang for the crime. Bremer's trial was Monday, he told me. It was Saturday now.

I thought about what Philip Preston had told me about the dark carriage in the middle of the night and the bundle they had taken from number 22. That bundle had likely been Jane. But had she been dead or alive? Had they taken her to a brothel or thrown her into the river?

A coach needed a coachman. From my inquiries about Horne and his household, I knew he'd kept no coach of his own, which meant he would have hired any he needed. So he would have had to hire a carriage and a man to drive it.

I thought of the coachman Nancy had found for me, Jemmy—who, in truth, worked for Denis. Denis had put him in place with the Carstairs, and I believed now that Denis had removed him as well. No doubt Jemmy had reported my inquisitiveness to Denis, his true employer.

I began making inquiries at coach yards, asking whether any remembered hiring out a coach to a gentry-cove in Hanover Square about a month previously. None did. I returned home as the sky darkened, and settled in to a cold supper of yesterday's roast from the pub and a loaf of my landlady's bread.

I returned to the subject of Denis. He had known all about me and what I wanted. Horne might have written him of my questions about Jane Thornton, but I doubted it. The only people who had known of my interest in Jane's abduction other than Horne had been Jemmy and Grenville.

I let my mind wander. Grenville had been eager to help, at his own expense. He'd been strangely interested in Charlotte Morrison's disappearance and had dragged me to Hampstead to investigate. Then he'd volunteered to travel all the way to Somerset to make further inquiries.

The night we'd spent in Hampstead, he'd disappeared from the inn, and he'd offered no explanation as to his whereabouts. He might have simply met an acquaintance, of course, or enjoyed walking about by himself, and he had no reason to inform me of his movements. And his night wanderings in Hampstead did not necessarily have anything to do with James Denis. But I still wondered why he'd tried to keep what he did secret.

A knock on my door startled me out of my contemplations. I had stared into the flames while I thought, and when I turned away, my eyes were dazzled, and I could barely see to cross the room.

A boy stood on the threshold with a letter and a hopeful look. I took the letter and gave him tuppence.

The note was from Grenville. "I traveled hard to reach home, and then I heard you had gone to see Denis without me. It was too bad of you. I imagine you learned nothing on your own. Call 'round at my club tonight. I have something to tell you and plans to make. I'll send my carriage at nine."

I pitched the crumpled ball of the letter into the fire. I was tired of Grenville summoning me like his errand boy. I had displeased him; he wanted me to grovel. To hang on his every word and order as the rest of London did.

I seated myself at my writing table and wrote a letter back, telling him that I would call on him at my own convenience. I let my annoyance seep into the letter, and I let myself imply what I thought of a man who could ruin an artist's success with a simple frown and a person's acceptability with a raise of his brows. I was tired of his charity, and I refused to give up my integrity for Grenville's exquisite brandy and fine foods. I ended by recommending that if he wanted to hear all about true living, he should attend Louisa Brandon's supper party. No doubt Brandon would regale all present with detailed accounts of our adventures during the war.

His message had said he'd send his carriage at nine. Shortly before nine, I left the note for Mrs. Beltan to post in the morning, and I went out.

I walked all the way to Long Acre, and then east and north, away from my usual haunts. Let Grenville's footman search the environs of Covent Garden for me in vain.

Cool had come with the darkness, but the bitter cold of winter had gone. The air had softened at last, and it was almost a pleasure to walk. Others must have felt the same, because the streets were crowded.

I went to a tavern I'd never entered before. The locals, working-class men with calloused hands, leathery faces, and good-natured banter, looked me up and down in suspicion as I entered. These were the carters and wheelwrights and hostlers and a large man with knotted muscles who must have been a smith, catching time with their cronies before going home to sleep. After I'd settled onto a low stool by myself and remained sitting quietly, they left me alone. I had a glass of hot gin, then a tankard of ale.

I was halfway through that and pleasantly warmed when Black Nancy danced into the room. She looked about with wide, eager eyes, swishing her hips, then spotted me and rushed across the room.

"There you are, Captain. I tried to follow you, but I lost you in Long Acre. I had to ask everyone if they'd seen a lame man walking alone. A gent told me he'd spied you coming in here, and here you are."

I set down my ale. "Very clever of you. I came here because I am not in the mood for company."

"I'm sorry to hear yer say that." She dragged a three-legged stool to my table, perched on it, and gave me a wicked smile. "I got something to offer yer."

I was not in the mood for her teasing. I said sharply, "Which I have refused before."

"Not that. I know I ain't got a chance. Listen, Captain, ye want to nab this bloke what nabbed your

Miss Jane or Miss Lily, or whatever her name might be, don't you?"

I nodded and sipped ale.

"Well, I can help ye there. Me and Jemmy. He thought it over, and he don't like that he was made to do it. That's why he were so blackish when you questioned him. But we thought of a way to get the bloke, and we need your help."

Alarm stirred inside me. "What the devil are you talking about, Nancy?"

Nancy rested her hand on my shoulder. "Don't fret, Captain, it will be simple. All I have to do is get myself nabbed, and you catch him doing it."

Chapter Twenty

My response was instant. "No."

She grinned. "I knew you'd say that. Me and Jemmy, we got it all planned."

"The man is far too dangerous, Nance. I don't want you near him at all."

"I won't get myself near him. We worked it all out. Jemmy'll volunteer to go out and nab me. He'll take me back to his master, and then you can come along with the magistrate and arrest him. Then you will make him tell us where your Jane is, and me and Jemmy split the ten guineas reward. I would be rich. You want me to be rich, don't yer?"

I shook my head at her simplistic ideas. "Mr. Denis is not a usual kind of procurer. He doesn't want street girls, and it's most likely that Jemmy still works for him, and he's only luring you, and me, into danger.

Nancy snapped her fingers under my nose. "That's all you know. We already done it, anyway.

Jemmy's not stupid. He's proper handsome, too." She flicked her gaze up and down me, as though finding me wanting in comparison.

"Nance, do not do this," I said sternly.

"Don't matter. I'm to meet Jemmy, going midnight, behind the Covent Garden theatre. You can come along, or Jemmy and I will tumble him on our own. We don't need you to get our reward."

I caught her arm. "You and Jemmy are a pair of fools. This man is too dangerous."

"Let go of me. You ain't my father."

Nancy's voice carried. Heads turned. The locals eyed me with disapproval.

"If I were your father, I'd lock you in the cellar."

She jerked from my grasp. "And I'd scream the place down. You ain't my protector, neither. If I was, I'd do everything you said, always."

Nancy fled from me. I threw a crown on the table and hobbled after her. The inhabitants watched me go, likely glad to be rid of me.

"Nance," I called into the night.

I heard her footsteps moving away through the narrow lane, but I could not see her in the darkness. I hobbled after her, though I knew I'd never catch her. She was expert at disappearing. I would simply have to get to Covent Garden theatre a little early and spirit her away before she and Jemmy could carry out their plan. I had no cellar to lock her into, but I had the keys to Mrs. Beltan's attics. I could put her in there until the danger had passed. She'd not thank me, but at least she'd be alive.

I went to another tavern closer to home and had another tankard in peace. No black-haired girls with ridiculous ideas burst in to bother me, and if

Grenville's lackeys were looking for me, they were not looking very thoroughly. At half past ten, I returned to Grimpen Lane. I did not see Grenville's carriage, or any of his efficient footmen, so I concluded they'd decided it not worth waiting for me and had returned, empty handed, to Grenville.

At half past eleven, I went to Covent Garden theatre, which reposed at the end of Bow Street. The carriages of the wealthy still came and went in the front of the edifice, but behind it, darkness was complete. I shone my lantern around the blackness of the narrow passages, but except for a rat and an old man who scurried away, I was alone. The rat remained.

The clock at St. Paul's, Covent Garden struck the three-quarter hour. Running footsteps sounded, and I set my lantern down and stepped back into the shadows. I recognized the light footsteps of Nance, and presently, she trotted into the lantern's feeble glow.

"Who's there?" she said, much too loudly for my comfort.

"Me."

Her teeth glittered as she threw herself toward me. "Aw, Lacey, I knew you'd come."

I seized her wrists and jerked her to me. Her eyes, close to mine, opened wide.

"What are you doing? Are you trying to kiss me?"

"No, I am restraining you."

She looked at me in alarm then, and drew in a long breath, preparing to scream. I clamped my hand over her mouth. She tried to kick me, but I pinned her against the wall with my weight. She bit my hand. I snarled at her. She went suddenly limp and silent.

I jerked her upright and began to tow her back to the street, scooping up the lantern as I went. She trotted along, sniffling.

At the corner of the theatre, four men stood waiting. None were Jemmy. I took a step back, but they followed.

I tossed the lantern in one direction, and Nance in another. She squealed as she fell among the rubbish, and the lantern rolled and extinguished, plunging the passage in darkness.

The men struck. I dodged swiftly and felt a breeze brush my face. I wrenched my sword from my walking stick and clenched the scabbard in my other hand. I heard a strike coming, and I lunged out. A man grunted in surprise and pain.

They grappled with me in the darkness, trying to get under the reach of my sword, trying to get behind me. I put my back to a rubbish heap and struck hard and fast. Sometimes I hit, sometimes I didn't, but it kept them at bay.

But for how long? I could not fight here forever; already I was tiring. I couldn't depend upon Nance to run for help. She was crying loudly off in the darkness, making no effort to get away. She might be hurt. One of them might have her.

A blow got through and landed on my chest. I exhaled sharply, but kept my feet and struck back with my fist and scabbard. I felt teeth. The man I hit cursed and spat.

A sudden light blinded me. A lantern shone in my face, dazzling my eyes. I quickly closed them and looked away, but too late. A sharp blow fell on my left knee, and hot fire streaked through it. I struck out. In the light, another blow landed on my sword arm, then three men closed on me and wrenched the sword from my grasp.

"Hurry."

I recognized Jemmy's voice and sensed his flat face behind the lantern. I fought on. Another kick to my bad leg wrenched a cry from my lips, and then my hands and face struck the pavement, rough cobbles stinging.

They kept pummeling me. I curled inward, protecting my face and belly. My knee was a mass of pain, and I could feel little else. When the numb haze receded a little, I realized they'd stopped hitting me. I moved my arm, and heard myself groan. Sticky blood tickled my cheek.

I opened my eyes. In the light of the bright lantern, I saw a slender foot in a soiled slipper inches from my nose.

"It's a fair turnabout, ain't it, Captain?" Nance asked softly, and then she kicked me in the face.

*** *** ***

When I came to myself again, a long time later, I lay on a thin mattress and had a blanket thrown over me. Light—daylight—trickled through the broken slats of a wooden-shuttered skylight. My limbs felt curiously heavy, and the fiery pain I'd expected was now a dull, distant throbbing.

I tried to move and discovered my hands joined behind my back, the cords that bound them tight and biting. My feet were likewise tied, my boots gone.

They had not covered my mouth. I licked my dry lips, and drew a breath to call out, but only a whispered creak emerged, like a breath of wind through branches on a summer afternoon. My bed — no, the entire room, rocked gently, and I smelled mud and brine and filth. Shadows danced below the skylight, up and down, up and down, telling me that I was afloat. Somewhere. The air held the stink of the city, not the clean smell of open water, so I assumed the Thames, still in London.

Was I alone? Or did someone man the tiller? Perhaps the boat would sink, taking me down alone to the bottom of the river, my body lost forever.

I was thirsty and hungry and terribly sleepy. Even in my alarm, my eyes drifted closed, my body seeking the oblivion from which it had risen.

When I opened my eyes again, the light was fading from the skylight. A day had gone by. Only one? Or two, or more? My befuddled mind had an inkling this was important, but I couldn't make myself care. At least the boat was still afloat. I heard a man's voice outside the cabin door, then another answering. So I wasn't alone. Perhaps they'd shoot me first, before they scuttled the boat.

I went through my fuzzy memories. I could not recall much of what happened after I'd been pummeled by the four men and Jemmy behind Covent Garden theatre. I did remember lying in a darkened carriage, groans escaping my lips, and I remembered a hand forcing me to drink something bitter and burning. Opium. That would account for my numb heaviness, my indifference as to my plight. When the opium wore off, I'd be wretched indeed.

My cracked lips formed a smile. I'd explain to Louisa, if I ever saw her again, that I'd missed her supper party because I'd been drowned while trying to rescue a sixteen-year-old prostitute from her own stupidity.

Nance had tricked me, and I'd walked right into it. She'd known I would not be able resist trying to keep her out of my business, and she and Jemmy had set a simple trap. Jemmy worked for Denis, and the four men who attacked me reminded me of the bully in Denis's library. Denis must have assumed I wouldn't be able to walk away from him without an attempt at retaliation. He must have seen in my eyes the stupid idea of trying to shoot him before it had even formed. So he'd struck first.

The rickety door opened, and two large men entered—I assumed to kill me.

They beat me instead. Soundly, thoroughly, with fists and cudgels, they pummeled my body until pain stabbed me even through the opium. Hoarse screams I could not control leaked from my mouth. I looked straight at one man, into the same flat, uncaring eyes that Denis possessed.

They departed, and I lay in a daze.

They say that opium promotes clarity of thought. Poets and musicians are said to use it to inspire great works. I read little poetry, but music gave me joy, and it seemed to me that the strains of violin and pianoforte slid through my brain now, circling my thoughts. The drug lifted my mind above the pain, divorcing feeling from thought. While my body soiled itself and I lay there in the stink of my own blood and urine, the events of the last days sorted themselves out and lined up neatly and clearly.

Philip had told me everything I'd needed to know. I'd focused my wrath on Denis, the man who discreetly acquired things for his customers; his only consideration being how much they were willing to pay and how desperate they were. No matter how Denis dressed himself up, he was filth, and I knew it. But through my disgust with him, I had blinded myself to a simple truth—that not *one* person had visited Horne's house that day, but *five*.

Bremer had nothing to do with Horne's death, had been as surprised as anyone to find him. I'd always known that in my heart. But among those five people—Denis, Denis's bully, two men making deliveries, and one woman with a basket—was the culprit. Mrs. Thornton had carried a basket the day her husband had been shot in Hanover Square. Alice no doubt had a basket for shopping in the markets. And who noticed a maid?

Who noticed a man who delivered things, for that matter? If Mulverton, Horne's cousin, had been in a hurry for his inheritance, he could have dressed himself as a working-class man and come to the house with a bushel of turnips simply to see how things lay.

That was far-fetched; I did not suppose for a moment that a gentleman from Sussex would conceive of putting on shabby clothes and dirtying his face simply to see if he could put his cousin out of the way. But I turned the possibility over in my mind, because what I truly believed was terrible, and I did not want to examine that belief too closely. Bremer was a better culprit. An old man, who'd been willing to do his master's disgusting bidding, who would achieve fame on his way to the gallows.

I still did not know where Jane Thornton was, but I had a good idea of what had happened to her. Philip had seen someone take her away that night, and I feared in my heart that she was dead. I also knew who would know for certain, and my wrath moved to that person and smoldered there for a time.

As the light faded, I thought about the secondary problem of Charlotte Morrison. I thought about her letters, and I thought about the look I'd seen in her cousin's eyes, and I realized what she'd feared. I'd known it in Hampstead, but I'd not wanted to believe the loathsome conclusion, and so had not let myself draw it.

The opium helped me to see clearly what I had already known. Just as it had happened years ago when I'd concluded which officer and his sergeant had decided to rid the army of Arthur Wellesley, I'd known the solution right away and had not wanted to look it in the face. A night alone, fearing for my life, had forced me to acknowledge the truth. During that chill night in Portugal, I'd not had the comfort of opium to dull my fear, but my life had been just as much in danger then as it was now.

But the secrets of Jane, Horne's death, and Charlotte's disappearance would die with me. No one would find them in my water-rotted brain when they fished me from the bottom of the Thames. My own fault for avoiding painful truths and keeping my confidences to myself.

I lay in twilight now, my eyes open, watching the last shadows drift across the scarred and tar-encrusted floor.

Sometime later, the door opened. The flare of a rag light pierced my widened pupils and sent fingers of pain into my head.

Black Nancy closed the door and moved to the bunk. She set the lamp on the floor and smoothed my hair from my forehead. Her fingers smelled of tar and mud. She may have bathed all over for me a few days ago, but she certainly hadn't since. "Don't worry, Captain. Nance will take care of you."

I said nothing, still too weak to speak.

She continued to stroke my hair. "He's going to give you to me, did you know that?" she crooned. "I help nab you, he said, and he fixes it up so you'll always do everything I say. Black Nancy will always have what you need."

She leaned down and kissed my lips. I lay, unresponding. She thrust her tongue into my mouth, forcing my blood-caked lips open, but I didn't answer her insistent pressure. Her hand snaked down to touch my arm, my chest, my groin. Her smile widened. "There now, I knew you was awake. You like me in truth, don't you?"

The drug that suppressed my pain seemed to heighten my physical response. I grew stiff under her hand, but the excitement stopped there, never reaching my head or heart. My trousers were damp where I'd wet myself, but Nancy did not seem to notice or care. She flashed a satisfied smile at me and began popping open the buttons.

On a sudden, the door thumped firmly shut, and a bolt grated into place. Nance gave a shriek, whipped her hand from me, and scurried to the door.

She stared at the barricade for a stunned moment, then she pounded her fist on the door. "'ere. You let me out."

No answer came. Nance pummeled the door again. I rolled onto my side and tried to force myself into a sitting position. Nance shouted and screamed until her voice went hoarse.

"They are not going to let you out, Nance," I said. "They are going to kill me, and you with me."

She whirled. "No, they ain't. They promised."

I shook my head, which only made it pound with nasty pain. "They used you, Nance. They aren't going to let us go. They will likely scuttle the boat."

Tears streaked her dirt-caked cheeks. "They can't do that. I just wanted you, that's all. I'd a done anything to get you."

I wanted to hate her for doing this to me, but the only thing I could feel for her was pity. Denis had used Nancy's silly childlike need to get to me. I'd used her desire to please me to find Jemmy the coachman. I knew who was to blame for landing her square in this business in the first place.

I tried to speak sternly. "Come here and untie my hands."

Her eyes went wide. "If I untie you, you'll beat me."

"I wouldn't do that, Nancy. I promise. Untie me, and I'll think of a way to save us."

"You're lying. You'll beat me."

I lost my patience. "Damn you, girl. Come here."

She put her hands to her face and wailed.

I clenched my teeth and tried to gentle my voice. "I haven't the strength to beat you, Nance, even if I wanted to. If you don't want to drown, you will untie me, and I will take you out of here."

Her hands came down. "How?" she sniffled.

"I will think of something. Please."

She watched me fearfully for a few moments, then she stumbled back to the bed. I rolled over to give her access to my hands.

It took a long time. Nancy picked at the tight knots and sobbed under her breath. Her tears dropped onto my bleeding hands, stinging them. She cried that she could not do it. I bullied her until she was incoherent with weeping.

At last the knots loosened. I tugged at the bonds until one broke, and I quickly unwound my hand. I tried to push myself up, but my fingers were wooden, lifeless, and would not support me. I heaved with my legs and shoulders to roll over again and finally raised myself to a sitting position.

I leaned against the wall and cradled my hands in my lap, closing my eyes as hot pins and needles spiked my flesh. I would have to wait until my fingers became deft enough to untie the cords that bound my ankles.

The act of sitting up had nearly drained my strength. I wondered how the devil I would get both myself and Nance off the boat and all the way to shore.

She rubbed her nose on her sleeve. "If you'd only took what I offered, we'd not be in this fix." Her eyes filled. "I'd not have chased you, and I'd not have believed them when they told me I could have you. You'd have been mine, and I'd have done you so good, you wouldn't have wanted to go to no one else." Her throat worked. "I'd have taken care of you and not complained when you knocked me about, and I wouldn't have gone to no other man unless you said I could." Tears spilled from her eyes. "I'd a done anything for you. Why don't you want me?"

I suppressed a sigh. She still could not understand that all this was about more than desire. But she was hurting, and afraid, and I was responsible for dragging her into this danger.

I gave the bed beside me a clumsy pat. "Nance. Come and sit here."

She shot me a distrustful look, but she shuffled to me and sat down. The bunk sagged, spilling my leg onto her thigh.

"I've told very few people this, Nance," I said. "Once, long ago, I had a daughter."

Nancy looked surprised. "Ya did?"

"Yes. When I was very young, I took a wife." The word choked in my throat, and I had to swallow and wait before I went on. "And we had a daughter. One day, my wife—she took my daughter, and went away."

I had not spoken much about it for fourteen years. The words hurt. Oh God, they hurt.

Nancy stared. "She left you? The old cow. Was she mad?"

My temper heated to hear that white and gold girl from long ago called an "old cow," but I reminded myself that Nancy did not and could not understand. "She disliked the army and following me about. I don't blame her; it was a hard life, and she was of a delicate nature."

"So where is she now?" Nance asked, frowning. "And your little girl?"

"I don't know. They went to France, long, long ago, and I never was able to find them. I don't even know if my daughter is alive or dead. But if she is, she'd be, oh, about as old as you."

She stared at me, fascinated. "Did she have black hair, like me?"

"No. Her hair was fair as a field of buttercups. Like her mother's. When I last saw her, she was only two years old. She could barely say my name."

My heart wrenched, and the intensity of the wrench surprised me at little. I'd thought that all the years between had taken away the worst of the hurt. Perhaps the opium in my veins had broken down the shield I usually kept over that memory.

"You don't know even if she's alive?" Nance asked.

"I wonder sometimes, if she is. And whether she is safe, with friends who care for her. Or if she is . . ."

"Like me," Nance finished. "A game girl. Having to go with flats that are as likely to knock her about as pay her for kicking her heels to the ceiling."

I touched Nancy's matted black curls. "Yes. And when I look at you, I think of her. And wonder."

"If she's like me?"

"Yes."

"So poking me would be like poking your daughter? Some coves like that."

I pretended to ignore that revelation. "I want nothing to hurt you. You are so young, and yet, I've seen girls like you die when they're not much older than you. I want to keep you safe."

Silent tears spilled down Nancy's cheeks. "You can't keep me safe. If I don't go with flats, me dad whips me 'til I bleed."

"You have to let me try." I continued stroking her curls. "What color is your hair, really?"

Nance dashed the tears away with the back of her hand. "Brown."

"I'd like to see it. Let it grow back without dying it."

She snorted. "A right fool I'd look. With half of it a different color."

"Cut it off, then. Some ladies of fashion still lop off their curls."

She gave me a look that told me I was hopelessly old and likely insane. "Ain't much I can do about it here. How are we going to get away, then?"

She sounded a bit like her old self, and some of the feeling had returned to my hands. I leaned down and worked loose the bonds that held my feet. I rubbed my bare ankles, wincing as the blood flowed its way to my feet. This took a long time, and Nance fretted with impatience.

I doubted I could stand or walk or fight or swim. But I would not sit and tamely wait to be killed. The boat was quiet, but the occasional thump of footsteps on boards outside told us Denis's men still inhabited the decks.

I managed to stand at last, though my legs shook like new branches in a spring breeze. I refastened the buttons that Nancy had opened on my trousers, my fingers still clumsy. "Give me the candle," I said.

Nance retrieved it from the floor and handed it to me. The light was little more than a rag soaked in grease, twisted into a wick at the top. The feeble flame burned blue and did not give off much light. But the rag was soaked, enough for my purpose.

I hobbled to the rickety wooden door. My left leg buckled, pain throbbing through it, and I had to pause three times, easing my weight from it, before I could resume.

I rubbed my hands in the grease, and then onto the doorframe, near the latch. I repeated this several times, being careful not to douse the lamp, then I touched the flame to the wood.

The grimy doorframe sizzled, and a thin band of smoke rose and stung my eyes. I held the flame to it, rubbing on a little more grease. The wood grew warm. The grease melted. After a long time, the flame crawled up the damp wood, found fuel, and clung there.

"What are you doing?" Nance cried.

"Setting the door alight."

She sprang to her feet. "Are you mad? You'll kill us."

"I imagine Denis's men will not want to remain on a boat that is going up in flames."

"No, they ain't stupid. They'll light for shore."

"Not if they have no way to get there. They will not want to go down with us."

"Why don't we just duck out the skylight?"

"We will. But Denis's men are out there. And maybe you're right."

I tossed the candle to the bunk. The flame nearly went out, then it caught on the dirty sheet. The linen crackled and smoked.

Nance stared at me, round-eyed. "Right about what?"

"That I am mad. Up you go."

I caught her 'round the waist and boosted her toward the skylight. She pushed on it. "It's fastened."

"Pound on it, then. The wood's old."

"You should have done this before you set us on fire." She beat her fists against the frame, but to no avail.

I lowered her to the floor. I stripped off my coat and wadded it around my hands. While she hunkered in the corner farthest from the bunk, I reached up and slammed my hands, at the top reach of my arms, against the slats above.

The bunk was burning well now, and the wall behind it caught. Flame snaked up and down the doorframe, and smoke hung heavy in the air. I heard shouting. They'd seen. They were coming.

I pounded the boards. With a loud crack, they broke. I continued beating them, smashing the wooden slats away. Splinters rained down on me, and slivers cut through my jacket to tear my hands.

I flung the jacket aside and grabbed Nance. "Up you go."

She squealed. I shoved her through the broken skylight, pressing my hand on her backside. "Once you're out there, you run for the side and go over and cling to the boat. I'll be right behind you."

She wailed. "I can't swim."

"Damn you, I can. I am a strong swimmer. I'll tow you to shore."

I had no idea if I could walk across the deck, let alone get myself and one sobbing, wretched girl to the bank of the Thames, but I'd galvanized Nance. She wriggled herself upward and caught the edges of the skylight. Nancy cried out softly as the slivers cut her hands, then I pushed her through. She landed on her stomach and rolled away.

I couldn't follow. My leg made it impossible for me to jump, and the only piece of furniture I could have stood on, the bunk, was bolted to the wall and ablaze.

A splash of water hit the door. They were trying to put out the fire without entering the cabin. I smiled. Futile. Flames licked the roof, eating toward the skylight from which Nance had fled. This boat would burn.

I caught up my coat, wrapped it around my arm and shoulder, and charged the burning door. The wood, weak and smoldering, gave way at once, and I fell through. My bare foot slid on the wet deck, and I fell hard to my knees.

I scrambled to right myself. One of Denis's huge brutes charged me, and I ran, gritting my teeth on the pain. I wondered whether Nance had gotten away, and if so, where she had gone over the side.

In the shadow of the cabin a grappling hook bit into the planks of the deck. A taut rope drew a rowboat alongside. A bulky shadow of a man crouched in the stern, but in the bow, one foot on the gunwale, stood Lucius Grenville. Firelight glinted on his dark hair and his glittering eyes. In his hand he held a pistol, and he pointed it straight at me.

Chapter Twenty-One

I took one step back then dashed forward and flung myself over the side. Grenville shouted. The bitter cold water of the Thames took me, sliding greasily over my body. The cuts on my face stung as the grimy water closed over my head.

I kicked hard, and surfaced. Above me, Grenville fired. The spark flared in the night, and the roar deafened me. A thin spiral of smoke drifted upward, white against the darkness. On the deck, one of Denis's thugs fell, groaning.

A rope snaked across the space between me and the rowboat and slapped the water. I grabbed the line, wrapping it around my numb wrists. It tightened, dragging me toward the boat. I realized that the bulky figure behind Grenville, towing me to safety, was Aloysius Brandon.

I grabbed the side. Brandon reached down, seized me beneath the arms, and hauled me into the boat. I landed on the gunwale and rolled in, a crash of water following me. Grenville fired another pistol. Brandon abandoned me to slice the rope that bound us to Denis's boat.

"Wait." I climbed to my knees, my teeth chattering. "We must find Nance."

"What?"

"Nance. I told her I'd take her to shore. She can't swim."

"I can't make out what the devil you're saying, Lacey. Sit down. We're going."

"No," I choked.

Grenville swung around. "Are you talking about the girl? I saw her climb out of the cabin and go over the side. You came out just after."

My jaw shook hard with cold and reaction. "Where? Row 'round the boat."

Grenville dropped to the seat and grabbed the oars. I thought, hysterically, that I supposed I should take it as a compliment that he was ruining a pair of fine kid gloves to rescue me.

He competently pulled around the stern of Denis's boat. The cabin was completely ablaze now, and Denis's men had turned their efforts to dousing the fire. I expected any moment to see Nance clinging to the side, her black head above the water, but she did not appear. Grenville circled close, turning the boat on one oar.

I peered into the blackness, shading my eyes against the glare of the fire. "Nance!"

I heard nothing above the crackle of the flames. Other boats, attracted by the blaze, were moving toward us, coming to the aid of the ailing craft.

"Nance!"

My eyes stung, and my opium-fogged brain wanted to slip back to sleep. But the drug was wearing off enough for me to feel the wounds Denis's men had inflicted, along with the cuts from the skylight and the torn mess of my bare feet.

A pistol roared, and a ball whizzed by my head. Brandon ducked, cursing.

"Devil take it, Lacey, we have to go."

"I won't leave her."

Grenville rowed, breathing hard. I scanned the surface near the boat and the water beneath it. I saw nothing. We slid all the way back to our starting point.

"Go 'round again," I shouted.

Grenville bent over the oars. Brandon rose. "No. Leave it. Pull for shore."

"I'll not leave her!"

"We have to. There's no time."

My chest was hot, my belly clenched. "Go 'round again, Grenville. Do it."

"Damn you, Lacey. I'll make it an order if I have to."

I swung on Brandon. "I'm not leaving her here to rot, you bastard, like you left me. Grenville, row."

Another pistol shot whistled past us. Brandon seized me. "Do I need to knock you down?"

My rage came forth in a wash of madness. I hit him, hard, in the gut, and then in the jaw. Brandon cursed and spat blood. Then his head came up, and his eyes sparked all the fury and hatred he'd bottled up behind politeness for the last two years.

"Fuck you," he said.

I lunged for him. I beat him, the man I'd loved best in the world once upon a time, beat him with all

the anger and rage and helplessness I'd felt when
Denis's men had pummeled me. I beat him for
Nance, drowning under the dark waters of the
Thames, for Jane Thornton, who'd likely had gone to
the same fate. I beat him for Aimee, broken and
scarred by a monster, and for Louisa, who cared far
too much for both of us. I beat him for myself and the
ruin of my life.

Grenville grabbed me from behind. "Enough.
Lacey, stop it. He's right. She's gone."

Brandon disentangled himself from me. Blood
smeared his face and spattered his neckcloth.

The fight went out of me. Grenville held me for
another moment or so until my rage washed away,
and my legs buckled. I sank to the bottom of the boat
and buried my head in my hands.

The other two fell silent. Brandon's breath gurgled
in his throat. The fire on Denis's boat roared into the
night.

Across the water came a muffled sobbing, quiet
and soft, accompanied by faint splashing. I raised my
head.

Grenville was on his feet, balancing against the
pitch of the boat, sighting into the darkness. "There!"
He pointed. I followed the line from his outstretched
finger to a tiny patch of deeper darkness, bobbing in
the current.

I got to my knees and grabbed an oar. Grenville
dropped to the seat, snatched the oar from my grasp,
and bent his back to turn the boat. Brandon half
stumbled, half crawled to the tiller, seizing it as it
began to slap against the water.

We slid across the current to the girl who
floundered weakly in the shadow of Denis's boat, her

cries growing fainter as we neared. I held the rope ready. Grenville competently turned to drift alongside Nance, just as her head went under.

I tossed away the rope, leaned hard over the side, and grabbed. Nancy's shoulder slipped from my grasp, but her hair tangled my wrist. I buried my fingers in it and hauled her upward. She came, all limp and heavy, and I got my hands under her arms and pulled her over the gunwale. Nance fell to the bottom with a wet slap, her skirt in shreds, her legs cut and bleeding.

Her eyes were closed, her skin cold and clammy. I rolled her onto her belly, and pressed hard on her ribs. I pushed and pushed, while my opium haze receded and pain ground through me.

At last, Nancy groaned and vomited up the dark water of the Thames. I pulled her into my arms, holding her, rocking her, kissing her wet face. Tears spilled from her eyes, but she clung to me, kissing me back, her lips weak.

Grenville took up the oars again and rowed us away from the conflagration and the boats zigzagging through the river, and toward the shore.

*** *** ***

I awoke to warm sunshine, a sweet-smelling bed, and a cool hand on my brow.

"Louisa."

I caught her hand and gripped it, tight, tight. She returned the pressure, and our eyes met, and held.

I lay in a featherbed with cool sheets over me and lavender-scented pillows under my head. My body ached all over, my face stinging with healing cuts.

"Where am I?" I croaked. "This isn't your spare bedroom."

Louisa smiled. "No, it's Mr. Grenville's. He insisted you be brought here, and he sent for his own surgeon."

Damn good of him, but I felt a twinge of worry. "What about Nance? Where is she?"

"At my house, being fussed over by my cook and housemaid, hating every minute of it."

My face hurt too much for smiles. "She does not much like women."

"So I understand from her unfortunate language. Who is she?"

I let Louisa disentangle her hand from mine. "A street girl whose well-being I foolishly care about. Please don't cart her off to a workhouse. Or one of those horrible houses of reform."

"Don't worry. She may stay in my attics until you decide what's to be done for her."

"I hope you have a stout lock on your attic door."

A smile crinkled the corners of her eyes. "She has tried to run away twice. Until I told her you wished her to remain there. Since then, she's been curiously compliant. The things she says about you are—quite interesting."

I grunted. "Don't trust her."

Louisa smiled again, then she dropped her gaze, watching her hand smooth my sheet. "Aloysius wants to apologize to you. For something he said out on the river, I gather."

My head began to ache. "I am far too tired to face Aloysius."

"A moment only, Gabriel. Please."

I stared at her until she looked up and met my gaze. I wanted to tell her that I much preferred Aloysius's candid curses to that damned public politeness he hid behind while he hated me with his eyes. But I was not certain she'd understand. She wanted me to forgive him all his past sins, and I was not yet ready.

"Tell your husband and his apology to go to hell," I said.

Her eyes filled with tears. We eyed one another for a few heartbeats of silence before she turned and rustled across the cavernous room and out the door. She did not say good-bye.

My fogged brain still swam with the aftereffects of opium, and whatever else Grenville's surgeon had given me for pain. I remembered the conclusions I'd formed while on board the boat, and I groped for them through the haze of my thoughts. I was missing one piece of information about Horne's death—the identity of one person—but I knew now what that person had done.

As much as I tried to think it through, my eyes closed, and when I awoke again, the shadows slanted sharply on the huge carpet.

Grenville's spare bedchamber must have been about thirty feet across and as much high. The canopied bed I lay in could have held five people, and the cost of the damask hangings could have bought them all food for a year. I felt like an insect waiting to be stepped on.

I rubbed the blur from my eyes as Grenville himself tramped into the room. He was dressed in a costly suit and a pristine cravat, but he wore soft, flat shoes and no jewels in his lapels, so I assumed he was spending the evening at home.

When he saw that I was awake, he pulled an armchair next to the bed and plopped down on it, resting his elbows on his knees.

"Where did you learn to row like that?" I asked.

"Quebec. And the Nile. I'll tell you all about it someday. I never thought I'd have adventures in staid and boring London, but that was before I met you."

"Grenville, about that letter I sent you—" My face warmed, remembering the haughty phrases I'd used.

Grenville held up his hand. "Say nothing of it. I had no right to be such a highhanded prig, and I deserved everything you said. Well, most of it. I might have to box you over one or two things. But it's a mercy you told me to go to Mrs. Brandon's supper party. When my servants came home without you, I worried a bit, but when I received your letter next morning, I understood you were simply annoyed with me. When I called on you in person, and you weren't home, I still supposed you avoiding me. But when I told Mrs. Brandon of your absence, she became alarmed at once." He shuddered. "Damn it, Lacey, Denis might have killed you and we still wouldn't know."

"He didn't mean to kill me."

"No? Those pistol shots came damned close for someone who had no intention of killing you."

I shook my head against the pillow. "If Denis had wanted me dead, he'd have had me killed at once. He could have done so at any time, easily, and you'd still be wondering where I'd got to. No, he meant to frighten me away from crusading against him. He wanted me to escape, and probably watched to see how I'd do it. The shots were made by his hired men, who were understandably annoyed at me for setting the boat on fire."

"Perhaps." He looked skeptical.

"How did you know where to find me, anyway?"

Grenville's dark eyes lit, as though he'd been eagerly awaiting the opportunity to tell me his part in the adventure. "As I said, Mrs. Brandon grew alarmed when I said I hadn't been able to find you. So I told Brandon—and his wife, because she refused to leave the room—about Denis and my fears."

Grenville paused to smile. "Your Mrs. Brandon must be one of the Furies. As soon as she heard my tale, nothing would do but that we went out at once and searched for you. She was prepared to come with us to the end. Nothing her husband said could persuade her otherwise, even when he shouted at her to obey."

I could picture the scene exactly. "Louisa is the most stubborn woman I know."

"I pointed out that Mrs. Danbury had arrived and needed looking after, and that seemed to persuade her. But looking into Mrs. Brandon's eyes, I knew how the Spartans felt. We'd better bring you back alive, or not come back at all."

"Mrs. Danbury?" I remembered the elegant blond woman I'd met at the viewing of the painting. "Dear God, she didn't see me, did she?"

"No. I brought you directly here and sent word to Mrs. Brandon."

"Thank you for that."

Grenville lounged back in the chair. "Do you want to know how I found you?"

He seemed anxious to impart the rest of the tale. I nodded, not really caring.

"I started searching for you around Grimpen Lane and Covent Garden. One of my footmen found your walking stick — in pieces — behind the opera house. In pieces. The scabbard was broken, but I'm having another made for you."

"Good of you."

"Not at all. The trail was easy to follow after that. Large men in a scuffle leave overturned rubbish and annoy people, and that is remembered. Someone saw them carry you into a carriage and head toward the river. I remembered that Denis kept two boats on the Thames — which I'd learned when he'd procured the painting for my friend — and I went there. One of the boats was gone, and several boatmen on shore had seen it taken out. So I hired a boat, and Brandon and I went after you." He stopped. "Is it true you started that blaze on board?"

"Yes."

"Good lord, man. You might have killed yourself."

"I know. But I would have taken Denis's men with me. They meant to frighten me, and I wanted to frighten them back."

"Good God, Lacey, I sincerely hope he calls a truce. And that you honor it."

I lay quietly for a moment, my aching head demanding a rest. I had slighted Grenville in my proud anger and still he'd made a dangerous and difficult attempt to rescue me. True, part of his impetus had been to satisfy his sense of adventure, but his actions told me that he forgave my momentary peevishness and thought it of no consequence. There was just a chance that I might have made a friend.

I opened my eyes again. "You said in your letter that you'd found interesting developments in Somerset."

Grenville's eyes sparkled. "I found much more than that, Lacey. What I found was the missing Charlotte Morrison."

Chapter Twenty-Two

I nearly sat up, but pain drove me back down. "Found her?"

"Yes, safe and sound, and married to a vicar."

I stared. "Did you say married to a vicar?"

"Exactly."

"Then she has nothing to do with Jane Thornton."

"I could see no connection, no."

I rubbed my pounding temples. "Damn. Then you went for nothing."

"Not necessarily," Grenville said. "I believe the problem more complex. Her curate became a vicar with a living, and a rather good one; I can't imagine the Beauchamps opposing the match."

"Why the mystery, then?"

Grenville tapped his fingertips together, a habit, I noticed, he had when interested in a problem. "That is what I wondered. Miss Morrison wouldn't speak much to me, and neither would her husband. They thought at first I'd come from Bow Street to drag her back to Hampstead. When I finally convinced them I had not, they unbent a little, but still did not want me to tell the Beauchamps where she was. I pointed out to Miss Morrison that she'd worried her cousins exceedingly, but this did not appear to move her. She seems very frightened of something, and I could not get her to tell me what."

I thought about the letters she'd written to her friend, which had hinted at some fear. "Did you speak to her friend, Miss Frazier?"

"I did. She is a lively woman, a spinster of about thirty, and apparently Miss Morrison's greatest friend. When I asked her about what Charlotte Morrison had written to her, she looked down her fine nose at me and told me to mind my own damned business. She said she would do nothing to interfere with Charlotte's happiness, and the best thing I could do was return to London and pretend I'd never come."

"She certainly sounds firm of purpose. What did you do?"

Grenville lifted his hands. "I returned to London. I suddenly realized she was right, that the lives of Charlotte Morrison and the Beauchamps were none of my damned business. So now I have a dilemma. Do I tell the Beauchamps that their cousin is safe and relieve their fears? Or do I pretend I never went to Somerset, as Miss Frazier commanded, and let them sort it out themselves?"

I lay quietly for a time, thinking. The conclusions my drugged mind had drawn flitted just out of reach, what had seemed so clear then now foggy and muddled.

"I believe I know why she went," I said.

"Do you? Well, I am baffled. I might understand her actions if she'd run away with some roué, but she married a stolid, respectable vicar with gray hairs. Why should she fear telling her family of it? Unless he's a highwayman in disguise." He laughed a little at his own joke.

"I'm certain the vicar is as respectable and steady as he seems. But I have an advantage. I read the letters, and you did not."

"But you told me what was in them," Grenville pointed out.

"I know. But I couldn't convey the feelings I got from them. There was so much Miss Morrison did not say."

Grenville regarded me impatiently. "So what do I do, Lacey? Tell the Beauchamps to find her themselves?"

"Tell them nothing for now. I would like to go to Hampstead myself and speak to Lord Sommerville."

"Why? Sommerville already told me he'd discovered nothing about his kitchen maid's death."

Weariness weighted my limbs, and I needed to sleep, but I answered. "Charlotte disappeared soon after the maid's death. So soon that my first thought upon hearing the tale was that the body found was Charlotte's."

"I thought the same. But it wasn't."

"No. Charlotte is alive and well."

Grenville shot me an impatient look. "You're being damned cryptic, Lacey."

"Forgive me, I'm still half-dead on opium. I mean that Charlotte no doubt knows who killed the girl. That knowledge made her flee back to the safety of Somerset."

Grenville stared at me a moment, clearly curious. Then he shook his head. "Our trip to Hampstead will have to wait in any case. I doubt you could walk across a room just now."

He was right. I sank a little farther into the mattress. "It was good of you to put me up. I will remove to my own rooms as soon as I can."

"Nonsense. Stay until you are healed. You need warmth and I have plenty of coal. My chef is happily inventing menus for you. I think he's rather bored with me."

"I suppose you won't let me argue."

"Suppress your pride for once and do what's good for you, Lacey. We'll go to Hampstead when you're better, but only when you're better. Or I'll fetch Mrs. Brandon, who will no doubt tie you to the bed."

I smiled and subsided. I prepared to let myself drift off to sleep again, then I remembered something. "What day is it?"

"A fine and fair Monday afternoon."

I tried to sit up. "Bremer's trial is today. I can't in all conscience let him be condemned for murder. I must talk to Pomeroy."

Grenville shook his head. "It will keep. In fact, it no longer matters."

His somber look alarmed me. "Why not?"

"I'm sorry, Lacey. I heard yesterday that the wretched Bremer is dead."

*** *** ***

I convalesced at Grenville's for five days. His chef did prepare some delightful and hearty meals for me, and it was probably thanks to his cooking that I healed as quickly as I did. His valet also seemed to enjoy waiting on me, and the footman who lugged coal bins about always stopped to chat about sport and give me a few tips on the races.

And all I could mull over was that I had not saved the stupid and frail Bremer.

Grenville had a friend who was a barrister, a silk, and he, knowing of Grenville's interest in the case, had relayed the news of Bremer's death. There'd been nothing sinister about it. Bremer had caught a chill, which settled in his lungs, and he'd died quickly.

Grenville told me, "My friend said that the magistrate believed Bremer to be guilty and that a gentler justice was served him by the hand of God. Butler went mad and killed his master, the magistrate said, was arrested, and died in gaol. End of story. Public and justice satisfied."

But I was not satisfied. I lay in Grenville's sumptuous guest room, too ill to move and too frustrated to rest. I had failed Bremer in my idiotic pursuit of Denis.

Grenville did his best to keep me cheerful, reading stories to me out of the newspaper and giving me the gossip from his club. I learned who was wearing the wrong-colored waistcoat, who had been snubbed, and who had lost a fortune at whist, and I didn't care about one word of it.

Louisa Brandon came to see me every day and threatened me with dire fates if I tried to get out of bed too soon. On one occasion, she brought her husband.

As the sun was descending behind Grenville's elegant, silk-draped windows, Colonel Brandon entered my chamber alone. He walked halfway across the carpet then stood with his hands behind his back in the attitude of parade rest and looked at me. I wondered if he'd come to force his apology on me, but the spark in his cold blue eyes told me that he was tired of being polite.

"You look bloody awful," he said.

I gave him a nod. "I imagine I do."

A cut ran from the corner of Brandon's mouth to his chin. I dimly remembered pounding my fist just there when we'd fought in the rowboat.

"Thought you'd like to know," he said. "I was speaking the other day with Colonel Franklin, Gale's commanding officer. He said he got the order about Hanover Square from Brigadier Champlain himself."

Champlain had been one of Wellington's most trusted generals. I propped myself up on my pillows, waiting for him to go on.

"I saw Champlain at a card party yesterday," he said. "He imparted to us that he'd sent for Franklin in response to a message from a friend. This friend was afraid that the house of an acquaintance in Hanover Square would be set alight by a mob. Champlain owed the friend a favor and agreed to assist."

"And the name of the friend?" But I'd already guessed.

"James Denis."

Of course. Denis would hardly want the father of the abducted girl drawing attention to Horne. I wondered if Denis had ordered Mr. Thornton to be shot, or if that had been Cornet Weddington's own idea.

"Louisa ferreted it out of him," Brandon said. "Franklin gave the orders to Lieutenant Gale, and

Gale took out a squad of his best men." He hesitated. "According to Grenville, this Denis is the same gentleman who had you dragged out to that boat."

"Yes."

"Good lord, Lacey, he has one of the highest generals in England owing him favors. And you've pitted yourself against him."

"I have."

Brandon stared at me a moment longer, his anger palpable from where he stood. "You always were a damned fool."

He knew better than most what I fool I had been.

So Denis had a general in his pocket. I wondered how many other men in high office owed Denis "favors." Perhaps I should have gone through with my plan to shoot Denis after all.

"Thank you," I said tiredly. "That does help. Thank Louisa for questioning Champlain on my behalf."

Brandon should have simply said, "Not at all," and left the room. I wished he would. But he remained fixed there on the carpet as though he still had plenty to say. Every muscle in my body tensed.

Brandon cleared his throat, and my muscles tightened all the more. "Out on the boat," he said. "You might have killed us all, trying to save that girl."

"I know."

"That is why I tried to stop you."

"I know."

He cleared his throat again, looked uncomfortable, and clenched his fists at his sides. "It was well done, Lacey. Even if it was bloody stupid."

My lips cracked as I smiled. "High praise from my brave commander."

Brandon glared at me, his face reddening. Again, I wished he'd go away. I was too weary to fence with him and wanted to sleep. I hoped to God he did not intend to offer his forgiveness for my sins past and present. I did not think I could stomach it just now.

His lip curled. "Such things are why you never rose higher than captain, Gabriel. As admirable as you may be."

I felt my temper stir beneath my hurt and tiredness, but I closed my eyes and willed it to silence. "Are you finished?"

When I opened my eyes again, it was to see Brandon's face a mask of undisguised fury. Had he come here hoping to provoke a reconciliation? If he had, he was a fool.

Brandon breathed heavily in the silence. "The way you have played it, Gabriel, we will never be finished."

I waited for him to explain what he meant by that, but Brandon snapped his mouth shut and turned on his heel. He said nothing more, not a good-night or best wishes for my health. He simply stalked away, letting the slam of the door behind him tell me what he thought of my rudeness.

I slid my eyes closed, threads of pain winding through my head. It took a long time for me to drift again to sleep.

*** *** ***

Staying with Grenville gave me time not only to heal and think, but also to come to know him better. He was a complex man who took three hours to dress for supper, yet could practice philanthropy in meaningful and useful ways. He had acquaintances across all classes and held prejudice only against a man who would not think for himself.

He admired beautiful women and had had discreet affairs with duchesses and actresses alike, but Grenville had never found a woman he'd wanted to marry. I told him dryly that it was just as well; his bride would have no room in his house for her own mirror, and he laughed and supposed I had hit upon a truth.

The evening before I returned home, Grenville entered my chamber looking rather bewildered.

"I've just had a visit from your Marianne Simmons."

I came alert, remembering how I'd told her to apply to Grenville for her ten guineas. "I'm sorry, Grenville, I ought to have warned you about that. She brought me some interesting information, and I sent her to you so she would leave me alone. I'd forgotten about it."

"It is no matter. She is rather—overwhelming, is she not?"

"It's how she survives."

Grenville looked troubled. "And yet, I found myself giving her twenty guineas."

"Twenty? I told her ten, the wretch."

"She asked for ten. But then I saw that her shoes were cheap and shabby. No one should go about poorly shod, Lacey. I told her of a shoemaker in Oxford Street and instructed her to tell them I'd sent her."

"What did she say to that?" I asked.

"She told me I was a gentleman. And then she said a few things that brought a blush to my cheek.

I'll admit to you, Lacey, though I've traveled the world, I've never met anyone like her."

"You may count yourself fortunate for that."

Grenville gave me a sharp look. "There is nothing between you, is there?"

"Between Marianne and myself? Good lord, no. She likes only wealthy gentleman. I would have a care, were I you."

He looked at me a long moment. "I believe that is good advice. Thank you, Lacey."

Grenville rang for wine and shared it with me, but he drank deeply of his and sat in silence most of the evening.

*** *** ***

I returned home to find that, despite her twenty guineas, Marianne had taken all my candles, and I was obliged to visit the chandlers to acquire more. The quietness of my return and the fact that I went from candle shop to pub and back home without being accosted reaffirmed my idea that Denis had abducted me not to kill me but to show me where I stood in his world.

I understood his message. I was to stay out of his way.

My mind spun with things I needed to do, but my body was too tired to do them. I'd written to young Philip Preston with my apologies for missing our appointment for riding instruction, and I needed to write again to set another date. On the weekend, Grenville and I would travel to Hampstead, where I would speak with Lord Sommerville. I'd pay a visit to the Beauchamps as well, having made my decision as to what I'd tell them. As to the whereabouts of Jane Thornton and the identity of Horne's killer, my mind balked. I knew who had killed Horne and why, but I did not want to know this. The world was happy with Bremer as the culprit; let him satisfy the world.

I also wasted time missing Janet. I wished for the hundredth time I'd never gone to Arbuthnot's to view that damned painting—I'd met an attractive woman there, Mrs. Danbury, who made it plain she had no interest in me, and I'd chanced upon Janet. God had been amusing himself with me that night.

I should have stayed longer at Grenville's, I reflected as I lit a candle in the darkness of my rooms. He at least diverted me with talk and food and drink. Here I was alone with my thoughts, my memories, and my past. I needed action.

Pomeroy had told me I was mad. Brandon agreed with him. Grenville thought so too. Louisa understood me a little better, but even she was fond of telling me how imprudent I was. All of them were right about me.

I changed into my regimentals, hobbled to the hackney stand in Covent Garden market, and took myself to the house of James Denis.

Chapter Twenty-Three

"You'll forgive my precautions, Captain." Denis touched his fingertips together and regarded me calmly from a brocade wing chair. "I assume you did not call on me to apologize for setting my boat alight."

Upon my arrival, two of his thugs had thoroughly searched me for weapons and had taken away my walking stick, which Grenville had had repaired for me.

But the fact that Denis would not let me near him without searching me satisfied me a little. I did not make him feel safe.

"You are curious as to why I came," I said. "Or you never would have let me in."

He gave a single nod. "I admit, I am slightly curious. But I have an appointment in a half-hour's time, so please be brief."

I had no intention of being brief. "I've had much time to think this past week. It occurred to me that Josiah Horne was a man of sordid and vulgar taste."

Denis raised his sleek brows. "Please do not tell me that you traveled all the way to Mayfair to inform me of this obvious fact."

"The abduction of Jane Thornton smells of his vulgarity. To lure an innocent girl from her family, to take pleasure in her ruin — that fits with Josiah Horne and his way of life."

Denis looked pained. "Indeed."

"It occurred to me, however, that such a mode of business is not typical of you. You work for the rich and the discreet. You steal precious paintings from under Bonaparte's nose. Your business is a subtle one; you have networks scattered far and wide. You make wishes come true with seeming ease."

"You flatter me."

"I've had time to mull over the risk and the foolish theatricality of Jane Thornton's abduction, put together with what I've learned about you. I wondered why a man with your exactitude would want to do such a thing. And then it struck me. *You had nothing to do with it.*"

Denis did not move, but his eyelids flickered. "I told you this when you called the other day."

"You actually told me nothing. You let me run on in my anger, and you denied just enough to put me off the scent. You knew about Horne's abduction of Miss Thornton, and it angered you. So much so that you went to see him to tell him this. But it did not anger you in the same way it angered me. You cared nothing for Miss Thornton's welfare. Instead, you worried that Horne's stupid actions would endanger something else in which you were involved. What was it, I wonder?"

Denis brought his steepled fingertips to his chin. "It cannot matter anymore, can it? Horne is dead."

"And you could be his murderer."

"I could be. But I was not."

"I believe you. You didn't lie to me when you said he was worth more to you alive than dead. What did he ask of you? What did you give to him that put him so deep into your power?"

Denis watched me a moment, and at long last I saw some emotion in the cold blue depths of his eyes. That emotion was irritation.

"When I first met you, Captain, I told myself that someone like you could be useful to me. I have revised my opinion. You are too hotheaded. I would not be able to trust you."

"You owned him body and soul, didn't you?" I asked. "I think that once upon a time, vulgar Mr. Horne wanted a seat in Parliament. He came to you and behaved as though he were doing you a favor asking you to buy up votes for him. He disgusted you, but you must have seen an opportunity. No doubt you own other men in the Commons, and perhaps even in the Lords, people who owe you favors, as Brigadier Champlain did. But one more wouldn't hurt. You could have eyes and ears in all parties and manipulate whichever would benefit you the most.

"So you helped Horne get his seat, and your price was that he obeyed your every order. I can imagine a man like Horne would not even resent you. He had a seat; who cared that he made no move without your permission? But his stupidity over Jane Thornton could have jeopardized his position, especially when you discovered that her father had tracked her to his doorstep. When Thornton tried to accuse Horne of ruining his daughter, you called in a favor and had five cavalrymen ride to Hanover Square to shut Thornton's mouth. So they obeyed orders and shot an innocent man who was only grieving for his daughter."

Denis regarded me coolly. "You seem to have worked everything out to your satisfaction."

"If it is not the truth, it is very near."

His gaze drifted to the clock on the mantel. "My appointment is in ten minutes, Captain. I must bid you good evening."

I didn't move. "You don't fear me or my revelations. Horne is dead, and I can prove nothing. I imagine many men of power owe you favors and would make sure that you were not hurt even if I tried to speak. I imagine they, like Horne, are grateful to you for what you've done and don't mind helping you."

"It is the way of the world, Captain. Do not pretend you do not know that. You were in the army."

"I admit I have done things I would not care to have closely examined," I said. "But my promises were made on the right side of honor."

"Yes, I have heard all about your honor. It has put you where you are today: poor and of no consequence."

"I must live with that."

Denis shrugged. "I am pleased to meet a man who values honor so highly. There are few these days. But

I must insist you leave now. I have many things to do this evening."

I rose to my feet, and he stood up as well. I was a fraction taller than he, but the cool stare from Denis's blue eyes told me he cared nothing for that.

"Good evening, Captain. Next time, remember that I see no one without an appointment."

I remained in place. "I came for a second reason. I would be most interested in speaking again to your coachman, Jemmy."

Denis looked thoughtful. "I am certain you would. And I'm certain I know why. Very well, I will deliver him to you. Please remember, however, that murder is against the law."

"Jemmy is of more use to me alive than dead," I said.

"Not to me." The chill in Denis's eyes could have frozen oceans. "Be so good as to tell him that for me when you speak to him."

*** *** ***

By the week's end, I felt well enough to accompany Grenville to Hampstead. He took me to the estate of Lord Sommerville, an elderly viscount, and listened curiously while I asked his lordship about his kitchen maid.

Lord Sommerville reiterated what he'd told Grenville earlier, that he'd found no satisfactory culprit in his kitchen maid's death. He directed me to the housekeeper, who had known the girl better, with the instruction that he wanted to know anything I discovered about the girl's murder. The housekeeper restated what Lord Sommerville had told me and let me talk with the kitchen maid's sister, who also worked in the house.

The sister was still very upset about Matilda's death, but she spoke with me readily. She wanted to find the culprit more than anything and bring him to justice. Yes, she believed it had been a man, the same man who had turned Matilda away from her other young man. Matilda had not told her sister who she'd taken up with, but she'd shown her little trinkets the man had bought her and bragged that she was moving up in the world. Matilda had slipped out in the middle of the night, probably to meet this new suitor, and had never returned.

I gave the woman my condolences, and Grenville and I took our leave.

"Was that helpful?" he asked as we rolled away in his luxurious coach. "I first believed that the person who killed the maid also killed Charlotte Morrison, but Miss Morrison is alive."

"Miss Morrison is alive because she ran away. And she ran away because of the maid's death."

"Because she feared for her own life?"

"Because she knew who killed the maid. And it upset her so much that she fled."

"If that is the case, why didn't she go to Lord Sommerville and tell him what she knew?"

I contemplated the green meadow on our right. "She was afraid. Or so horrified by what she knew that she could only think to get away. She was wrong to go, but I understand why she did. Sometimes it is easier to turn your back on the truth than to face it, especially when it is more painful than you can stand."

Grenville had nothing to answer to this, and we traveled in silence for a time. Then Grenville cleared his throat. "There is something I've wanted to ask you, Lacey, about you and Brandon. On the rowboat, you fought him hard, and he looked at you as though he'd cheerfully kill you. I'd thought you the dearest of friends."

"We were. Once."

Curiosity flickered in his eyes, but I shook my head. "I might be able to explain someday. The same day you explain to me why you disappeared from the inn when we visited Hampstead the first time."

Grenville started, then laughed. "And I thought I was utterly discreet." He turned to look out the window, his gaze fixing on something far from here. "Let us say that I have a friend who once met a lady. But what was between them could not be. And so he agreed to go away. Much time has passed since then. And then the friend heard the lady was in Hampstead, and so he searched for any excuse to go there." He slanted me a wry look. "Unfortunately, his damned curiosity led him to an interest in other problems, and he went all the way to Somerset to satisfy it."

Grenville looked embarrassed, an expression I'd never seen on his face. His sangfroid had slipped, and I had the feeling that few people had ever seen it slip.

I tapped my walking stick on the scarred, square toe of my boot. "I have a friend," I began, then stopped. I should say nothing, but somehow I wanted Grenville to know, to understand, the depths of my anger, and why I'd never forgiven Brandon, nor he me. "This friend knew another man, a man of pride and wealth whom the friend deeply respected. My friend followed his every order without question. One day," I said, my voice slowing, "this respected man made the decision to put aside his lady. She could not give him children, you see, which was a severe blow to him. The great man's family and name meant much to him, and he saw his lineage trickling away to weaker and lesser branches. And so he decided, with great reluctance, that she must be sent away." I studied the tip of my boot with great intensity. "My friend objected in the strongest possible manner to the dishonor such a thing would cause this lady. If she were put aside, she would be ruined, reviled, and this the friend could not allow. He found himself in the situation of having to choose between his love for the lady and his love for the great man. And so he chose. Things grew complex from there. Suffice it to say, the two gentlemen nearly killed one another over it."

I stopped, tired of the memories. Still vivid in my mind was the night Louisa's golden head had rested on my shoulder when she'd come to me in anguish. I remembered with perfect clarity, as though it had happened yesterday, the silken texture of her hair beneath my palm, the heat of her tears on my cheek. Also vivid was the look on Brandon's face when he'd walked in and found her crying on my shoulder — the anger, the chagrin, the utter heartbreak.

I said nothing about the rest of it, how Brandon had let anger simmer inside him until the day he could take his revenge. After Vitoria, he had sent me to take up immediate command of another unit, neglecting to inform me I'd journey alone right through a pocket of French troops. They ambushed me, stole the papers I carried — which were false anyway — and then amused themselves torturing me.

An English troop at last swooped down upon them, and I was left with the dead. The English did not see me, and I crawled away from the scavengers, broken and barely alive.

After many days, I had regained my regiment, my leg a ruin. The look on Brandon's face when he saw that I was alive told me everything.

Our commander had not been best pleased with either of us. A scandal between officers was not what he wanted in his regiment. He had made me realize that if I raised a stink, if Brandon were court-martialed as he deserved, the disgrace would stain all of us—Brandon, me, Louisa, the regiment.

We three had agreed to leave the army and return to London.

When I looked up from my muddy boot I found Grenville regarding me in stunned surprise. "Forgive me, Lacey. I had no idea." He drew a breath. "I am honored that you told me this. I swear to you it will never cross my lips to another soul."

I had no doubt that he would keep his silence. Grenville kept staring at me as though he thought me even more a wonder than he had before, until I grew irritated.

"You make too much of it," I said, and turned to look out the window.

We said nothing more until we reached the well-bred house of the Beauchamps, Charlotte Morrison's cousins.

Chapter Twenty-Four

"I'm so pleased to see you again, Captain." Mrs. Beauchamp shook my hand. "Do you have news?"

"I'm happy to tell you, Mrs. Beauchamp, that Miss Morrison is alive and well. In Somerset."

Eyes widened, brows rose. Mr. Beauchamp spluttered, "Somerset?"

"Good heavens, why has she not written us?" his wife said at the same time. "Did she return to her family's house?"

Grenville glanced at me. I hadn't told him what I'd intended to say, but he followed my lead. "I saw her," he said. "She is safe. And married."

Mrs. Beauchamp gaped. "Married?"

"But why not write to us?" her husband demanded. "Why disgrace herself by running away?"

"It doesn't matter," Mrs. Beauchamp said. "She is safe, thank God. Do you have her direction, Mr. Grenville? I must write to her and tell her that of course we forgive her. She must be worried that we'll be angry with her. No, we should make preparations to journey there and tell her ourselves."

I held up my hands. "I believe she doesn't yet want visitors. No doubt she'll write to you when she is ready."

Mrs. Beauchamp lost her smile. "I don't understand. We're her family."

"That is all I know, madam. I myself care only that she is safe and well."

Beauchamp's ruddy face held a mixture of relief and anger. "I thank you for coming in person to tell us, Captain." He held out his hand. "It was good of you."

"Yes." Mrs. Beauchamp sounded subdued.

I shook both their hands. "I bid you good afternoon."

Grenville, who'd kept his composure well throughout the entire exchange, bowed and murmured his good-byes, though I could see him bursting to ask me questions.

Beauchamp followed us out. He waited until the footman had given us our hats and gloves, and he accompanied us out into the soft rain.

"My wife is understandably upset," Beauchamp said. "But we feared the worst. No doubt we will rejoice that Charlotte is well when the surprise wears off. It was kind of you to journey all this way to tell us."

"I had another errand in the area," I said. I took a parcel from my coat. "And I wanted to give you this."

Beauchamp frowned at the parcel, but he took it, bemused.

Grenville's footman helped me into the carriage, and Grenville sprang up behind me, the door slamming as the carriage rolled away. Beauchamp remained in front of the house, staring at the brown paper, rain pattering on his bare head.

Grenville contained himself until we'd gone half a mile. "I've kept my peace long enough, Lacey. What the devil did you give him?"

The road curved, bending through the flat land behind the Beauchamps' house. "Ask your coachman to stop."

"Would it be futile to demand to know why?"

"I will tell you in a moment."

Grenville look was aggrieved, but he rapped on the carriage roof and gave the order to stop.

We waited. The damp air rose, fresh and green-smelling, the earth rich and virgin, awaiting the first spring planting. A muddy path led to a stile, and over this to the meadow behind the Beauchamps' home.

The horses, bored, snorted and moved in the traces, rocking the carriage slightly. The light rain grew heavier.

A rider appeared at the bottom of the meadow, on a small horse, trotting fast. Both horse and rider were rotund, the master rivaling his mount for squat body and stout belly.

Grenville lowered his window. "It's Beauchamp."

At the stile, Beauchamp dismounted. He did not tie his horse, but it seemed content to lower its head and crop grass. Beauchamp climbed the stile and scrambled down the other side, his face streaming perspiration and rain.

He approached the coach. I opened the door and climbed to the ground to meet him.

He thrust the parcel at me. "What is your game, Lacey? What is this?"

"Lord Sommerville's housekeeper gave it to me," I said. "It's the remains of the gown a servant girl wore the night she was killed, sometime at the end of February. A man bashed in her head and tried to bury her in the woods. Were you not at the inquest? The entire village turned up, I've been told."

Beauchamp glared at me, flushed and angry. "My wife and I stayed away. It was a sordid affair."

I opened the paper and smoothed the blue worsted strips. "Likely it was her best dress. She must have been excited, knowing she was going to meet a lover. Not the solid, hardworking young man who'd hoped to marry her, but an older man, well off and respected, who would give her presents. Maybe jewelry and gowns finer than this."

Grenville climbed down from the carriage and his coachman watched from above. Beauchamp looked from me to Grenville. "What do you want of me?"

I ignored him. "Perhaps, as the mistress of a wealthy gentleman, the kitchen maid began to give herself airs. Perhaps she threatened to tell her young man about her lover, or your wife."

Beauchamp took on a hunted look. "She was a silly girl, a maid, for heaven's sake. What did she expect me to do? Put aside my dear wife for her? You gentlemen understand."

"Your cousin, Charlotte, knew who killed her," I said.

Beauchamp began to stammer. "Matilda wasn't murdered. It was an accident. She fell and hit her head."

"Or perhaps Charlotte did not know; I cannot say. But your attentions must have frightened Charlotte. So much so that she fled you, in a manner that makes it impossible for you to pursue her and bring her back."

Beauchamp gave me a pleading look. "We took Charlotte in, we gave her a home. How could she have done this? We were her family."

His bleating was pathetic, but I hardened my heart. "I imagine your wife's pretty young cousin was a great temptation for you. An intelligent and beautiful girl would be much more satisfying than a silly maid. And close at hand, under your own roof. You'd need no secret trysts in hedgerows. Did you seduce Charlotte? Or threaten her if she did not comply?"

Beauchamp sucked in his breath. "How do you know this? Charlotte must have told you."

"Your wife gave me her letters. You sent a boy after me to steal and destroy them. You feared that Charlotte might have written some hint, left some clue of what you had done to her."

Beauchamp clasped his hands against his ample belly. "You must not tell my wife. She is a gentle creature. It will break her heart. Please, I beg of you."

I went on ruthlessly. "What happened in the woods that night? Did you tell Matilda you'd found better? Perhaps Matilda did not want to leave so quietly. Perhaps she threatened to make a fuss. And you grew alarmed, and struck out."

Tears trickled down his cheeks. "No, it truly was an accident, I swear it. Matilda wanted me to run away with her. She started to screech and cry. I tried to make her stop. She started to run away, but she stumbled and fell. I heard her head crack on a rock. I tried to help her, but her head was covered with blood, and she had stopped breathing. I could not take her home; could not explain."

I thrust the parcel back into his hands. "Explain it to Lord Sommerville. He is a reasonable man."

Beauchamp wiped his eyes. "Will I ever see Charlotte again?"

"I rather doubt it. Tell your wife the truth, all of it. She will understand why Charlotte isn't coming back."

I turned away from him. Grenville, his face white, waited while I climbed back into the carriage.

"Please, gentlemen."

Grenville ascended behind me, and his footman, shocked and trying to hide it, shut the door. I looked out of the window at Beauchamp, weeping beneath me.

"Go home," I said.

Grenville rapped on the roof of the carriage, and the coachman drove on.

*** *** ***

"Are you going to tell Sommerville?" Grenville eyed me sternly. "If you don't, I will."

I leaned back against the sumptuous cushions, suddenly exhausted and wanting to be done with it. "I'll write Sommerville tonight and post it in the morning. I want to give Beauchamp time to confess. If he has an ounce of honor, he will take the blame and leave his wife out of it."

"If he has any honor at all, he will already be dead," Grenville said.

I wondered if the man with the rabbity eyes would have the courage to put a pistol to his own head and save his wife the pain of his trial and the public knowledge of his betrayal. "I wish I knew if he had. It is up to him now."

As we made our way back to London, my tiredness lifted somewhat, and I told Grenville about my second visit to Denis and what I'd decided about his involvement in Jane Thornton's abduction. I did not much want to talk about it, but I'd learned my lesson. If I hadn't written Grenville that rude and angry letter, and if he hadn't been magnanimous enough to forgive my idiotic pride and come looking for me, I'd probably be resting at the bottom of the Thames, Black Nancy with me.

Grenville was eager to interview Jemmy with me, but I told him I needed to run another errand, one I'd rather do alone. He did not ask me what, but he regarded me sharply as I descended the carriage.

What I had to face next pained me beyond thought. I left home shortly after dark and traveled to the house near St. Paul's Churchyard. As before, I was shown to an upstairs parlor, and Josette Martin met me there.

She came forward and took my hand, lamplight shining on the thick braids of her nearly black hair.

"Captain Lacey. I am pleased to see you again. Will you sit?"

I remained standing, holding her hand. "When do you leave for France?"

She looked at me in surprise. "A week today. Why?"

"Can you leave tomorrow? Will Aimee be well enough to travel?"

"Tomorrow? I am not certain."

"Even if she isn't, I advise you to take Aimee and start for France immediately."

"Why, Captain? I do not understand."

I led Josette toward the worn divan and drew her to sit facing me. The room smelled faintly of old flowers, overlaid with the slightly stuffy scent of a room whose windows had long been closed.

"Because I know who killed Josiah Horne," I said. "In all conscience, and following duty, I ought to tell someone everything I know."

Josette's face drained of color. "Please explain what you mean."

"The Runners arrested Bremer, the butler. He went to Newgate, but he died before he came to trial. They are satisfied. But Bremer didn't kill Mr. Horne."

Her beautiful eyes shied from mine. "You cannot know that. How can you?"

I held her hands gently. "Alice must have told you that she believed Aimee was a captive in Horne's house. She had no proof, but you did not let that stop you, did you? Going to the front door would not help the Thorntons and Alice, so you decided to approach through the kitchens. You began making deliveries to the Horne household, possibly offering a greengrocer or seamstress your services."

"I did nothing, sir," she said weakly.

"I'd been so concerned about who'd entered Horne's house through the *front* door that day, that it never occurred to me to worry about who went in through the scullery. But the lad who lives next door to Horne saw you. You'd started making deliveries, he said, about four weeks earlier—right after Alice and Mr. Thornton discovered that Jane was living with Horne.

"The lad next door spent the day of the murder looking out of the window, waiting for his tutor, who never arrived. He told me that two delivery men and a woman with a basket had gone down the kitchen stairs and entered the house. I thought nothing of it, and neither did he. That day, at last, you must have been able to go from the kitchens to the study upstairs. I imagine that no one in that chaotic household noticed you. Am I right?"

Josette pressed her hands to her face, tears leaking from her beautiful eyes. "She did not mean to do it. Aimee was so frightened. And so desperate. She just struck out. She did not even know."

Chapter Twenty-Five

I waited, my heart heavy, until Josette's weeping quieted. When she looked up at me, her black lashes were wet with tears.

I said quietly, "You found Aimee in the study when you entered it."

She nodded. "He was on the carpet, with the knife in his chest, and Aimee lay in a swoon beside him. It had happened only moments before I arrived. Aimee did not even realize what she'd done. He'd taken her from the wardrobe where he'd locked her that day. The knife had been lying on the desk—I suppose he'd used it for opening letters or cutting open books. She simply picked it up and struck him with it. There was very little blood. A little on her hand; that was all."

"If it is done correctly, a blow like that does not bleed much."

"But I knew that if Aimee was found there, she would hang. No matter what the man Horne had done to her, it would be Aimee who paid." Fire burned in the depths of her beautiful eyes. "I could not let that happen."

"No," I agreed. "You could not. So you wiped off her hands, renewed the bonds on her wrists, and locked her back into the wardrobe. Aimee was frightened enough and confused enough to obey you. You knew that she would likely be found after the murder was discovered, and of course no one would suspect her, when her hands were tied so tightly and the wardrobe was locked from the outside. If they didn't find her, you would return to the house as the concerned aunt, looking for her. It must have been difficult to leave her."

She nodded fervently. "It was, oh, yes, it was. But if I'd taken her away then, we might be discovered. They'd find Mr. Horne, and Aimee would be accused of the crime. I had to leave her."

"It was wise of you." Locking Aimee back in the wardrobe would have served two purposes—the obvious one of making it seem that Aimee could not possibly have committed the murder; and second, the discovery of her in the wardrobe would expose Horne for the bastard he was. A man having sport with a maid was one thing. Making a slave of her was something else.

Josette swallowed. "I had to make certain that the bonds cut into her flesh, and then I had to walk away from her. I had to go home and wait, not knowing who would find Aimee and when. It was the next morning before Alice sent word that she was safe. I had no idea, all that night, if I'd done right. No way to know— " More tears spilled from her lovely eyes.

I pressed Josette's work-worn hand between my own. "But your deception worked. I voiced my opinion loudly to everyone who would listen that it was impossible for Aimee to have killed Horne. It wasn't until I speculated that two people might have been involved that I realized Aimee could very well have stabbed him. Her accomplice would have to have been coolheaded, brave, and utterly devoted to her. And I remembered that Aimee had an aunt who had raised her and was preparing to take her away to France."

"You are right," Josette said softly. "I am devoted to her. And I'm as guilty as she."

"You did one more thing before you left that room."

She whitened. "I barely remember it."

I smoothed my fingers over the back of her hand. "I would have been in a howling rage myself."

"I was." She raised her head, words angry. "He had hurt Aimee so deeply, and there he lay, dying, beyond my reach. I wanted to hurt him back. He'd already taken down his trousers, and there he was, exposed for the world to see. I am not certain what happened then. But the knife was in my hand, and I—"

I saw again the yellow carpet bathed in blood, smelled the pungent odor of it. I saw Josette of the beautiful eyes, the knife in her hand, rage twisting her face, savagely cutting the man who had raped her beloved niece. Blood had poured from his body, exposing his sins. He had bled the same as any other man would bleed, though his soul was foul and black.

"What will you do, Captain?" Josette asked in a quiet voice. "If you go to a magistrate, please, I beg you, let me take the blame. Tell them I killed Mr. Horne. Let Aimee go."

I stood, leaning heavily on my walking stick. "In two days, I will confess what I know to one other person and then decide what is best to do. If I wait longer, I will be tempted to hide it forever, and let the innocent Bremer be labeled the culprit. In two days, you can be in France. I advise you to tell no one exactly where you are going."

Josette looked at me for a long time before she nodded. "It will be as you say. I believe Aimee will be well enough to leave tomorrow." She paused. "You must think me hard, Captain, to do what I have done. But she is my only family. And what he did was unforgivable."

I cupped her cheek. "I think you are courageous, Josette. And quite beautiful." I leaned down and pressed a kiss to her parted lips. "God bless you," I whispered, then I left her.

*** *** ***

The next day, James Denis sent a carriage for me, and when I climbed into it, I found Denis himself waiting for me.

"Upon reflection," he said, settling a rug with fine-gloved hands, "I decided I wanted to be present when you interviewed my former coachman."

I was not pleased at this turn of events, but I had no choice. If I wanted to find Jane Thornton, I needed Denis's assistance.

"To prevent Jemmy from telling me the wrong things?" I asked.

"Something like that."

Denis did not much like sharing the carriage with me either, if his fidgeting with his gloves and his walking stick were any indication. Also, he'd squeezed one of his massive footmen into the seat next to me, and this man watched my every move.

We went to a house in a lane that opened from the Strand. I realized as I entered the house's dark interior that this might well have been the house to which Jane had been lured by the procuress.

Jemmy sat behind a plain wooden table in a ground-floor room. Two of Denis's large men stood near him, waiting for us. Jemmy started when he saw me, then sank back into his chair, his face pasty white.

A fire had been lit, and the room was warm, but the only light came from the flames on the hearth. When I sat down opposite Jemmy, red light illuminated his pocked face and glinted on his filed teeth.

"Where is Jane Thornton?" I asked him.

Jemmy looked, not at me, but over my shoulder to where Denis waited. "Why is *he* here? I don't understand this."

"Answer his question," came Denis's voice, smooth as silk.

"I don't know. I don't know nothing."

"Horne must have met you in his dealings with your employer," I said. "Perhaps he asked you if you wanted to make a little extra money doing a favor for him."

"What of it? No harm in making a bit of the ready."

Denis broke in. "If you needed more money, you should have told me. I would have found extra work for you."

His quiet, matter-of-fact tone made Jemmy blench.

"You contacted the procuress," I said. "You thought of the girl you'd abduct—the young friend of Mr. Carstairs's daughter—and let the procuress make the plan. She lured away Jane and her maid, probably with the help of an accomplice, and after the fervor had died down, you returned to help carry them to Horne. Horne paid you, and you thought no more of it. Until the night he sent for you again."

Jemmy clenched his hands. "I won't listen to this."

I don't know what look Denis gave him, but Jemmy subsided at once. Behind me I heard Denis walk softly to the window.

"That night, about four weeks ago, you drove whatever conveyance you had to hand to Hanover Square," I continued. "You carried Jane Thornton from Horne's house. Where did you take her?"

Jemmy wet his lips. "I can't be sure. A place he directed me to."

"Where?"

"I don't remember, I tell you."

I started over the table for him. Jemmy slammed back in his chair, giving me a half-belligerent, half-fearful look.

Denis turned from the window. "Tell the captain what he wants to know, Jemmy."

Jemmy swallowed nervously, firelight gleaming on his sweating face. "I can't explain it. I'd have to take you."

"Take me then."

Jemmy's gaze darted to Denis as he stood up. I moved aside to let him around the table, and we left the room. One of Denis's thugs led the way, then Denis himself, then me, then Jemmy, the second large man bringing up the rear.

When we reached the street, Jemmy tried to bolt. The two servants locked themselves on either side of Jemmy and manhandled him to the top of the coach. While they held him there, Denis and I were assisted inside by Denis's stone-faced footman.

Denis instructed the coachman to follow Jemmy's directions, but I asked that we stop by the Thorntons' nearby house first. I needed to ask Alice to accompany us. I wanted there to be no mistake in Jane Thornton's identity.

Alice looked nervous about joining me and Denis inside the carriage, but she came all the same, hope in her eyes. I asked her about Mr. Thornton.

"He's mending, sir. But slowly. If we could find Miss Jane, it might make all the difference."

The ride was tedious through snaking traffic and the rain. The coach was as sumptuous as Grenville's with velvet walls, gold leaf on the windows, and cushioned stools for our feet. Denis looked out the window as though Alice did not exist, and the bulky footman watched her with his cold, blank stare.

The carriage wound its way to London Bridge, and thence across. We entered Southwark.

"Where the devil is he taking us?" I asked, peering out at the gloom.

Denis shrugged, with the air of a man who is always surrounded by a bubble of safety. I fully expected a gang of toughs to be waiting at the end of the journey, Jemmy taking us straight to them. Or

Denis might have recruited Jemmy to lead me into the lion's den, but I didn't think so. The terror in Jemmy's eyes had been real, and Denis and I seemed to have called a truce of sorts.

The stink of the river hung heavily in the air, as did the smoke from an ironworks. Stagnant pools of noisome water reflected the black of coal smoke and the dreary sky. The carriage ground to a stop in a back lane that fronted the river. From here, steps led down to the shore of the Thames, where fishermen clung to their trade.

The footman assisted me down, and I handed Alice out myself. A wave of rain swept over us. Alice tented her shawl above her head. Jemmy had descended from the top of the carriage and now stood uncertainly between Denis's two servants.

"Down there," he said, pointing to the river.

"Where? Show me."

He didn't want to. But his fear of Denis overcame his fear of me, and Jemmy plodded down the muddy, slippery steps. I followed with Alice.

Denis remained inside the carriage. He could easily tell his coachman to drive away and leave us stranded, and I think the same thought occurred to Alice, because she melted close to me and stayed there.

Jemmy led us to a fishing shack that looked no different from the others that dotted the shore. The Thames rolled away beyond us, the far bank lost in the mist and rain.

Before he reached the door, Jemmy stopped suddenly. "It's the beaks!" he shouted into the shack. "Run!"

A man came boiling out and sprinted down the beach. A woman followed him, but too slowly. One of Denis's men leapt forward and caught her as she slipped on the rocks. He dragged her back to us. Hanks of gray hair hung limply about her face, which was lined and worn.

Her eyes were frightened, but defiant. "We didn't do nothing. Makes no difference what 'e said."

"Where is Miss Thornton?" I asked.

She looked bewildered. "'oo?"

"This way," Jemmy said.

He tramped around the shed and down a path that led to the shore. Jemmy led us along this, myself and Alice trailing him, Denis's servant following with the woman, who kept up a constant patter about nothing being her fault.

At the end of the path, behind a stone staircase that led back up to Southwark, lay a pile of debris, looking like nothing more than a caved-in shed and a tarp held down by rocks. Jemmy made for the tarp.

"No!" the woman shouted. "It weren't me."

Jemmy lifted pieces of the debris and hurled them aside. One of the footmen stepped in and helped him. After a space had been cleared, Jemmy reached down and tugged back a fold of tarp.

Beneath it lay a small, white hand, palm up, fingers curled in supplication to the uncaring sky.

Alice gave a sharp cry.

"It weren't us," the woman bleated. "He brought her to us, told us to hide her. We wanted to dump her in the river, but he said no, we had to hide her. She were already dead when she came."

I moved to the debris as Alice clung to my coat. I slid my walking stick under the tarp and turned it back.

A woman's body lay there, covered in muck and mud. What had once been a nightdress clung to her chest, which was sunken with time and the piles of board that had rested atop her. Her face was pale, serene, eyes closed, mouth limp, but the skin of her neck was puckered with decay.

Alice sank to her knees beside me, a wail tearing from her. The fisherman's woman darted back, as though afraid of the sound, and pointed a thin finger at Jemmy. "'*E* brought her 'ere. 'E's the murderer."

"I didn't murder no one," Jemmy said. "She were dead already when he sent for me."

I believed him. I'd seen what Horne had done to Aimee. Possibly Horne hadn't meant to kill Jane; possibly it was pure accident. Perhaps when Horne had seen what he'd done, he'd panicked. He'd sent for Jemmy, remembering the young man's help abducting the girls in the first place, and bade him get rid of her. Young Philip Preston had told me someone had carried a bundle, like a carpet, to the dark carriage that night. A carpet, yes, but with Jane's body rolled inside it.

Alice's sobs turned to a wordless keening. I covered Jane's body with the tarp, then I straightened and faced Jemmy.

Jemmy stepped back in alarm. I stared him down, the man who'd caused Jane Thornton's ruin and death, even if indirectly. Jemmy had made the abduction possible and was as much to blame as Horne.

I unsheathed my sword. The blade rang, and raindrops glittered on the bright steel as bitter anger burned through me. I wanted nothing more than to press that sharpness through the terrified coachman's heart and watch him bleed until he died.

Behind me Alice sobbed. "Please don't, sir. It won't bring her back."

It was as though my conscience had spoken aloud. I pressed my anger down, slid the blade back into its sheath, and helped Alice to her feet. In silence, I led her back up the path to the stairs.

Not until we approached the waiting carriage did I realize that Jemmy and Denis's two footmen had not returned with me. I glanced back through the rain to the bank below, but I couldn't see them.

The footman who'd remained with the carriage opened the door and hoisted both Alice and myself back inside. Alice huddled, damp and miserable, into a corner. I took the seat next to her, forcing the footman to sit next to Denis.

We rode in silence back through Southwark, winding into the traffic heading across the bridge to the City. Denis studied me in the soft lantern light, the only one of us dry and unmussed.

"Revenge, Captain, is usually a waste of time," he said. "I don't deal in it."

"Jane was avenged," I said quietly.

"With the murder of Horne by the butler? I suppose she was, indirectly."

"But it will not be enough. I want the procuress and anyone else who helped them."

Denis shook his head. "You are a hard man, Captain Lacey."

"If Horne had taken an innocent child and dashed out its brains, it would have been no different. All she'd ever known was happiness and people who cared for her. Suddenly all that was ripped from her, and she faced a monster. I cannot even begin to imagine her terror. She must have found it unbelievable that such a thing could happen."

Alice whimpered. I wanted to pat her hand, to comfort her, but I had no comfort to give. Sometimes there is no comfort, only the knowledge that the worst has happened.

"I want everyone who was a part of that to face a magistrate and be punished for their sins."

Denis gave his head a slight shake. "Jemmy will not face a magistrate. He will face me. He had no business dealing directly with Horne without my knowledge."

I looked into his blank, handsome face and cold eyes, and my anger grew hot and heavy. "You are filth."

Denis held up his hand in its immaculate, expensive glove. "Have no doubt, I will make him name his accomplices."

"And send them to a magistrate? I want them tried before God."

He looked idly out the window. "It will do you no good to take them to court. First, you would have to prove what you say. I told you, I will not give you Jemmy, and without him, you will have no eyewitness. Second, you would have to tell the story of your Miss Thornton in all its sordid details, a story that would be sensational enough to be printed in the newspapers for all the world to see. Her family will always bear the stigma of having a daughter abducted, ruined, and murdered. Is that what you want?"

My lips moved with difficulty. "No."

"I know you want vengeance, but the conventional way is not the best in this case. I will obtain your revenge for you, as a favor."

"I do not want to owe favors to you."

"You already owe me favors, Captain. You will get nowhere without Jemmy, and I will not give him to you. You will have to let me do this my way."

I met Denis's eyes, clear, cold, and unforgiving. He knew I was dangerous to him, and he'd already begun taking precautions against me. I knew I would not win.

*** *** ***

"So I let him," I said.

Louisa twined her cool fingers through mine. She reposed next to me on the low divan in my sitting room, where she'd sat for the last three hours while I poured out my story.

Five days had passed since I'd discovered Jane's fate. Four of those I'd spent sunk in melancholia, unable to rise from my bed, barely able to eat the broth Mrs. Beltan forced upon me. Even today, every movement of my limbs hurt me, every motion was made with the greatest effort.

I had gone to the Brandons' Brook Street house after I'd helped Alice break the news to Mrs. Thornton that her daughter was dead. Louisa had been out, but her husband had been there, and I'd made him tell me where she was. He insisted on accompanying me to the card party at Lady Aline's, where Louisa was happily gambling and chatting with friends.

Louisa's mirth had evaporated when her husband and I entered to pull her from the sitting room. I explained what had happened, barely able to speak, my mind already pulling away from me. I was never sure what happened after that, because after a long, long time traveling back through London and the hour it took to climb my stairs to my rooms, I'd had strength enough only to crawl into bed and lie there.

I learned later that Louisa had gone to the Thorntons and given them what aid she could, including arranging for Jane's body to be retrieved and decently buried in a churchyard with the proper service. She told me that Mr. Thornton would survive his gunshot wound, but she suspected he would always be weak. The heart had gone out of him.

I never did discover what had happened to Jemmy and the procuress and anyone else involved in the matter. I came across a terse letter from Denis as I leafed through the post that had piled on my writing desk in the intervening time. In brief sentences, he told me that everything had been taken care of, giving me no details. From that day forward, I heard nothing, not from Denis, not in newspapers, not in rumor.

I told Louisa everything, the words tumbling from my lips, as though she were a papist confessor and I a contrite sinner.

"So I turned my back on Jemmy and left him to Denis's mercy. God knows what he did to him."

Louisa lifted her head, and firelight glistened on a sleek, golden curl that fell to her neck. "I confess that I do not feel much sympathy for him. Not after spending these past days with Mrs. Thornton. Not for Horne, not Jemmy, not the procuress."

"You didn't see Denis's eyes. I have never seen anything so cold. It's as though he's not even alive, Louisa."

She shivered. "I think I never want to meet this man. Although I am *very* angry about what he did to you, and I would like to tell him so."

I smiled at the image of Louisa Brandon scolding James Denis, her finger extended, then I sobered. "He wanted to punish Jemmy himself, not because Jemmy had done a terrible thing, but because he'd disobeyed Denis. And, Denis sees it as a way to have power over me."

"Mr. Denis also could not let Jemmy in court for fear of what he might confess in the dock — or on the scaffold," Louisa pointed out.

"Denis does have the magistrates in his pocket, but gossip and public opinion can still ruin him." I ran my hands through my hair. "But I did the same, didn't I? I let my own will prevail over the law and justice."

"By letting Aimee's aunt take her to France?"

I rested my head against the back of the divan. "Ease my conscience, Louisa. Was I right to let her go?"

Louisa met my eyes, hers clear gray and filled with compassion. "What Horne did was unforgivable. Aimee took his life in desperation, and in defense of her own. He never would have paid for what he'd done, if she hadn't."

"But does one crime negate another?" I asked. "I've shot men who were doing their best to shoot me, I've plunged my saber into men who were trying to plunge their bayonets into me. Does it make me — or Aimee, or Josette — any less guilty?"

"I cannot answer that, Gabriel. Please don't ask me to. What was right for Aimee, and what was wrong, I do not know. Perhaps the choice was neither right nor wrong, it simply existed." Louisa laid her hand on my knee. "I am afraid that, in this case, you'll not have the comfort of knowing you did right."

I closed my eyes. "If I let Aimee and Josette escape to France, then I say that murder under certain circumstances is perfectly acceptable. And who are we to judge what those circumstances are? But if I go to Bow Street and tell them all I know, they'll go after them and drag them back. And they both would likely die a horrible death."

"What will you do, then?"

Louisa watched me, expectant.

I stared at a point beyond the flaking plaster arches that climbed to my ceiling. The firelight softened the once-gilded walls to a mimicry of their former glory.

"I must let them live."

Louisa looked relieved. "I'm glad."

"May God forgive me."

Louisa leaned to me, fragrant with lemon and silk, and pressed a soft kiss to my forehead.

"Even if he will not," she whispered, "I will."

End

Please turn the page
for a preview
of Captain Lacey's next adventure

A
Regimental
Murder

Captain Lacey
Regency Mysteries
Book 2

Chapter One

London, July 1816

A new bridge was rising to cross the Thames just south and east of Covent Garden, a silent hulk of stone and scaffolding slowly stretching its arches across the river. I walked down to this unfinished bridge one sweltering July night through darkness that belonged to pickpockets and game girls, from Grimpen Lane to Russel Street through Covent Garden, its stalls shut up and silent, along Southampton Street and the Strand to the pathways that led to the bridge.

I walked to escape my dreams. I had dreamed of a Spanish summer, one as hot as this, but with dry breezes from rocky hillsides under a baking sun. The long days came back to me and the steamy rains that muddied the roads and fell on my tent like needles in the night. The warmth took me back to the days I had been a cavalry captain, and to one particular night when it had stormed and things had changed for me.

Now I was in London, Iberia far away. The damp warmth of cobblestones caressed my feet, soft rain striking my face and rolling in little rivulets down my nose. The hulk of the bridge was silent, a dark presence not yet born. That is not to say it was deserted. A street theatre distracted passersby on the Strand and game girls stood at the edges of the pavement. A threesome of burly men, arm-in-arm and smelling of ale, pushed through singing a happy tune off-key. They slithered and dodged among wheeled conveyances, never loosening their hold on one another. Their merry song drifted into the night.

A woman brushed past me, making for the tunnel of darkness that led to the bridge. Droplets of rain sparkled on her dark cloak, and I glimpsed beneath her hood a fine, sculpted face and the glitter of jewels. She passed so close that I saw the shape of each slender gloved finger that had held her cloak, and the fine chain of gold that adorned her wrist.

She was a furtive shadow in the midst of the city night, a lady where no lady should be. She was alone—no footman or maid pattered after her, holding slipper box or lantern. She was dressed for the opera or the theatre or a Mayfair ballroom, and yet she hastened here, to the dark of the incomplete bridge.

She interested me, this lady, pricking the curiosity beneath my melancholia. She might, of course, be a high flyer, an upper-class woman of dubious reputation, but I did not think so. High flyers were even more prone than ladies of quality to shutting themselves away in gaudy carriages and taking great care of their clothes and slippers. Also, this woman did not carry herself like a lady of doubtful morals, but like a lady who knew she was out of place and strove to be every inch a lady even so.

I turned, my curiosity and alarm aroused, and followed her.

Darkness quickly closed on us, the soft rain our only companion. She walked out onto an unfinished arch of the bridge, slippers whispering on boards laid over stones.

I quickened my steps. The boards moved beneath my feet, the hollow sound carrying to her. She looked back, her face pale in the darkness. Her cloak swirled open to reveal a dove gray gown, and her slender legs in white stockings flashed against the night.

She reached the crest of the arch. The rain thickened, a gust of wind blowing it like mist across the bridge. When it cleared, a shadow detached itself from the dark arms of scaffolding and moved toward her. The woman started, but did not flee.

The person—man or woman, I could not tell which—bent to her, speaking rapidly. The lady appeared to listen, then she stepped back. "No," she said clearly. "I cannot."

The shadow leaned forward, hands moving in persuasive gestures. She backed away, shaking her head.

Suddenly, she cried out, turned, started to run. The assailant lunged at her, and I heard the ring of a knife.

I ran forward. The assailant—male—looked up, saw me coming. I was a large man, and I carried a walking stick, within which was concealed a stout sword. Perhaps he knew who I was, perhaps he'd seen me and my famous temper at work. In any event, he flung the woman from him and fled.

She landed hard on the stones and boards, too near the edge. I snatched at the assailant, but his knife flashed in the rain, catching me across my palm. I grunted. He scuttled away into the darkness, disappearing in a wash of rain.

I let him go. I balanced myself on the slippery boards and made my way to her. To my left, empty air rose from the roiling Thames, mist and hot rain and foul odors. One misstep and I would plunge down into the waiting, noisome river.

The woman lay facedown, her body half over the edge. Her cloak tangled her so that she could not roll to safety, and her hands worked fruitlessly to pull herself to the firm stones.

I leaned down, seized her about her waist, and hauled her back to the middle of the bridge. She cringed from me, her hands strong as she pushed me away.

"Carefully," I said. "He is gone. You are safe."

Her hood had fallen back. The jewels I'd glimpsed were diamonds, a fine tiara of them. They sparkled against her dark hair, which lay in snarls over her cloak.

"Who was he?" I asked in a gentle voice.

She looked about wildly, as though unsure of who I meant. "I do not know. A—a beggar, I think."

One with a sharp knife. My hand stung and my glove was ruined.

I helped her to her feet. She clung to me a moment, her fright still too close.

Gradually, as the rain quieted into a soft summer shower, she returned to herself again. Her hands uncurled from my coat, and her panicked grip relaxed.

"Thank you," she said. "Thank you for helping me."

I said something polite, as though I had merely opened a door for her at a soiree.

I led her off the bridge and out of the darkness, back to the solid reality of the Strand. I kept a sharp eye out for her assailant, but I saw no one. He had fled.

Our adventure had not gone without attention. By the time we reached the Strand, a small crowd had gathered to peer curiously at us. A group of ladies in tawdry finery looked the woman over.

"Why'd she go out there, then?" one remarked to the crowd in general.

"Tried to throw herself over," another answered.

"Belly-full, I'd wager."

The second nodded. "Most like."

The woman appeared not to hear them, but she moved closer to me, her hand tightening on my sleeve.

A spindly man in faded black fell in beside us as we moved on. He grinned, showing crooked teeth and bathing me with coffee-scented breath. "Excellent work, Captain. How brave you are."

I knew him. The man's name was Billings, and he was a journalist, one of those damned insolent breed who dressed badly and followed the rich and prominent, hoping for a breath of scandal. Billings hung about the theatres at Drury Lane and Covent

Garden, waiting for members of the *haut ton* to do something indiscreet.

I toyed with the idea of beating him off, but knew that such an action would only replay itself in the paragraphs of whatever scurrilous story he chose to write.

The curious thing was, the lady seemed to recognize him. She pressed her face into my sleeve, not in a gesture of fear, but betraying a wish to hide.

His grin grew broader. He saluted me and sauntered off, no doubt to pen an entirely false version of events for the *Morning Herald.*

I led the lady along the Strand toward Southampton Street. She was still shaking and shocked and needed to get indoors.

"I want to take you home," I said. "You must tell me where that is."

She shook her head vehemently. "No." Her voice was little more than a scratch. "Not home. Not there."

"Where, then?"

But she would not give me an alternate direction, no matter how much I plied her. I wondered where she had left her conveyance, where her retinue of servants waited for her. She offered nothing, only moved swiftly along beside me, head bent so I could not see her face.

"You must tell me where your carriage is," I tried again.

She shook her head, and continued to shake it no matter how I pleaded with her. "All right, then," I said, at my wit's end. "I will take you to a friend who will look after you. Mrs. Brandon is quite respectable. She is the wife of a colonel."

My lady stopped, pale lips parting in surprise. Her eyes, deep blue I saw now that we stood in the light, widened. "Mrs. Brandon?" Suddenly, she began to laugh. Her hands balled into tight fists, and she pressed them into her stomach, hysteria shaking her.

I tried to quiet her, but she laughed on, until at last the broken laughs turned to sobs. "Not Mrs. Brandon," she gasped. "Oh, please, no, never that. I will go with you, anywhere you want. Take me to hell if you like, but not home, and not to Mrs. Brandon, for God's sake. That would never do."

*** *** ***

In the end, I took her to my rooms in Grimpen Lane, a narrow cul-de-sac off Russel Street near Covent Garden market.

The lane was hot with the summer night. My hardworking neighbors were in their beds, though a few street girls lingered in the shadows, and a gin-soaked young man lay flat on his back not far from the bake shop. If the man did not manage to drag himself away, the game girls would no doubt rob him blind, if they hadn't already.

I stopped at a narrow door beside the bake shop, unlocked and opened it. Stuffy air poured down at us. The staircase inside had once been grand, and the remnants of an idyllic mural could be seen in the moonlight—shepherds and shepherdesses pursuing each other across a flat green landscape, a curious mixture of innocence and lust.

"What is this place?" my lady asked in whisper.

"Number 5, Grimpen Lane," I answered as I led her upstairs and unlocked the door on the first landing. "In my lighter moments, I call it home."

Behind the door lay my rooms, once the drawing rooms of whatever wealthy family had lived here a century ago. The flat above mine was quiet, which meant that Marianne Simmons, my upstairs neighbor, was either on stage in Drury Lane or tucked away somewhere with a gentleman. Mrs. Beltan, the landlady who ran the bake shop below, lived streets away with her sister. The house was empty and we were alone.

I ushered the woman inside. She remained standing in the middle of the carpet, rubbing her hands as I stirred the embers that still glowed in my grate. The night was warm, but the old walls held a chill that no amount of sun could leach away. Once a tiny fire crackled in the coals, I opened the windows, which I'd left closed to keep birds from seeking shelter in my front room. The breeze that had sprung up at the river barely reached Grimpen Lane, but the open window at least moved the stagnant air.

By the fire's light, I saw that the woman was likely in her late thirties, or fortyish as I was. She had a classic beauty that the bloody scratches on her cheek could not mar, a clean line of jaw, square cheekbones, arched brows over full-lashed blue eyes. Faint lines feathered from her eyes and corners of her mouth, not age, but weariness.

I took her wet cloak from her, then led her to the wing chair near the fire and bade her sit. I stripped her ruined slippers from her ice-cold feet then fetched a blanket from my bed and tucked it around her. She sat through the proceedings without interest.

I poured out a large measure of brandy from a fine bottle my acquaintance Lucius Grenville had sent me and brought it to her. The glass shook against her mouth, but I held it steady and made her drink every drop. Then I brought her another.

After the third glass, her shaking at last began to cease. She leaned against the worn wing chair, her eyes closing. I fetched a cloth, dampened it with water at my wash basin, and began to wipe the blood and grime from her hands.

Sitting this near to her let me study her closely. Her hair, now tangled and loose, was darkest brown, bearing only a few strands of gray. Her mouth was regal and straight, the mouth of a woman not much given to laughter.

She was a lady, highborn and wealthy, who had been to a ball or soiree or opera. Who had managed to get herself away from her carriage and servants to walk alone to the unfinished bridge at the Strand for her secret errand.

I still did not know who she was.

Grenville would know. Lucius Grenville knew everyone who was anyone in London. Every would-be dandy from the Prince of Wales to lads just down from Eton copied his dress, his manners, and his tastes in everything from food to horses to women. This famous man had befriended me, he'd said because he found me interesting, a relief from the ennui of London society. Most Londoners envied me my favored position, but I had not yet decided whether I should be flattered or insulted.

"Will you tell me who you are?" I asked as I worked.

"No." The voice was matter-of-fact, the timbre rich and warm.

"Or why you went to the bridge?"

Her closed eyes tightened. "No."

"Who was the man who accosted you? Did you have an appointment to meet him?"

She opened her eyes in sudden alarm. Then she focused her gaze on my left shoulder, holding it there as if it steadied her. "He was a beggar, I told you. I thought to give him a coin, because he was pitiable. Then I saw he had a knife and tried to flee him."

"Happy chance I was there to stop him." My palm still throbbed from the cut he'd given me, but it was shallow, my glove having taken the brunt of it. "That still does not answer the question of why you went to the bridge in the first place."

She lifted her head and bathed me in a haughty stare. "That is my own affair."

Of course she would not tell me the truth, and I had not thought she would. I wondered if the women at the bridge had been right, that she'd gone there to end her life. Suicide was a common enough means of ending one's troubles in these times—a gentleman ruined by debt, a soldier afraid to face battle, a woman raped and abandoned.

I was no stranger myself to melancholia. When I'd first returned to London from Spain, the black despair had settled on me more times than I cared to think about. The fits had lessened since the turn of the year, because my sense of purpose was slowly returning to me. I had made new friends and was beginning to find interest in even the most wretched corners of London.

She offered nothing more, and I carefully touched my cloth to the scrapes on her cheek. She flinched, but did not pull away.

"You may rest here until you feel better," I said. "My bed is uncomfortable, but better than nothing. The brandy will help you sleep."

She studied me a moment, her eyes unfocussed. Then, with a suddenness that took my breath away, she lifted her slim arms and twined them about my neck. The light silk of her sleeves caressed my skin, and her breath was warm on my lips.

I swallowed. "Madam."

She did not let me go. She pulled me into her embrace and pushed her soft mouth against mine.

Primal blood beat through my body, and I balled my fists. I tasted her lips for one heady moment before I reached up and gently pushed her from me. "Madam," I repeated.

She gazed at me with hungry intensity. "Why not? Does it matter so much?" Her eyes filled and she whispered again, "Why not?"

I could easily have accepted what she offered. She was beautiful, and her lips were warm, and she had quite entranced me. It was devilish difficult to tell her no.

But I did it.

She sat back and regarded me limply. I picked up the cloth I had dropped and resumed dabbing the blood from her face. My hands trembled.

Silence grew. The fire hissed in the grate, coal at last warming the air. My lips still tingled, still tasting her, and my body absolutely hated me. None would blame me, it said. She had come here, alone, deliberately forsaking protection, and had offered herself freely. The censure would go to her, not to me.

Except the censure from myself, I finished silently. I had already tallied too many regrets in my life to add another.

After a time, her eyes drifted closed. Her breathing grew steady, and I thought she slept. I returned the cloth to my washbasin, but when I came back to her, she was watching me.

"They killed my husband," she announced.

About the Author

Award-winning Ashley Gardner is a pseudonym for *New York Times* bestselling author Jennifer Ashley. Under both names—and a third, Allyson James—Ashley has written more than 35 published novels and novellas in mystery and romance. Her books have won several RTBook Reviews Reviewers Choice awards (including Best Historical Mystery for *The Sudbury School Murders*), and Romance Writers of America's RITA (given for the best romance novels and novellas of the year). Ashley's books have been translated into a dozen different languages and have earned starred reviews in *Booklist.* More about the Captain Lacey series can be found at the website: www.gardnermysteries.com. Or email Ashley Gardner at gardnermysteries@cox.net.

Books in the Captain Lacey Regency Mystery Series
The Hanover Square Affair
A Regimental Murder
The Glass House
The Sudbury School Murders
The Necklace Affair (novella)
A Body in Berkeley Square
A Covent Garden Mystery
A Death in Norfolk

And more to come!

CPSIA information can be obtained at www.ICGtesting.com
Printed in the USA
BVOW08s0546100416

443678BV00007B/265/P